THE ISLAND BOY PRESIDENT

THE STORY OF ACHIEVEMENT-MOTIVATED LEADERSHIP

TOM,

THE 21ST CENTURY RADICAL

Order this book online at www.trafford.com
or email orders@trafford.com

Most Trafford titles are also available at major online book retailers.

Printed in the United States of America.

ISBN: 978-1-4907-1889-7 (sc)
ISBN: 978-1-4907-1888-0 (hc)
ISBN: 978-1-4907-1890-3 (e)

Library of Congress Control Number: 2013919784

Trafford rev. 10/30/2013

 www.trafford.com

North America & international
toll-free: 1 888 232 4444 (USA & Canada)
fax: 812 355 4082

About the Author

The author considers himself a radical. Radicals think outside the box and not limited by the Status Quo box. My career was in medical education. My time was spent in doing medical research, administration, and teaching, in that order. Thus, much of my career involved the use of the Scientific Method. The methods and procedures of the Scientific Method have been used since the seventeenth century to characterize natural science. The Method involves observation, measurements, and experimentation. One generally forms a hypothesis from known data and designs experiments to test the theory. The process leads to the discovery of new knowledge. Price pointed out in his book titled *Little Science, Big Science,* published in 1960, that most of the scientists, who have ever lived are alive today. This is because of the rapid growth of population. The percentage of scientist in the population has increased and the population has increased. Both changes in our population contribute to the large number of scientist who are alive today. The study of logic, decision-making, and problem solving have occupied much of my career time.

I have always believed that the success in decision-making and problem solving by any institution is directly related to their organization. The organization chart and the ability to use the chain of command have a major effect on their ability to make creditable decisions and solve problems.

Observations have shown that the nearer the decision is made to the people involved, the less the adverse effects on the companies' operations.

It does not take a genius to know that when governments are reduced in number and size, the cost of government is reduced. When the cost of government is reduced, there are funds for the purchase of items needed or used by society. When such items are purchased, there is an improvement in the nation's economy. When there is an improvement in the nation's economy, employment is increased, and the salaries are higher. When there is an increase in the number of people employed and the salaries, the tax base is increased, and the government can collect additional tax dollars. Thus, reducing the number and size of governments improves efficiency and provides effective results for society.

Acknowledgments

The author thanks his wife, Eunice, for putting up with an achievement-motivated radical for sixty-nine years. That has taken a lot of patience. Many thanks to those who have helped the author publish this novel.

Foreword

As we know, the current constitution of the United States of America was adopted in 1791. The first national census taken at that time listed the population of the United States as almost four million people. The five cities with the largest population were New York with 33,954, Philadelphia with 28,522, Boston with 18,320, Charleston with 16,359, and Baltimore with 13,503. The populations of Virginia, North Carolina, South Carolina, and Kentucky were between one fourth and one half slaves. The number of slaves reduces the total population of free persons.

President George Washington and Secretary of State Thomas Jefferson believed the 1790 census was an error. They believed the population of the nation was more than the count indicated. An undercount could have been due to several problems at that time. The population was dispersed. The population of the five major cities would indicate the dispersion. Many people lived on farms and plantations. Transportation was very slow and lacked many links. Contemporary technology left much to be desired. It was believed that many people just failed to collaborate.

The founders of the nation and the members of the Constitution Convention were interested in forming a union of the colonies. They were living at the end of the Age of

Enlightenment—1791. They were residents of the middle of the Industrial Age. Their knowledge of organization, problem solving, and administration was very limited as compared to the citizens of today. Democracy as a method of government was totally a new idea. Their experiences with governments were as their experiences with the governments of Europe. As one could see from the population numbers for cities and the number of cities, the colonists were essentially closely related to the old European Feudalism. There were very few industries in the southern colonies, and just a few northern colonies had industries. Most of the families produced what they needed and were totally independent.

They produced a constitution that met their needs and not a constitution that provided the much-needed method of government that was effective and efficient. In 1913, the congress realized the fact that the growth of the population was providing a House of Representatives that needed to be prevented from growing further in membership. They limited the House of Representative to the then 435. That did nothing to improve the method of government. We have benefited greatly from the Electronic Age brought on by the Kennedy space program and the development of the Internet. Our knowledge of management techniques and the use of the chain of command have allowed many companies with large employee populations and large incomes to operate effectively and efficiently.

The author believes it is time the nation took advantage of the knowledge of today and called for a Constitutional Convention that provides a method of government that is efficient and effective. The State governments and the governments within the States should merge to reduce the number of governments and the size of the government. Reducing taxes would serve as a needed enhancement to the economy.

The author hopes everyone will learn from Albert Sabin Martin and Paul Harvey Collins. It is past the time for the citizens to benefit from improvements in our methods of government.

Dylan Johnson, a very well-known and respected presidential biographer, entered the Paul Harvey Collins Presidential Library on the campus of the University of South Carolina. He was there to interview the former president. Dylan was always impressed by the structure of the presidential libraries. He thought it was an excellent idea to preserve history and store the important documents related to the history of the president's tenure in office. He passed under an arch that was inscribed with the following words: *The freedoms granted by the 1791 Constitution are timeless.* He thought it was a nice touch. He decided to stroll around the library and have a look at the building. He knew he would be spending a lot of time reading the documents stored there. After his stroll, he approached the former president's office and was greeted by a receptionist near the door.

She said, "Mr. Dylan Johnson, I presume?"

He replied, "Yes."

She said, "I will announce your presence to President Collins."

At this time, the former president appeared at his office door. He greeted Dylan by saying, "Dylan, I hope you do not mind me calling you by your first name. I am very happy to meet you."

Dylan Johnson replied, "It is indeed a pleasure to meet you, Mr. President. I do not mind being called by my first name. In fact, I prefer to be called Dylan. Mr. Johnson is far too formal for me."

The former president said, "Please come into the office, and let's sit near the window."

Dylan looked out the window at a Rose Garden that was very similar to the Rose Garden outside the Oval Office at the White House. Dylan commented, "That garden is a very nice touch."

The former president said, "I think so too. I enjoyed sitting in the Oval office and looking out at that Rose Garden."

Dylan said, "The Arch with the inscription about freedoms is another nice touch."

The former president said, "I wanted that near the entrance so that everyone who entered would read those words. There is another arch inscribed with these words—*The method of government is time-dependent*—just down the hall."

Dylan said, "I took a stroll around the library and saw that arch. With the things you have accomplished, that is a very fitting inscription for your library."

The former president said, "Where shall we start, and what can I do to help you with this project?"

Dylan said, "Everyone knows that you have always been a worker and interested in getting the job done. Your last remarks only assure me that your reputation is well deserved."

The former president said, "I do have the reputation of being an achiever, and I am correctly accused of being in a hurry to get things done. Go-getters like to get things completed so they can take pride in the accomplishment."

Dylan said, "You should tell me about your life." Dylan took a yellow pad and a recorder from his briefcase. He placed the recorder on the coffee table between the former president and himself. He then said, "Mr. President, I hope you do not mind if I record our interviews."

Paul Harvey Collins said, "Since we will be spending a lot of time together, let's drop the formal language. Please call me Paul, and I will call you Dylan.

"The recorder is an excellent idea, and I think I will get one for myself. That way I can keep up with what we have and have not covered."

Dylan said, "Paul, you are living up to your reputation. Everything I have heard or read about you said that you like to be informal and hate the power-motivated symbols."

Paul walked to the door and asked his receptionist if she could get him a recorder. She returned within a few minutes with a recorder for him. He thanked her and placed it next to Dylan's recorder. He then said, "If I am to tell you about my life, I guess I should start with where and when I was born."

Dylan said, "That would be a good starting place, but please tell me about your father and mother first. Family life tells everyone more about an individual, and often, a person's family life tells us about the character of the person."

Paul said, "In my case, I think that is very true. Charles Collins was my father, and my mother's maiden name was Carolyn Watts. I was born in Chicago. My parents moved from South Carolina to Chicago shortly after my dad received his Master's Degree in Pharmacy Administration and my mother received her college degree in Education. She had sufficient math credits to graduate with a math major, but she preferred a degree in Education. My dad was a graduate of the University of South Carolina, College of Pharmacy. He received his Pharmacy license. My dad's degree in Pharmacy Administration was from the University of West Virginia. He was well informed in the manufacture and distribution of pharmaceuticals. His father wanted him to continue his education and get a Doctorate Degree. He had received an excellent job offer from a pharmaceutical manufacturing company just north of Chicago.

"When my mother knew my father would work in the Chicago area, she applied and received a teaching position in the area. That was the reason for the move from South Carolina to Chicago. My mother was a small-town girl who had gone to a small college, Presbyterian College in Clinton, South Carolina. She wanted to live on the lakeshore in downtown Chicago. This meant a commute for dad but he did not mind as long as Mom was happy with where she lived. I am told they were doing very well with their finance in Chicago. Dad had an excellent salary, a good stock option, and mom's teaching position helped. My dad had an excellent trust fund that was provided by my grandfather who had been very successful in business and had made money on the stock market.

"One thing my dad said he liked about Chicago was Paul Harvey's radio program. He never missed a program and had picked up on Paul Harvey's saying, 'Now you know the rest of the story.' Dad also liked another program that was broadcasted in Chicago, where the announcer would say, 'It is a beautiful day in Chicago' and would often tell the truth about how bad the weather was. In fact, my dad often used to say, when Mother went into labor before my birth, that it was a beautiful night in Chicago, when, in fact, the temperature was minus four degrees, it had been snowing for more than an hour, and the wind was thirty miles per hour off the lake.

"He said he had entered the waiting room at the hospital, and there were seven men in the room. He asked the man sitting next to him as to how long he had been at the hospital. The man took a quick look at his watch and said, 'Seven hours and about twenty minutes.' Dad said, 'You must have been one of the first ones here.' The man said no and that the men on the other side of the room had been there longer. Dad said he was ready for a long night when the door opened, and a nurse announced his name. He said, 'It cannot be my turn. These other gentlemen have been here a lot longer.' The nurse said, 'It does not work that way. You are the father of an eight-pound-fourteen-ounce boy.' He then entered Mother's room, and she was holding me. He said he took a look and said, 'Now we know the rest of the story.'

"Mother told me that she said, 'Charles, we have discussed a lot of names. We decided not to name a boy after your dad or mine because we thought the other one would be disappointed. I know the perfect name. We have not discussed it, but I think you will like it. Let's name this lovely boy Paul Harvey Collins.' Dad answered by saying, 'It is a perfect name. Now we know the rest of the story.' Mom said that she had heard that phrase so many times and that it would most likely be the first words of Paul Harvey Collins. Dad said, 'I like Paul Harvey Collins, and it has a good ring to it.'"

Dylan said, "I have often wondered how you came to be named Paul Harvey Collins, and now I know the rest of the story."

We had a good laugh, and I said, "Dylan, I thought I was going to enjoy these visits and the time spent with you, but now I am sure of it.

"My parents and I continued to live on the lakeshore front until the summer before my second birthday. They had summer vacation time and took a trip to South Carolina to see their parents and to show off the new addition to the family. I am told we went to Clinton first. They enjoyed the visit with my mom's family and friends, and her family and friends enjoyed seeing me. Dad said he took Mom to the place where he proposed to her. It was the Presbyterian College baseball field. He said they sat about halfway up the bleachers, and he asked her to marry him and gave her the ring he had bought. He said he did not deserve a wife as beautiful as my mom and with the perfect personality. She said she had loved him since the first time he had asked her to dance on the pavilion at Folly Beach. Mom always talked about how much fun she had when the family took a two-week vacation each summer at Folly Beach."

I asked Dylan, "How am I doing so far?"

He replied, "You are doing just fine. I am getting everything I need. When you get tired, let me know."

I said, "I am on kind of a roll, and I can go on for a while longer. The family left Clinton and went to Dad's home on Sullivan's Island, just north of Charleston. I have been told that I loved the beach and especially two tidal pools that were there at low tide. After two days at my grandfather's house, my dad told me he and Mom were talking in bed the third night. He said he had enjoyed growing up on Sullivan's Island and that he thought the lakeshore apartment was not a good place to raise a family. Mom said she agreed at once as she had been thinking about it for some time. I am told that the next morning, my grandfather had me at the tidal pools, and Mom and Dad were sitting on the porch.

"Dad said that he said to Mom, 'Isn't this a lovely view in the morning? Those big white cumulus clouds are beautiful against that blue sky.' Mom said that she loved the view and that the cool ocean breeze smelt so good. Dad said, 'Let's move back here.' Mom said that would be fine with her, but she would like a house of her own. Dad agreed and said the perfect house was just two doors down and was for sale. He said he knew the house inside out and that with just a few minor changes, it would be perfect for us. He said he loved the beachfront porch and would enlarge the one on that house. That afternoon, he had arranged for a tour of the house, and Mother fell in love with the place. On the walk back, she said that she could get a teaching job in the area. But what would Dad do? He said that he had been thinking about this for a very long time and that when they got back to the porch, they could talk about it.

"After dinner, Mom and Dad were sitting on the porch. He said he had his South Carolina Pharmacy license and thought he would open several pharmacies along the coast. He said he owned a large parcel of land off Interstate Highway 95 near the intersection with Interstate Highway 20. Where those two interstates crossed would be a great place for a pharmaceutical distribution business. Mom said she knew they had considerable money but that she did not know if they had enough for these big ideas. Dad assured her he did. He told her, 'The money and stock from my job and the trust fund are more than enough to buy the first pharmacy locations and the house we both like. I can fund my plan, and we will always have enough from the trust fund to pay for our standard of living. We should earn enough with the first pharmacy locations and the trust fund in order for us to live well and still have money to build the pharmacy distribution center on Dad's property. I intend to start small with the distribution center. I may rent space and services to major pharmaceutical companies. I will be able to increase the income with additional pharmacies. I plan to have prescriptions filled at the distribution center. I will have single dose packaging for assisted-living facilities and smaller hospitals.' Mom said that she should have known Dad would not plan to do something that he had not thought through completely. Dad said he would have to go back to Chicago to close down the apartment and get the furniture moved to the island. He needed to file his resignation letter and serve his two-week notice period.

"Mom said she asked how long it would be until they could buy the house they wanted. Dad said he would call his friend, Tom Murphy, and get him right on it. The next morning, he called Tom and asked him to come by for porch secession. Tom said he would be right down. His real estate office was on the Isle of Palms, the next island north of Sullivan's Island. When Tom arrived, he and Dad went to the porch. Mom brought out coffee, cups, and a plate of sweet rolls. Tom said that he always knew Dad would marry an angel. Dad asked about the house next to Granddad's, and Tom said he thought it was in excellent condition, but he thought the asking price was a little too high. He told Dad the two people who lived there wanted to move to the Franke Home at Seaside in Mt. Pleasant. The home had become very popular with active retired people. They had assisted-living and total-care facilities. Dad said he thought he would have to remember this. His mother and father were not getting any younger. Tom said the owners had kept the place up very well. Dad said that he remembered the house inside out. Mom said that she and Charles had visited the house and that she loved it.

"Dad said that he told Tom that we wanted the house and would pay cash at the closing. He also told Tom he wanted him to begin to look around for good places to open pharmacies. He said he needed at least three places. They had to be in different areas around Charleston. He told Tom he planned to open the three stores as part of a greater plan. Tom asked what Dad planned to do about the chain drug stores in and around Charleston. Dad told him he planned to open community base stores from Hilton Head in the south to Myrtle Beach in the north. He told Tom that his store model would be the Mt. Pleasant Pharmacy. 'I want the old soda fountains back,' Dad said. 'My stores will not be general merchandise stores. They will be the old-fashion neighborhood pharmacies.' He said that my grandfather owned land near the Interstate intersection of 95 and 20. He thought this land would be a good place for a distribution center. He planned to have many of the prescriptions filled and single dose packages assembled for nursing homes and assisted-living facilities at the distribution center. Tom said he always knew Dad was a big thinker and that he would be very successful.

"Tom said, 'It is great to have you and the family moving back home, and you are becoming a great customer.' Dad said he laughed and said, 'Tom, you do not know how great it is to be doing business with old friends. We Island Boys have always stuck together.' Tom said, 'That is true. There is something about the Island Boy friendships that make them better than most.' Dad said, 'Do you think it is because the surrounding water makes the island insulated? Island comes from the Latin root that insulate comes from.' Tom said, 'It is most likely the reason we were always a close-knit clique.'

"The Island Boys were much closer friends in high school than the boys in other high schools. Dad said, 'We sure had fun back in those days.' Dad told Tom he was going to be back in Chicago for at least two weeks. He had to close down the apartment and get the thing moved home. He would have to resign from his job and that required a two-week notice. Tom said, 'By the time you get back, I will have everything lined up. I will get you the best deal I can on the house and have the closing all set up.' Dad said, 'That would be great.'

"After Dad's secession with Tom, Mom joined him on the porch. He told her, 'The meeting with Tom was a success. By the time I get back from Chicago, everything would be in place. Tom will have set up the closing on our new home and should have a few places that are suitable for my new pharmacies.' Mom said that sounded good and that she would begin to look for a teaching job. She asked if Dad thought it would be difficult for us to find someone qualified to take care of me while they worked. Dad said his mom and dad would love to take care of me. He said he had learned a lot from his dad and that he wanted me to have the same opportunity.

"Mom asked when he was going back to Chicago. He said that Sunday afternoon he had his reservation. She said she had been looking around for furniture we would need in the new house. The Brick House had several things that looked as if they were made for the house. It was second-hand furniture, but it looked perfect. Dad said that it was going to be up to her. He was going to be interested in the porch. Mom laughed and said, 'You and the love of these oceanfront porches!'

"Dad was certainly right. I vaguely remember Dad being gone. But I remember the time I spent with Grandpa. I started to call him 'grandpa' while Dad was gone. I think it was his idea. But I do not remember when and how I started calling him grandpa. Dad commented on it when he got home—I do remember that. I remember Grandpa taking me to the fort, and I remember looking out at Fort Sumter. I remember this because it was my first visit, and I was very impressed by the difference from anything I had seen before. The dark halls and rooms made it seem as if you were deep underground. There was considerable earth on top of the fort. It made it hard to see the fort from the sea. Grandpa talked to me all the time. I am sure much of what I knew at that early age came from my experiences with Grandpa. I remember Grandpa asking me about things we had talked about. I thought he had a bad memory, but he was testing me to see what I was retaining.

"Dad said he dreaded the loss of time on his new project and the thought of leaving many good friends. Once he was back in the Chicago apartment, he worked for nights, filling boxes with valuable things from the apartment. He carried them to his office and sent them to Sullivan's Island by UPS. He elicited the help of the superintendent of the apartments and the lady who had worked for Mom in the apartment to get the furniture and the remaining items shipped. He arrived at his office ahead of time as usual. He composed his letter of resignation that he had thought about while on the plane and in the apartment. He gave the reason for leaving as family problems and the need to return to the South. He signed the letter and gave it to his secretary to send to his boss, the vice president for Research and Development.

"Things worked out as he thought they would. The first week was visits to his office by old friends and members of his team. All of them said how much they would miss him, and they hoped he would change his mind. The second week also worked as he knew it would. The vice president called him in and wanted to know what would change his mind. The president called him and questioned him about what he planned to do and how they could keep him.

"Then the CEO called him in and got down to business. He wanted to increase Dad's stock option and salary. Dad said he thought, *If I am worth that much now that I am leaving, why didn't they give me what I deserved when I was here?* The CEO interrupted his thoughts by asking, 'Have you looked around the area well? There are many good areas to live where you can raise a family.' Dad's answer was, 'Well, I guess I have always been a Southern boy, and I want Paul to enjoy the things I enjoyed when I was growing up.' The CEO asked Dad, 'What will you do when you get back home?'

"This was another question Dad said he was sure he would get, and he knew the answer before the CEO asked the question. Dad had been asked that question many times. He answered, 'I have had a South Carolina Pharmacy License since I finished college. I plan to open a pharmacy near my home.' The CEO said he would never be able to earn as much money running a pharmacy. Dad told him his father had provided a very large Trust Fund and that he will have a good standard of living back home. The CEO excused Dad, and he left the office. He had enjoyed his time with this company, and now he had mixed emotions. His thoughts turned to the increase in stock option and the raise in pay. Why do companies always leave you with the feeling you have been cheated when you leave the company?

"It was near lunchtime, and Dad started for the dining area. He needed a cup of coffee. It would be better if they served beer. Once again, he reflected on his time at the company. Yes, for the most part he had enjoyed his job. But when the new vice president for Research and Development had come on board, things had begun to change. The vice president had neither the experience nor the education needed to run R&D. He did not realize that the primary function of R&D was to protect the products in the marketplace because they were making money.

"The VP brought in someone he had worked with before who was less capable than he was. Dad was now glad he had decided to do what he always wanted to do. He wanted to get back home to see Carolyn and little Paul. He wanted to get to work on the project that had occupied his thoughts for a long time."

I said, "Dylan, I know that you know I do not remember any of this about Dad's departure from his job. He talked about it a lot over the years. I have heard the story about Dad leaving his job in Chicago many, many times. I am repeating what I heard."

Dylan said, "Do not worry about things like that. I will check every fact before we go to press. We cannot have errors in the final copy. It would make other things suspect. But we can check everything."

I said, "Well, it seems like this is a good place to stop for this time. At our next secession, I can start with our experiences on Sullivan's Island as I was growing up. How does that sound to you?"

Dylan replied, "I have plenty of material to keep me busy, and I want to do a little research in your library."

I said, "Shall we meet at my place on the island next time? I am sure you will enjoy the porch. We have plenty of room, and you could stay with us for as long as you like."

He said, "That sounds good to me. I have heard so much about those historic porch secessions that I want to get to one myself. When you are as interested in history as I am, you always want to see the places where history occurred."

I said, "Yes, that porch has become very famous. Shall we start on Monday morning?"

Dylan said, "That sounds fine. I will check the flight times and let you know what time I will arrive."

I said, "I will be waiting for your call."

Dylan packed up his yellow pad and recorder, and we said our good-byes. I placed the record I had put on the coffee table into my briefcase and headed for the door. I told the receptionist good-bye and that I would let her know when I would be back. I knew she knew how to get in touch with me if she needed to. There were staff members in the library and in the Charleston office.

When I got home, I told Jo Anne about Dylan and that I had enjoyed his company. I was sure she would enjoy meeting and visiting him. She asked, "Is he married? Does he have children?"

I replied, "I do not know."

Jo Anne said, "Men are never interested in the important things."

We had a good laugh. Then I said, "He will be here next Monday and may stay a few days with us. You can ask him yourself."

She said, "That will be fine, and I sure will ask him. It is time for my wine. Would you like a beer?"

I said, "I would love a beer."

The Secret Service man left the porch, and soon, Jo Anne had her wine, and I had my beer. There were also snacks. The service the former presidents get cannot be beat, but I hate the symbolism. They are the symbols of power. Thus, they are the things power-motivated people love.

Jo Anne said, "That look on your face says a lot, not only to me."

I said, "I am sorry I will just never be happy with a status of power."

Jo Anne said, "After eight years in the White House and now your former president status, I would think you would give up and live with it.

"It sure is not bad having all the attention and service. But I know you and your motivation."

I said, "It sure is different here now. Before I became president, people dropped by for a visit. Now getting in the gate from the street requires a lot of trouble. I wonder how Dylan will make out. I have notified everyone that he is coming. He has visited so many former presidents, so I guess he is used to the security."

Dylan called on Saturday and said that he would arrive on Monday at the house at about 10:30 a.m. I notified the security of his visit and the time and asked them to bring him to the porch. He arrived as planned and was shown to the porch by not one but two security guards. There were two on the porch with Jo Anne and me. After Dylan arrived, there were four. I called the one who stayed with me over and said that there was too much security. Two of them left, and the other two moved to the other end of the porch.

One would always be looking toward the beach and the other one would be watching us. They looked like two tigers ready to spring on any animal food that was available. I asked Dylan if he had trouble getting in the gate. He said not as much as the usual security—checks to make sure he was who he said he was.

I said, "I am glad you are familiar with the security. Many of my friends are not."

He said, "It comes with the territory."

I said, "I hated all the security while I was in the White House. I had a running battle with the head of the Secret Service. The twentieth of January arrived, and Randy Woods was sworn in as the president of the United States of America, and I became the former president. We moved out of the White House and back into my house here on the beach. On the last plane ride on Air Force One home, Jo Anne and I talked about security. When we were at home before we had the security, friends stopped by at any time. We wanted it that way again. Neither of us liked all the attention the security generated. I called the head of the Secret Service and asked him to take away the lead and chase cars when we went places. He did not like the idea.

"I bought a specially fitted SUV from Ford. It was bulletproof and bomb-resistant. It had seats for a driver and one other person in the front and two rows of three seats each that were comfortable. It blended into the traffic. The Secret Service thought the new SUV was grand and removed the need for the lead and chase cars. There would be two Secret Service members with us—a driver and another person in the back seat. When we had more people in the SUV, the second guard would ride with a shotgun.

"They would not reduce the number of guards at the house. They said that was a target, and they planned to change the appearance of the SUV at different times. I bought a second one so there would be a backup. We arranged an irregular schedule with an auto paint shop in Mt. Pleasant to change the colors and the designs. The license plates were changed almost daily. I argued that we were in friendly territory on the island. The head of the Secret Service insisted we needed the guards because we were exposed to the ocean. It was always a chance that if someone wanted to send a warning to the US, he or she could see me as an easy target. He played hardball. He used one of my lines. He said the primary purpose of government was to protect the lives of its citizens. He said that was especially true for the Secret Service."

Jo Anne asked Dylan if he would like coffee or something else to drink and added that we had breakfast food. Dylan said he was fine. Jo Anne then asked, "Dylan, are you married, and do you have children?"

Dylan answered, "Yes, my wife is named Marlene, and I have two grown-up boys, James and John. They have flown the nest. James, the oldest son, lives and works in New York, and John lives and works in Washington."

Jo Anne said, "I would love to meet Marlene. Can you bring her with you next time? We could have fun visiting Charleston and doing some shopping."

Dylan said, "I am sure Marlene would love that, especially the shopping. In fact, I plan to visit Charleston while I am here. I love history, and Charleston is the historic city."

Jo Anne said, "Paul and I will see to that while you are here."

I enjoyed the small talk, but as always, I was ready to get down to action. I had my briefcase with me, and I reached inside and took out my recorder. Dylan took the hint and got out his yellow pad and the recorder and placed the recorder between us. I said, "I guess I will always be the guy in a hurry."

As Jo Anne got up to leave, she turned and said, "There is no doubt about that."

Dylan said, "She is the wonderful person I have always heard about. She is a very gracious lady."

I agreed and said that I was a very lucky guy the day I met her.

Dylan said, "I hope I am going to hear about the day you met her."

I said, "I am sure you will."

I asked Dylan if he was ready, and he was, so I began. "When Dad got back to the island, Tom had everything in place."

Dylan said, "I see you have been listening to your tape recorder and know where to start. That is unusual as most former presidents used to ask me each time where to start."

I said, "You will not have that problem with me. Tom called and said they could close on the house the next day. Dad said that would be great. Tom had several stores and lots he wanted Dad to look at for possible location for the pharmacies. Dad was very happy that Tom was a person of his word and that he would not be wasting time. Dad and Mom went to the closing, and it went well. Larry Dodd, an attorney, was present. He said that the deed would be about a week to ten days in coming to the house we now lived in.

"There was a person Dad and Mom did not know. He was from First Federal of Charleston. There was a loan on the house, and he was there for the payment. They came home with the keys to the house they had bought. We all went down for a look. Dad wanted to enlarge the porch and put steps down from the middle of the porch to a path to the beach. There were steps on the right side of the porch. Dad said he preferred the way Grandpa's house was arranged. Grandpa's house faced the street, so the living area was on the street side. That put the kitchen next to the porch on the beach side. The new house faced the beach, and the living area was on the beach side. That means you had to go through the house to get food and drinks for the porch.

"Mom was ready for the big move. She had hired and interior decorator who owned the second-hand furniture store, to help with the furnishing of the house. The store was called the Brick House and was located in Mt. Pleasant. The furniture was displayed well in the store, and Mom had the several pieces she found, that were made for the house, just waiting to be moved in. Our things from Chicago had arrived and were in storage. The next day, all our furniture and the new things Mom had bought were in the house, and we moved in.

"Mom had good news for Dad. She got a teaching job in Mt. Pleasant. The pay was not as good as in Chicago, but the benefits were better. She had good health insurance for the family. Dad was glad for that. We were all delighted with the furnished house. I loved my room since the first time I saw it. Mom had done a wonderful job with my furniture, and she changed it as I grew up and my needs changed.

"The day after the closing on the house, Dad went out with Tom. He selected two areas west of the Ashley River from Charleston and one on the Charleston peninsular. He told Tom to buy all three locations. He was in a hurry to get the first one started. It was to be on River Road, and he called it the River Road Pharmacy. Both Mom and Dad had hit the ground running. I was having a great time with Grandpa and Grandma. I enjoyed all their attention, and they were enjoying teaching me things. Mom was very pleased with what I was learning and said so often.

"Dad called Al Kerry, who was an old friend and a good contractor. Tom had gotten Al and Durwood Churchill to inspect the house before Dad bought it. Al asked Dad how he liked the house and whether he wanted any work done. Dad thanked him for the good inspection and said he wanted the beachside porch enlarged. Al said he would get at it right away. Dad said that was not why he had called. He told him he was going to buy a property on River Road and wanted to turn it into a pharmacy. Al asked if he had any plans, and Dad said yes. Al made arrangements to come over and get the plans and to talk with Dad about the project. Al said he had not been on the porch since high school and would love to get back to the porch. Dad reminded him that we had moved into the house he had just bought. Dad said that he would use the porch the way he and his dad had always used the porch.

"I remember meeting Al when he came to the house. I was in the porch swing, and Dad was in his favorite porch chair. Al came over and shook my hand and told me I had a great Dad. Dad thanked Al for the letter with the inspection report on the house. He said he would follow all the suggestions, especially the things that were related to the air conditioning and the suggestion for maintaining the house. They talked business for a while before Mom showed up with drinks and snacks and orange juice for me." Al thanked Mom for her thoughtfulness. He told Dad he was a very lucky man. Mom said she had been very lucky when she met Dad on Folly Beach. Al said, 'We have all loved Charles for a long time. He has been a great friend.' He then added a thought by saying Folly Beach was the place many couples had met and married. To his knowledge, most of the marriages had worked out well. Dad said, 'The good old group of Island Boys has done well with the girls they met on Folly.'

"When Al left, Dad said he was really glad to be back on the island. It was much easier to get things done. He was happy to be getting his project off to a fast start. He said to Mom, 'When you need something done, get an old friend who is an Island Boy, and things will happen quickly.' As I remember it, they really did happen rapidly. It seemed to me that we had not moved into the new house very long before I was off to a preschool in Mt. Pleasant. Mom set a time each day when she would sit down with me and teach me things that I would need to know or learn when I got to school. I remember, at one of the lessons, Dad said I was a luck boy to have a teacher for a mother. I did not know it then, but I found out later that he was sure right."

"Dad got the first pharmacy opened, and we all went to the grand opening. I remember that day because there was what Dad called an old-fashion ice-cream counter at the front of the store. I had myself full of good ice cream. When I left for home, I asked if we could go to that store often. Dad said yes, and Mom said I would look like a giant hog. Dad said he had set up each store to make them look like a good old-fashion pharmacy. He did not have all the things the chain drug stores carry. He had mainly prescription medications, over-the-counter medications, and a few items people needed for a sick room or personal care. I remembered this from my later life when I went into one of his stores.

"He used the distribution center for storing the items that the stores carried. The store could call the center and order any product they did not have. There were several trucks, both for quick service and for regular delivery. Dad always said this cut down on the inventory in each store and at the center. As I grew up, I remember my dad saying, 'Thank God for the Computer Age.' It sure helped with running a business and kept down unnecessary cost like excessive inventory. He bought me a desktop computer when I was six and taught me how to use it. If I had a problem, I could always ask either my dad or my mom. They taught me early on how to use the search engines."

Dylan said, "It sounds to me as if you were a pretty precious boy."

I replied, "I guess you would say that I was. My mom and dad worked with me a lot. My grandparents also worked with me, seeing to it that I was learning things that I had to know. My mom's math background did not hurt. I was well advanced in math when I got to school, and Mom made sure I stayed that way."

Dylan said, "Is this a good time to stop for lunch?"

I said, "Yes, and I had planned for lunch at a local place. I think you will like it. Let me get Jo Anne, and we can leave."

We went to Dunleavy's Irish Bar and Grill. We were enjoying the food and the beer when a group of Island Boys arrived. They saw Mom and Dad and came to their table. The Island Boys were Tom, Elly, Donnie, and Horace. All were old friends of mine. I introduced them to Dylan and told them he was doing a biography. Tom said, "That should be quite a job with all the accomplishments I had achieved. We all knew he would be a great success, but he far exceeded anything we had ever thought he would do."

There was a loud "Here! Here!" from the other Island Boys. Dylan said that he had heard about the Island Boys from me and that he was glad to meet them.

After lunch, Dylan and I returned to the porch. Jo Anne when to visit a few of her friends. I said, "Well, Dylan, I think it is time I started telling you about my grammar school years."

He said, "I am ready when you are."

"My grammar school was on Sullivan's Island, an easy walk from my house. There were the remains of an old gun emplacement between the school and the beach. The cannons were long gone, but it was fun for us kids to climb around on the old fort.

"We played as if there were enemy ships trying to get into Charleston harbor, and we were firing on them. Now when I think back to those days, I know why we no longer have coastal forts and coastal artery. The defense was all on the ocean side. There were no defenses from the land side. If the enemy got behind you, the guns did not turn around, and there was nothing to protect the soldiers. It is funny, but I remember more about playing on that old gun emplacement than I do about much I learned in that school.

"I do remember Mrs. Purse. She was my third-grade teacher. She taught me how to learn. She made sure all of us had notebooks for everything. We copied our spelling words from the blackboard into one of our notebooks. When we got home, we used the dictionary to look up the words and to write down the meanings of the words. We also copied the sounds of the letters. We used flash cards with the definition on one side and the spelling on the other. The side with the word's meaning also contained the sounds for the letters in the spelling. I used this method during the rest of my education. The notebook and the flash cards sure improved my learning and retention of knowledge. I saved every set I made.

"The flash cards and the notebooks made it easy to review material and study for examinations. She made sure we recorded every important fact about each subject in the notebook and used the flash cards to remember the important facts. I am sure I still have some of those notebooks and flash cards from her class. I have a file of notebooks and flash cards from my years of education. They have come in handy very often over the years of my career. Her class was different. In that, we learned how to learn instead of just memorizing facts."

Dylan said, "I know why you remember Mrs. Purse. She made a real impression on you."

I said, "Mom and I were both very happy when I got her for my third-grade class. There were two third-grade classes at the school. I do not think the other class benefited the way Mrs. Purse's class did."

Dylan said, "Each former president I have worked with had teachers they remembered well. They were the ones who had the greatest effect on them. I had a few teachers like Mrs. Purse. I remember my college history professor very well. He had a major effect on my life."

I said, "I remember a quotation by Abdul Kalam who said, 'If a country is to be corruption-free and become a nation of beautiful minds, I strongly feel there are three key members who can make a difference. They are the father, the mother, and the teacher.'"

Dylan said, "I was told you like quotations and often used a quotation to support a point. In this case, you have picked an excellent one. I am making one of Mrs. Purse's notes of the author and the quote."

We both laughed and enjoyed the moment. Then I said, "Dylan, I think that is about enough of my early life. My memory of high school is much better. There is one fact I remember from my grammar school days, and that is, it was the first time I really noticed girls. When I was in the fourth grade, a girl was late getting back from vacation. We had been in class for a few days when she arrived. The teacher introduced her. Her name was Betty Watts. I thought she was a very cute girl. But before I could make a move, I saw her with a friend of mine named Marion Grooms. They were sitting on the foundation for the school flagpole. They looked like a couple, so I decided to let things pass. I told Mom about my experience, and she said I would meet a lot of girls and boys in high school and that there would be dances. I told her that I did not know how to dance. Mom said, 'When the time comes, we will see about that. I know a good dance teacher. She is Cecil Vaughn, and she has been teaching dance for a long time.'

"My next encounter with a girl I thought was cute was while I was in the sixth grade. Dylan, did you have and do you still get that feeling when you see a certain girl? I have asked several boys, and most of them said that they got the feeling. One said it was like having your heart jump into your throat."

Dylan replied, "Yes, and that description describes it well."

I said, "We had a slide on the playground, and I enjoyed climbing the latter and coming down the slide. It reminded me of sliding down the side of the ammunition storage site. One day, I was at the top of the slide, and I realized there was someone right behind me. I turned around and saw the most beautiful girl I think I had ever seen. She had a lovely face and long blonde hair. When I got to the bottom of the slide, I looked around for someone to talk to and saw my friend Donnie. I asked him if he knew the girl. He said yes and that she lived on Race Street near his house. Donnie lived on Sumter Street which was one block from Race. I asked if he could introduce me to her. He said he could but that Dick Hair lived right next door.

"I knew Dick almost as well as I knew Donnie, so I decided to ask him. I saw Dick across the park. I ran over and asked him if he would introduce me to the girl who lived next door to him. He asked if I meant Claire Risher. I said, 'I do not know her name, but Donnie said she lived next door to you. She is a very cute girl with long blonde hair.' Dick replied, 'That is Claire. I will introduce you to her, but do you know she is Mormon and her mother is very mean to boys?' I said that I did not know anything about her. I asked him what a Mormon was. He said it is a religion that is different from most religions. I thought about that, and I thought her religion should not be a problem. But her mother being mean to boys was likely to be a bigger problem."

"Dick and I went across the playground to where Claire and a group of girls were sitting. Dick said to Claire that I wanted to meet her. He told her I was his friend, Paul Harvey Collins. He said, 'Paul, this is Claire Risher.' Claire said she had seen me on the slide often. I said, 'Yes, I like that slide, and you were behind me a while ago.' She said yes and that was no accident. She said that she wanted to meet me. We both laughed. Dick said, 'Oh! Oh! It looks like I just became a matchmaker.' That brought a bigger laugh from everyone around. I liked the fact that Claire told her feelings and was very open with her thinking. Claire and I walked around the playground and talked. We got to know each other a lot better. I did not mention anything about religion or her mother being mean to boys."

"After dinner, Mom, Dad, and I were sitting on the porch. I asked them what they knew about the Mormon religion. Dad said that was a strange question coming out of me. Mom said she had known several people who were Mormons. She said she did not know much about the religion, but she thought the religion was started by a man named Smith. He was said to have found plates with inscriptions from God. He had trouble with people who did not believe his story, so he took the people who did believe across the country to open country in Utah. The religion is now located largely in Salt Lake City, and there is a beautiful church and a wonderful choir.

"She asked me why I asked. I told them about Claire and that Dick Hair had said she was a Mormon and her mother hated boys. Dad said that one thing about the Mormon religion was that the men were allowed to marry more than one woman. He said that might be one reason her mother disliked males. Mom said that a more likely reason was Claire was a cute girl, and she wanted to protect her from all the boys hanging around. That brought a laugh from Dad, and he said, 'Your mom is most likely right. Mothers are always very protective of their children, especially their girls.'

"Every Sunday afternoon, a group of us boys would meet at the playground and walk to different places on the island. On this Sunday, we decided to walk toward the Isle of Palms. Breach Inlet separated Sullivan's Island and the Isle of Palms. It was not safe to swim at Breach Inlet as the current was often very fast, and there were undercurrents. Many people went to the beach just a few hundred yards on the Sullivan's Island side of Breach Inlet. It was a much safer place to swim. While it was still a little cool for swimming, there would be kids from the islands, Mt. Pleasant, and some from Charleston on the beach at this point.

"When we got there, a crowd was on the beach. It was a good spot. The fort had barracks and other building in the area and along the beach during World War II. All the building of the army had been removed. There was a street near the beach and plenty for parking area. There were no houses near this spot.

"I saw Claire and a group of girls among the crowd on the beach. I asked Donnie, Elly, George, Horace, and Warren if they would mind going over and talking to the girls. They all answered at once, 'Are you kidding? We think we should be on our way over.'

"Claire saw us coming and walked out to meet us. She was one of the people who was the what-you-saw-was-what-you-got type. She said what she was thinking. She said, 'Hello, Paul, I am sure glad you came to the beach.' I replied, 'Hello, I am glad to see you again.' She said she had been hoping to see me again. The other Island Boys paired up with other girls in the group, and we all sat down in the sand. After we had talked for a while, Claire asked, 'Would you all like to come over to my house tonight? We can play games and have fun.' We all answered at once, 'Yes, we would love to come over.' She said that we should come at 7 p.m. We agreed.

"After a very enjoyable afternoon on the beach, I was at Claire's house at 7 sharp. Donnie and George were already there. Horace and Jinks arrived about the time I did. Elly was late arriving as usual. Claire had invited the group of girls over, and they were all present when I got there. Each boy paired up with a girl. When Elly arrived, Claire suggested we go inside and play games. We went into her dining room and arranged the chairs so we could play wink. Horace had the empty chair. Claire was sitting in my chair. He winked at Claire, and she went over. I winked at Claire, and she came back with a big smile on her face. Caroline said, 'Are we going to watch Claire move from one chair to another all night?' That brought a loud laugh. Claire's mother came out of the kitchen and had a mean look on her face. She said, 'Claire, I do not want any spin the bottle or post office played in this house.' Claire said yes to her mother in a little angry voice. She returned to the kitchen, and Claire said, 'Let's go into the living room.' We got up and followed her and sat boy next to girl. The seating caused the boys and girls to be seated very near each other. I was enjoying being near Claire when her mother showed up again, and she asked Claire to join her in the kitchen. When she got back, she said, 'Mom says it is time you boys leave for home.' We got up and went outside. The girls came out right after we left. Each boy joined the girl that he was sitting with and walked her home. Since Claire was home, I could only leave alone and head home.

"The next night, Mom, Dad, and I were on the porch. I told them about our experience the day before. Mom said that Claire's mother had called her during the day and told her that she thought Claire and I were getting too close to each other for our ages. I told her I did not agree with her and that it was only natural for boys and girls to be interested in each other. I told her, 'I do not agree with her. I would talk to you. I just do not like that lady.' While I liked Claire and thought she was not only cute but also had a very pleasing personality, I decided to stop seeing Claire. Once again, Mom said that I would have a lot of girlfriends in high school. Dad said he really enjoyed the high-school dances. I reminded them that

I could not dance. Mom said she would take care of that after my grammar school graduation during the summer break from school.

"Mom was as good as her word, and I started dance classes with Cecil Vaughn. I enjoyed every lesson. I met Louise Peden at the lessons. Mrs. Vaughn paired us up. She said we both had talent and would dance well together. This turned out to be very true. Louise made a great partner. She seemed to know what I planned to do next before I started any move. We learned a lot of different dance styles from Mrs. Vaughn, and she taught us a lot of step in each style. When I got to high school, I was ready for the first dance and knew Louise would be my date and dance partner.

"In my first year in high school, I had Mr. Jarvis for math. Mom had me ready for his class. He was a very tough teacher. If you did not bring in your homework, he would make you bring it in done ten times the next day. But that was not all. He made you write, While I am a student in Mr. Jarvis's class at Moultrie High in Mt. Pleasant, county of Charleston and state of South Carolina, United States of America, I will always do my homework on the day it is assigned one hundred times when you failed to do the work. He would take you to the back of the room. He had a paddle made from a palm branch that was very flexible. He had made holes in the branch. He would swap your work for licks.

"That palm branch gave you about six to eight licks for each swing. The students did their work and avoided the trips to the back of the room. Mr. Jarvis and I took a liking to each other. I always did my work and did it well. My grade in math was a good A+. He became my go-to guy for any trouble I had in any course while I was in high school. Once Donnie,

Elly, and I got caught cutting school. It was Spring, and we wanted to go to Folly Beach for a little fun. I was called to the principal's office. When I got there, the secretary had called Mr. Jarvis. I learned later that Mr. Jarvis had told her if certain boys showed up in the office, she should call him. Mr. Jarvis told Mr. Strawhecker, the principal, that he would take care of me. Mr. Strawhecker agreed quickly to suit me. I knew what was coming.

"When we were alone in Mr. Jarvis's room, he said I knew better than to cut school, that I was a very good student, and that I should be there every day, learning what I was being taught. He then said what I did not want to hear—he asked me to go to the back of the room and assume the angle over the desk. I went to the back of the room and leaned over the desk, exposing my butt. He said that this called for twelve licks. My butt was sore for more than a week. I sat on a pillow at the table. Dad said, 'Have you had a visit to the back of Mr. Jarvis's room?' I said that I had been to the back of the room. Dad wanted to know why, and I told him. He said he should beat me too for being stupid enough to have got caught. We all had a good laugh at that one.

"Well, Dylan, while I recall that licking, let me take a break until after dinner."

Dylan said, "I wonder what Mr. Jarvis would think about licking a future president of the United States."

I said, "Knowing him well, I would say he would be proud of the fact that he had a hand in teaching the president how to behave."

Dylan said, "I do not know him, but I think I should agree." Jo Anne arrived with wine for her and Dylan and beer for me. She had a plate of cheese and crackers too. Two security guards were carrying the wine, beer, and plates. I looked over at Dylan, and he was smiling. He said, "After all these years, and you still do not like it."

I said, "I never will too much of a symbol of power. A hired servant or two is not bad. But I hate to think of the expense of the security we have here."

Jo Anne said, "He likes to look as if it costs too much, but it is the symbol of power that really gets to him."

We had an excellent dinner in the dining room. Dylan and I rested for about an hour, and we met back on the porch. When it was time for us to start again, I said, "As Mom and Dad had said, the thing I liked best about high school were the dances. Louise and I were the best dancers in the school. The boys always wanted to dance with her, and a lot of the girls wanted to dance with me. But we enjoyed dancing with each other. Often, everyone would stop dancing to watch Louise and I dance. We got a lot of applause and comments about how well we danced together.

"In my second year in high school, Mrs. Vaughn came to my house and told Mom that she had taught me all she could and that she thought I should go to a dance class run by Mr. Sal De Maria. She said he taught a class at the Island Club on Tuesday night. She said that I had excellent dance talent, and Sal could teach me a lot. She said that he judged major dance competitions around the country. He was an excellent dancer, and he would enjoy having Louise and Paul as students. Mom asked how she could get in touch with him. Mrs. Vaughn said she would have Sal stop by.

"Mom got a call from Mr. De Maria, and he said he would stop by after dinner on Tuesday night. He was true to his word and arrived on time. He told Mom he had heard from Cecil.

She had told him I had a lot of dance talent. She had also told him that Louise and I made an excellent dance couple. He said he had talked with the Peden family, and Louise was joining his dance class. Mom said that she would love to have me join his class, and I was looking forward to the classes with him. He said that was great, and he could take me to the Island Club tonight, and we could start. Mom said that would be wonderful. She asked how he would like to be paid. He said he would send a bill once a month. Mom said that would be fine. Mr. De Maria and I left the house for the Island Club.

"Sal was a short Italian guy that was a little overweight. But he could really dance. He and his assistant put on a demonstration before each class. It usually covered moves we would learn during the class. But none of us could dance as well as they could. Louise and I got better and better after each class. Mr. De Maria complimented us often and said he was surprised at how much talent we had as a couple. He said he had never had a couple with as much talent. He said it was a real pleasure to teach us.

"We continued going to the Island Club on Tuesday nights for about six months. Then Mr. De Maria said he would like us to come on Thursday nights for an hour from seven to eight o'clock. He wanted us without the other class members as he had something special he wanted to teach us. Both Mom and the Peden family agreed, and we started the new period. It was unusual, in that, he was teaching us how to change tempo. The music would change from one dance tempo to another dance tempo, and we would change our tempo. He showed us ways to make the tempo change very smoothly. Louise followed my lead on the tempo change as if she had always followed my lead. After a few months of these special lessons, Mr. De

Maria called and asked if he could bring the Peden family over. He wanted to talk to both families. Mom said she would love to have him and the Peden family."

Dylan said, "I had heard that you were a good dancer, but I would have never thought you could be as good as what you are telling me."

I said, "Just wait. I have not gotten to the best part yet. Mr. De Maria arrived with the Peden family. Mom said she had refreshments on the porch and that since it was a nice night, we might like to sit on the porch. We all went to the porch, and Mr. De Maria said that he had something very important to ask the families as well as Louise and me. He said that he wanted to enter us in a dance contest in Columbia. This would be preparation for a large dance contest in Atlanta. He said the prize for the winners of the Atlanta contest was a trip to Brazil and lessons in Latin dances.

"He said he had been judging the Atlanta contest for several years, and with a little contest experience, Louise and I would have a good chance to win the Atlanta contest. He looked at Louise and me and said he had been working with us in preparation for the contest. The contest judged the way the couple changed tempo as the music changed tempo. Both families agreed to the contest experience and said we could be entered in the Atlanta Contest. Sal said he would not judge the contest that we would be dancing in, but he would be there for us.

"Louise and I won the Columbia Contest, and we were entered in a contest on Folly Beach and won that Contest. Mr. De Maria was very pleased and said he would enter us in the Atlanta Contest. We continued to go to the Island Club on Thursday nights and practiced the tempo changes. Mr. De

Maria continued to correct some moves and teach us additional ways to make the changes. It soon got to be old hat to both Louise and me. Mr. De Maria said, 'You got it made, and you cannot lose this contest.' He called Mom and Mrs. Peden and told them we could not fail to win the Atlanta Contest. He said he would go over early and get the hotel and a place for Louise and me to warm up. He would meet us at the airport in Atlanta and have an SUV to take us to the hotel. Mr. and Mrs. Peden brought Louise over to the house, and they discussed the Atlanta trip with Dad and Mom. They planned for Mrs. Peden and Mom to take us over. The dads would take us to the Charleston International Airport and pick us up when we got back.

"The day finally came for us to leave for Atlanta. We went to the Charleston International Airport in one car, and the Peden family came in their car. We met at the gate. Sal was a man of his word and was waiting when we got off the plane in Atlanta. He took us for a little sightseeing ride around Atlanta. He showed Mom and Mrs. Peden how to get into the underground shopping area. He suggested they go there this afternoon while he had Louise and me at a friend's dance studio. We checked into the hotel and went up to our room. We were to meet Sal at one o'clock for lunch. The Contest was the next day at one in the afternoon.

After lunch, Louise and I accompanied Sal to his friend's place. Mom and Mrs. Peden went shopping. Sal's friend had a room all set up for our practice. He even had a recorder that changed tunes and tempo without a break in the music. Sal had a similar machine at the Island Club. Sal worked us for a while, and his friend said he was very impressed with our dancing ability. He said that with Sal as our teacher, he guessed he should have known we would be great. Sal said, 'I am sure I have got a pair of Contest winners here.' The friend said he did not see how we could miss. Sal said, 'Do not give them the big head. They will have to be at their best.'

"We got back to the hotel ahead of Mom and Mrs. Peden. Sal suggested we go up to the room and rest. He said we would have dinner at six. He wanted us in bed and resting well early that night. When Mom got to the room, I told her what Sal had said. She said that sounded good to her. She was tired after the plane trip and the shopping. We went down for dinner. After dinner, Sal told Mom and Mrs. Peden the plan for the next day before the Contest. He said we should have breakfast at eight. Around 9:30 a.m., he would take us over to his friend's studio for a warm-up. He said we would have a light lunch at about eleven-thirty. He did not want us to be overloaded with food before the contest.

He said we would arrive at the contest at about twelve-thirty. He said the contest was to be held on a basketball court and that the bleachers would be full people. He said the number of couples was limited, but the court and some of the surrounding area would be taken up early in the contest. An area would be marked off for each couple. He said, 'The music will start, and each couple will begin to dance. The songs will change, and the tempo will change too, but you are familiar with that. Each time the music stops, the couples will be removed from the floor, and the dance areas will become larger. When there would be twelve couples left, the finals will start. The music will stop, and the head of the contest will ask each judge if he is ready, meaning whether he has chosen his couples. If any of the judges says no, the music will start again, and you have to start dancing again. When all the judges have made their selections, they will be turned in to the head judge. He will add up the points and will announce the first couple, and that will be the couple that won third place. He will then announce the second couple that will be second place. The last couple number and names he announces will be seventeen, that is, Louise and Paul's number.'

"Mom said, 'You sure seem certain.' Sal said, 'I am, and when they get the cup and trip, I will tell you I told you so.' That brought a laugh from the group. Well, Dylan, I am going to run this like a game show on TV, and it is time for a commercial. You will have to wait until tomorrow to find out who won."

Dylan laughed and said, "I think I know."

We retired to our bedrooms. The next morning was a beautiful day on the island. The sky had just a few white fluffy clouds. They were almost on the horizon. The ocean was a bright blue. There was breeze, but it was soft. The ocean was very calm; you could hardly hear a sound. We had breakfast on the porch. Jo Anne sat with us. The house servants and the security guards served us.

Dylan said, "You may find it hard to get used to this life, but I do not think I would mind at all."

Jo Anne said, "It is not the life or the service. It is his problems with the power-motivated people during his career. He watched them add on the symbols of power, and he hated it."

I said, "The family all laughed at my expression the first time I heard 'Hail to the Chief' after I became president."

Dylan said, "Most of the former presidents I have interviewed were power-motivated individuals. When they were out of the White House, they could not get enough of the symbols of power. They missed their glory."

I said, "Yes, they say the president of the United States is the most powerful office in the world. I can easily see how a power-motivated individual wanted the office."

Dylan said, "They wanted the office, but not the job. None of them came near accomplishing the things you accomplished during your eight years as president."

I said, "That is exactly the way most of the power-motivated people I have known acted. They wanted the power, but they had no idea what to do with it after they received the power. Albert and I reached our lifetime ambition when we entered the offices. We had planned on improving government from the time of our early-in-life meeting."

We had finished our breakfast, so Jo Anne said, "I have got something I want to do in the house and then I am going to the Isle of Palms to see Scott at the beauty shop."

I said, "Oh yes! This is the day of the week that you get your hair done. Say hello to Scott for me, and ask him to tell Annette that I said hello."

She said, "I will tell Scott, and I will see you two at lunchtime. Come over, and we will have lunch at the shopping center. I will wait for you at the beauty shop."

I said, "We will see you there." She then left, and I said to Dylan, "I guess that was her manner of saying we needed to get to work. Shall we start?"

Dylan said, "Give a second to get out my recorder and pad." I had my recorder on the coffee table, and I turned it on.

I said, "I was telling you about our Atlanta Dance Contest experience. Mom and Mrs. Peden went to the contest with us. They were seated in the bleachers. Sal said, 'You two wait right here, and I will get your number.' He returned quickly with placards that he put on our backs. Our number was seventeen. He said our space was on the other end of the gym. We walked through the large group of contestants to our spot on the floor. Sal said, 'I am going to join your moms. Do not be nervous. You will do well. In fact, I expect you will win. Just be yourselves, and dance as if you are really enjoying a high-school dance.' Louise said, 'I am not nervous, and Paul will give me great leads.' I said, 'I am just going to dance with my great partner.' Louise smiled and said, 'I like that.'

"Sal then left, and the head judge announced from his stand, 'You will have a short warm-up period. When the music starts, you dance. I will announce when it is time to start the contest.' The music started, and it was a quick tempo. Louise and I started to dance. It was a very short time before the song and the tempo changed. This kept up for about five to seven minutes. The music stopped, and the announcer said it was time to start the contest.

"The music started again, but this time, each song and tempo went on for a longer period of time. We must have danced for fifteen minutes. I thought that was a little too long. The music stopped, and the judges walked around the floor and removed a large number of couples. That created a much larger dance floor. The announcer said that we were ready for the second phase of the contest. Again, we danced for about fifteen minutes. The songs and the tempo changes were more frequent this time. The music stopped, and the judges removed more couples. Louise and I were still on the floor. I looked into the bleachers and saw Sal. He gave me the thumbs-up sign.

"The announcer said that the remaining couples can sit on the chairs at the left end of the gym from his stand. He said this would be a rest period. It must have been for fifteen or twenty minutes, but it seemed a lot longer. He requested the dancers to return to the floor. We were given a good-sized space in which to dance. The music started, and we began to dance. During this time, the periods between the song changes and the tempo changes varied. After what seemed like more than fifteen minutes, the music stopped, and the announcer asked if any of the judges needed more time. Two judges raised their hands. The announcer said we would go for about ten minutes longer.

"After that dance period, the announcer said, 'Now for the thing we have been waiting for. We will announce the third-place winner first followed by the second place winner and then the winner will be announced.' Couple twelve was third-place winner. Couple number eight was the second-place winner. My heart stopped because I thought we had not even placed in the completion. The announcer then said, 'The winner is couple number seventeen, Louise Peden and Paul Harvey Collins.' We almost fainted. Sal was the first one to come to us. He said, 'I told you so.' Mom grabbed me and gave me a big hug. Louise's mom did the same. The head judge arrived, and he had a large cup with our names on it. He gave Louise the packet with the tickets and hotel reservation. He gave me the cup and handed my packet to my mom.

"We went back to the hotel a very happy group. Sal said we had a late checkout time, but we needed to get our things and head for the airport. We made out flight, and we enjoyed the flight to Charleston. Many people and the flight attendants wanted to see the trophy. We were congratulated by a large number of the passengers. Dad and Mr. Peden were waiting at the gate. When we approached them, Dad said, 'You do not have to tell us. We can see it in your faces that you have won.' Sal said, 'They were wonderful. I do not think I have ever seen a better couple.' I gave the trophy to Mr. Peden, and he and the family left for home. We enjoyed the ride to the island."

Dylan said, "That is the first time I have heard about that point in your life. I would have never thought you were a dance-contest winner."

I said, "We had about three weeks before we left for South America. Sal arranged everything as usual and made it easy for Mom and Dad. Dad said he had too many things on his plate for the trip, but Mom could handle it. Mom agreed and said that with Sal's help, it would be a piece of cake. We arrived at the airport in Brazil, and Sal was at the gate. He took us for a ride around the city, and we had a great sightseeing tour. I was surprised how much Sal knew about the city and the beach areas. He showed us where we would go for the dance classes, and it was a short walk from the hotel.

"He said, 'Your teacher is an old friend of mine. He has a very good dance studio.' We enjoyed the swimming and the hotel near the beach. We walked to the studio and had two days of lessons. We learned all the Latin dances and a few moves that were new to Louise and me. It was very enjoyable, and Sal's friend was very complimentary to Louise and me. He said he could see why Sal loved to teach us. He said we were the best students of all the students who had won the Atlanta Contest. We returned to the island, and Louise and I continued as students of Sal's. We went to every dance in the area and to a couple of the clubs that had dancing.

"When it was time for school to start, we were sitting on the porch on a quiet night. I said that I would have an American History class that year. I said I was very interested in the class, and I thought it would be good to learn about the War Between the States and the role Charleston and the fort played. Dad said

41

he had something he wanted me to see and left the porch. He went into his office and came back with a document he wanted me to read. Here is a copy of that document. I do not think you have a copy of this document. It is called Declaration of the Immediate Causes Which Induce and Justify the Secession of South Carolina from the Federal Union."

Dylan said, "I have read this document and the ones from the other southern states. As a History major, I was very interested in each of these documents."

I said, "I should have known I could not get one up on you when it comes to history." We both laughed.

Confederate States of America—Declaration of the Immediate Causes Which Induce and Justify the Secession of South Carolina from the Federal Union.

The people of the State of South Carolina, in Convention assembled, on the 26th day of April, AD 1852, declared that the frequent violations of the Constitution of the United States, by the Federal Government, and its encroachments upon the reserved rights of the States, fully justified this State in then withdrawing from the Federal Union; but in deference to the opinions and wishes of the other slaveholding States, she forbore at that time to exercise this right. Since that time, these encroachments have continued to increase, and further forbearance ceases to be a virtue.

And now the State of South Carolina, having resumed her separate and equal place among nations, deems it due to herself, to the remaining United States of America, and to the nations of the world, that she should declare the immediate causes which have led to this act.

In the year 1765, that portion of the British Empire embracing Great Britain undertook to make laws for the government of that portion composed of the thirteen American Colonies. A struggle for the right of self-government ensued, which resulted, on the 4th of July, 1776, in a Declaration, by the Colonies, "that they are, and of right ought to be, *free and independent states*, and that, as free and independent States, they have full power to levy war, conclude peace, contract alliances, establish commerce, and do all other acts and things which independent States may of right do."

They further solemnly declared that whenever any "form of government becomes destructive of the ends for which it was established, it is the right of the people to alter or abolish it and to institute a new government." Deeming the Government of Great Britain to have become destructive of these ends, they declared that the Colonies "are absolved from all allegiance to the British Crown and that all political connection between them and the State of Great Britain is, and ought to be, totally dissolved."

In pursuance of this Declaration of Independence, each of the thirteen States proceeded to exercise its separate sovereignty, adopted for itself a Constitution, and appointed officers for the administration of government in all its departments—Legislative, Executive, and Judicial. For purposes of defense, they united their arms and their counsels, and in 1778, they entered into a League known as the Articles of Confederation, whereby they agreed to entrust the administration of their external relations to a common agent, known as the Congress of the United States, expressly declaring in the first Article "that each State retains its sovereignty, freedom, and independence, and every power, jurisdiction, and right which is not, by this Confederation, expressly delegated to the United States in Congress assembled."

Under this Confederation, the war of the Revolution was carried on, and on the 3rd of September, 1783, the contest ended, and a definite Treaty was signed by Great Britain, in which she acknowledged the independence of the Colonies in the following terms: "Article 1—His Britannic Majesty acknowledges the said United States, via: New Hampshire, Massachusetts Bay, Rhode Island and Providence Plantations, Connecticut, New York, New Jersey, Pennsylvania, Delaware, Maryland, Virginia, North Carolina, South Carolina and Georgia, to be *free, sovereign, and independent states*; that he treats with them as such; and for himself, his heirs and successors, relinquishes all claims to the government, propriety, and territorial rights of the same and every part thereof."

I read through the document and said, "It is very interesting. I now know I am going to enjoy that history class. I know a lot more about how the people of South Carolina felt at the time before the war. Dad said, 'Just think what it was to write a constitution that formed the union in the first place. Most of these feelings were present when the Constitutional convention was held—Washington and the others had a hard job trying to form a union of the independent states. Each state and each person was enjoying the freedom from the rule of the tyrant kings in Europe. They were not ready to give up any of their individual rights to any government. The States loved their independence and did not want to give up any rights.

'The members of the convention had to assure the states and the citizens that they could maintain their rights, but they needed to have a federal government that was functional.' I said, 'I can see how that was a problem for the founders of the union. I have heard you and Grandpa complain about situations where there were two or more groups in charge of a situation.' Dad said, 'That is very true when the groups in charge are controlled by power-motivated individuals. When they are controlled by individuals who are achievement-motivated, they work together in order to achieve their goal.'

"I said, 'You remember when you told me I would have a lot of fun at dances and meet a lot of girls?' Mom answered, 'Yes, why do you ask?' I said, 'When you told me that, I remembered how you and Dad met. I want to be able to dance well enough to impress a girl.' Mom said, 'Well, it is good to be able to dance well enough to impress a girl, but when your dad asked me to dance, and I looked up at him, he was the most handsome man I had ever seen. Even if he could not dance, I would have followed him wherever he went.' Dad said, 'This is the first time I know that. I thought it was my dancing ability.'

"I said, 'I think I can dance well enough to impress any girl. The school year looks like I have a lot of subjects that interest me. I am going to have to spend a lot of time on the subjects, so if it is all right with you, I will not take dancing when school starts. I am not going to make a career out of dancing.' Dad said, 'I am glad to hear you are interested in your schoolwork and are planning to study.' Mom said, 'I am too. I will call Sal tomorrow. I will miss Sal. He has been a good friend.' I said, 'I will miss him as well.' Dad said, 'I am sure we can keep him as a friend. We can invite him over once in a while.'

"School started, and the classes I was assigned to were very much as I had thought. The math class was easy since I had Mom's help. The computer and the search engine helped with the history. My history teacher liked it when I brought up things I had learned about the period we were studying. He called me aside and asked how much time I spent on the search engine. I told him, 'A lot. I use the search engine to help me with all my subjects.' He said he liked to use the search engine himself. He told me to keep up the good work.

"About the middle of the first semester, Dad told me the Masonic Lodge was starting a Chapter of DeMolay for high-school boys. He said he thought I would like the organization. It was like a Key Club, but the boys ran their own organization. He said the chapter had a Masonic adviser, but he only advised that the boys made their own decisions. He said it would be a good experience. I knew Dad enjoyed his Masonic experience. I asked him if he would sign me up. He said no because it was I who had to do that. He said he would take me to the first meeting but that he could not stay. Only the adviser would be at the meeting. The adviser, I found out, was called the 'dad' of the organization. At the first meeting, there were three Masons there. They told us the Savanna Chapter of DeMolay would come up to initiate us into the Order of DeMolay. That was to be in two weeks. After the initiation, we were to elect our officers and run our organization.

"The boys from Savanna came up, and a few stayed in a hotel in Charleston. We had three boys stay with us. Other families too had some boys stay with them. Walter Kessler was one of the boys who stayed at our house. Walter and I hit it off at once. He was from South Carolina, but he lived near the Georgia broader, close to Savanna. He lived on a farm, but his dad was a shrimp boat captain. Walter and his two older brothers ran the farm.

"The initiation went well, and after we had learned about the organization, they held an election of officers for us. Horace Smith was elected Grand Master, and I was elected as Senior Master, which was the job just under Grand Master. The election process elected the other officers. We enjoyed our conversations with the boys from Savanna and the knowledge they gave us about running a chapter. Dad Lands was appointed as our Chapter Dad.

"At our next meeting, Horace said to me, 'I want you to arrange a dance for our chapter.' He said the Grand Master from Savanna had told him that was a great way to get the chapter off to a great start. The dance would bring in new members. I said, 'We could use the new members.' But a dance cost money, so I said to him, 'I might be able to get Dad to give the money.' Horace said, 'No, I want this to be on our own. Let me know when you think we have enough money.' I said, 'I think I can get Francis Cole to ask his dad if we could use the church activities hall. That would save us some money. We would need to rent a jukebox and decorate the hall. As I think about it, maybe it will not cost us very much to put on a dance.'

"The next afternoon, I went over to see Francis. I told him what we were planning and asked him whether he would like to join DeMolay. He said that sounded good and that he would take me to his dad. Reverend Coe was in his study. Francis introduced me to his dad and said I was a very good friend of his. I said that I was sorry for interrupting him in his study, and he said that was all right as he spent a lot of time in his study. I told him about the Order of DeMolay, and he said he was familiar with the organization. I asked him if we could use the church activities hall for a dance. He said that he and the church members liked to have young people around the church and that we could use the hall.

"At the next meeting, I told Horace to announce the dance and for the members to invite friends who might become DeMolay members. He made the announcement and that the dance would be at the church on the corner of Rutledge and Sumter streets in the activities hall. Several of our members, like me, had been to dances in the hall. Horace appointed several people who were to help me with the dance preparation. These were all my friends to whom I had talked about the dance.

"The next day, Tom, Donnie, and Elly went with me to the jukebox rental office. We got the price for the jukebox, and that was fine. He asked if the dance was going to be held at the second floor activities hall at the church. I said yes, and he said it would be an extra ten dollars to put the jukebox on the second floor and to bring it down. Tom said we could move it up and take it down. He said he did not want inexperienced people handling his jukebox. Donnie asked him if he could put it in the basement and take off the ten dollars. That brought a laugh from all of us, including the manager of the jukebox company. He said, 'Oh hell! I will put it in the activities hall for nothing.' We told him we planned to have lots of dances, and he would get all of us busy. He said that would be fine.

"On the morning of the dance, we were all set to decorate the hall. We decided to use fall colors of black and brown with some yellow crape paper rolls. We decided to get some palm branch, a few flowers, and a few corn storks to put around the hall. That was when we had made the worst mistake of my life to this point. We got the palm branches and some limbs with leaves in color, but when we stopped at a field to get a few corn storks, a policeman drove up. He got out of the car and said, 'You are under arrest for stealing corn.' We explained to him what we were doing, but we got nowhere. He said he was taking us down to Mr. Dalton's farmhouse, and he would decide if he wanted to press charges. We followed him down, and Mr. Dalton came out. The policeman told him he caught us in his field stealing corn. Mr. Dalton asked him, 'What are you doing with them at my house? They should be in jail.' I said, 'Just a minute, Mr. Dalton. We were just getting a few storks of corn to decorate a dance hall for a fall dance. I think your daughter Evelyn plans to attend the dance. We thought it would be good to have the corn to remind the people attending the dance that the start of school was not the only thing that happened in the fall. We wanted them to know that fall was harvest time and was an import time to each of us.' Mr. Dalton said that we had a truckload of corn. I asked him to come over and see. I told him that the corn was on top of other things we had gotten. He walked over and saw we did not have much corn. He then said, 'Why didn't you come down and ask me if you could go into my field?' I replied, 'I am very sorry I did not come down and ask, but the corn was near the road on the north end of the field, and I thought you would not mind us taking a few stalks.' He said, 'Next time, make sure to ask before you go onto anyone's property.' I assured him I would. I said, 'I have learned a good lesson here today, and I will remember it all my life.' He let us go, and every time I saw him after that day, I thanked him for letting us go and for the great lesson I had learned. His daughter was at the dance, and she had a big laugh at our expense."

Dylan said, "That must have been quite an experience. Was this the first time you had been arrested?"

I answered, "It was not only the first but also my last time. I have never been arrested. I have felt like a lot of people would have liked to have me arrested."

Dylan laughed and said, "I do not know about that. Everyone I have talked to tells me what a wonderful leader and person you are, and I have found them to be right."

I thanked him for his comment and said, "Albert and I tried our best.

"I had invited Kessler to the house and to the dance. I told him I would have a date for him. I asked Capitola Owens if she would go to the dance with a good friend of mine from out of town. I was very surprised when she said yes, she would go to the dance as a double date with me and my partner. I wished at that point that I had asked Tola as we called her to go with me. She was a beautiful girl. She had black hair and a lovely complexion that was olive-colored. She had blue eyes that captivated you, and in my case, she brought my heart into my throat. I usually had trouble talking around her. She lived on Folly Beach, and every boy for miles around was in line for a favor of a date with her.

Kessler was happy with his date as he should have been. I had Louise as my dance date. We had a wonderful time, and I got to know Tola much better. Walter said he was in love with her. I said, 'Join the line. Every boy who has ever seen her is in love with her. She has dated a few, but she is very picky. She rules all the girls who live on Folly or visit Folly.'

Since Tola lived on Folly, it was a twelve-mile drive each way. The dance lasted until eleven. It was about eleven-thirty before we got out of the dance hall. The drive to Folly and then to Sullivan's Island meant that I did not get Louise home until almost one o'clock. I knew I would have to apologize to her mom and explain the reason we were so late.

"The dance was a success. We got eight new members and a lot of comments about how much they enjoyed themselves. Louise and I put on a demonstration of the Latin dances we had learned. That brought a lot of applause and congratulations. The one I liked the most was when Louise told me Tola was very impressed with my dancing ability. Louise told me this on the drive back to Sullivan's Island.

"At the next meeting of the chapter, the officers decided we should have a dance once a month. I said that would mean we needed more dance halls. Reverend Coe said we could have the hall every fourth month. We found three other churches who allowed us to have their activities hall once every four months. My friends, the Island Boys, worked on the manager of the Island Club, and we got it twice a year. We had Sal come and work with the couples, and Louise and I gave demonstrations of what we had learned from Sal. He got a lot of new couples for his dance classes."

Dylan said, "I have about enough for this time. We can start here next time. What do you plan to cover next?"

I said, "I plan to cover the start of a DeMolay Chapter in Greenville and how I met Albert."

Dylan said, "That will be very interesting. I have been wondering how a boy from Charleston had such a good friend in Greenville." We cut off our recorders, and he packed his briefcase, and we said our usual farewells. Dylan was going home for a few weeks. He had a couple of speaking engagements and wanted to work on my biography. Jo Anne asked him to bring his wife next time, and he said he would.

Dylan was true to his word. On Monday, two weeks after our last meeting, he and his wife arrived at the house. He had called and asked if a Monday arrival would be all right, and we had said yes. Marlene and Jo Anne enjoyed each other's company. They planned to go to Charleston on Tuesday. Dylan said he hated to miss that trip. While Jo Anne showed Marlene around the Islands, Dylan and I got down to work.

We were back on the porch. He had his recorder ready, and I had mine turned on. He had his usual yellow pad. We were ready to go when Dylan said, "What a stunning day! The ocean and the sky are beautiful. You always have a breeze, and it smells so fresh."

I said, "We are spoilt. We have gotten so used to it that we fail to notice. The breeze is a blessing, in that, it keeps one cool. But sometimes, it gets too strong. It blows the papers around the porch and prevents you from enjoying the surroundings. We have wind blinds around the porch. You may have noticed we have hurricane shutters. My grandpa put this house in shape to withstand a hurricane. We spend a lot of time on this porch."

Dylan said, "The porch and your secessions here are well known in Washington."

I said, "If you are ready, I can start."

He said, "If you are ready, I am."

I said, "During the summer between my junior year in high school and the senior year at a meeting of DeMolay, Dad Lands said Greenville wanted a Chapter of DeMolay, and we had been selected to initiate the new chapter. There was a motion for us to go to Greenville and initiate the new chapter, and there was a second. There was no discussion, and the motion passed with everyone voting yes. After the vote, Dad Lands asked who would go to Greenville. Horace asked how many we would need. Dad Lands said about six to ten members. Horace said the officers would all go, and he appointed three other members. The group going to Greenville began to meet every night. We had to learn what we needed to know and what we needed to do. By the time of the trip, we were all ready.

"When I got to Greenville, I was assigned to stay with a family named Martin. The father was a pediatrician and well known in Greenville. He had a son I met and liked the moment I arrived. His name was Albert Sabin Martin. I said, 'We have something in common. We are both named after well-known people.' He said that his dad was a great admirer of Albert Sabin. His father's father had polio and was left crippled. I said I was sorry to hear that. Albert said that his dad thought Albert Sabin saved and helped a lot of people. I said I was sure he had.

"Albert said, 'I guess you have had the same hard time I have had living with this name.' I said there were a lot of bullies that I had left with a sore nose. He said he had left his share in the same fix. Tom, who was staying with the Martins, said he and the Island Boys had helped save me so many times. Albert and I gave each other a big hug. That was the start of a friendship that has lasted all our lives. After the initiation,

Albert and I agreed to visit each other. He came to the island several times over the next months, and I went to Greenville often.

"When school started, we were both in a civics class. My teacher took the class on a field trip to Columbia to see the legislature in action. When we arrived in the Capitol, I was surprised to see Albert. His teacher had brought the class to the Capitol for the same reason. We sat together in the balcony and watched and heard the action. You will never believe this, but it is the truth. They were debating on what time the alcohol beverage stores should close. In South Carolina, you could not buy a drink. You had to buy a bottle from the alcohol beverage store. Some of the legislature members wanted a late closing time. The others wanted to shorten the hours the store could be open. Albert leaned over and said it was easy to tell who was getting money from the store owners and which ones were in the pocket of their preachers. I said that I was thinking the same thing, and I wondered who would win.

"Well, shortly after that, there was a motion that the stores would close at sundown. There was an argument that the sun went down at different times each night. There was a motion that the bill be amended to read that official sundown was eleven o'clock at night. I know you do not believe it, but it is true. The side that wanted short hours was glad to get a bill that allowed them to fix the store hours. The side that wanted the longer hours was happy with the eleven o'clock time.

"In a very short time, the balcony began to fill with ministers from Churches in the Columbia area. There was a bill introduced that said that each store could place a large clock or sign in the window of the store that announced the time for sundown that day and that the stores would close at sundown. This bill was then passed. The eleven o'clock time was on the books only for about one hour.

"The next weekend, Albert came down to the island. Walter came up from the farm, and Tom also came over. We were sitting on the porch, and Albert told the other two boys about our experience in Columbia. Tom said that he had always heard the legislature was a crazy place and that he now believed it. Albert said money seemed to be a big problem for the members of the legislature. Walter said he had heard about a bar near the Capitol on Main Street where all the money changed hands. Albert said he would like to sit in that bar for a while.

"I said, 'You are getting very interested in politics.' He said yes and that he was thinking about becoming a politician and trying to give the people a better government. I said that was a noble ambition. He then asked me, 'Why don't you join me? We would make a great team.' I replied, 'I guess we could help a lot of people if we improved the government.' I asked Walter if he would join Albert. He said he would not. He was a farm boy, and he intended to remain a farmer. Albert asked Tom and me if we would join him. Tom said no as he was interested in medicine. He thought he could help a lot of people with a career in medicine. I said, 'Albert, I will join you.'"

Dylan said, "So that is how it all began. You and Albert were out to improve governments. We all sure benefited from your careers. You both are world famous today."

I said, "Yes, that is how it began. I talked with my mom and dad that night, and they said it was up to me, but they agreed the government needed improvement. Dad said that the government was a waste and that the government efficiency should be changed. Mom said, 'That was spoken like the true achiever you are. Your son will have his hands full and many a plate full in order to be the great achiever you are.' I said, 'Grandpa and Dad have had a great impact on my life. I like to achieve, and I am proud of accomplishments.' Mom said, 'You will have to learn how to love, not like achievements.'

"I went to Greenville the next weekend. Albert and I talked a lot about a career in politics and the efforts we could make to improve the government. I said that I thought the legislature was too large an organization to be effective. Albert agreed and said there were too many governments. I thought about that and realized he was right. I began to count the governments around the island, and I was surprised by how many there were for the number of people in the Charleston area. Charleston County's population was largely located in the Charleston area, but the county area covered a large area of the South Carolina coast."

Dylan said, "Are you telling me you and Albert were thinking about governments like that when you were still in high school?"

I said, "Yes, we had many discussions about governments before we were out of high school. We were also talking about decision-making and how it could be improved."

Dylan said, "Now I am really impressed."

"Albert and I spent a lot of time on the computer, working with our search engines. He worked more on the number of governments, and I worked more on decision-making. When I had learned a little about decision-making, I went to Mr. Jarvis and asked him about it. He said his math background made him more of the kind of a person who wanted to digitalize all data and use math to make decisions. He showed me the matrix system for deciding on a problem where there are multiple choices and multiuse. He said the defense department often used that system for making their decisions.

"He said if I was interested in decision-making, I should take every logic course offered in college. He said, 'You have a great math background. Your mom has been a great help to you.' I thanked him and told him I would take every course in logic I could get. I went home and looked up logic on the search engine and began to learn more about logic.

"The high-school work, having fun learning with Albert, and DeMolay kept my plate full. The chapter had so much fun at the dance. Several of the members wanted one every week. As I told you, we settled on one a month, and that took time. I enjoyed my courses during my last year of high school. I spent a lot of time on the search engine, looking up additional information about the subjects. I found a lot of quotations by famous people and filed them. I used many of them in answer to questions in class and on exams. I became known as the quotation kid.

"Albert and I talked every chance we got. We would share information about everything we had learned since our last meeting. We decided to go to the University of South Carolina and room together. We both graduated from high school at the top of our class. We were admitted to the university. Our dads got involved, and they found us a house in Shannon near the five-point area. They thought it was a good investment. We lived there longer than they thought we would. We went to law school after we finished college.

It turned out the house was a good investment. They bought when prices were down and sold when prices were high. They more than doubled their money over the about eight-year period we lived in the house. Mom and Mrs. Martin spent time furnishing the house. Mom got us a lady who came in twice a week and cleaned the house. We had a laundry room, but Albert and I only washed the things we had to wash. We took some to the laundry and cleaners and the other things home. We used the kitchen about as often as we used the laundry room. There were a lot of good places to eat near the house. We both had cars, and it was a short drive to the university. Like most colleges and universities, the students at Carolina spent a lot of time looking for parking spaces.

"Albert decided to major in Pre-Law. I decided to major in History and minor in English. Mom got me math books and gave me math assignments. She always purchased two books—one for me, and one she kept at home. She made sure I understood everything she assigned me. I most likely had a better math education than most of the Math majors. Mom also kept me up on Chemistry and Physics. Now you know what she wanted me to major in while I was in college.

"The Capitol was right across the street from the university, and Albert and I spent a lot of time watching the legislature and talking with members. Our moms had set the house up so we could study individually or together. We both had our desktop computers and laptop computers. We did not want for anything while we were in college. I guess you think we were a couple of spoiled brats."

Dylan said, "No, I think you both were lucky enough to have had loving parents. I have a question for you. Did you have a favorite professor at Carolina?"

I said, "Yes, that is an easy one. It was Doctor Steadley. He was about medium high, a little on the chubby side, and was bald-headed. The bald-headed part was the part I liked. When you asked him a question, he would rub his bald head for a few times. He would then ask you a question. If you did not know the answer, he would rub his head again and then he would ask you another question. He repeated this process until you got the question right. He would build from there until your question was answered. He would build the background you need to answer and understand the answer."

Dylan asked, "Did you have a professor you did not like?"

I said, "That is even easier. I had Doctor Wideman. He seemed to start in the middle of everything and work toward both ends. His blackboard was always full. He never erased the board or cleaned it. He would walk to the nearest blackboard, erase a small place with the side of his fist and then write in the space. If you were taking notes and missed where he was writing, when you looked up, you could not find where he had written. We offered to clean the blackboards, but he said it was a waste of time. I walked out of every class totally confused. It was always a wild guess what he was going to ask in the next quiz, and the final was like nothing I had ever seen. I got a grade of B, but not from what I learned in his classes. Doctor Steadley helped me often, and Mom was also a big help. I burned the book for that class in the backyard of the house.

"I followed Mr. Jarvis's advice and took three courses in logic. They sure came in handy during my career. Both Albert and I joined the debate team. There was a lot of fun. When we were at the house, we would debate each other on a particular subject. I continued my search engine work for each subject. I also looked up quotations on the subject matter. I saved those quotations in my file cabinet. When I included a quote in a test answer, it was generally received well by the professor."

Dylan said, "What did you do for fun while you were in college?"

I said, "I remembered what my dad said about all the fun he had on Folly beach, so I went there often. Several of the students at the university liked to go to Folly, so we rented cabins for the weekends. They still had a pavilion with a jukebox and lots of boys and girls hanging out there. We had very good dances at Carolina. I often had Louise come up for a dance, and we put on quite a show."

Dylan said, "Did you have another girlfriend other than Louise?"

I said, "I dated several girls while I was there. Some were Carolina students and some were from Columbia College. Columbia College was an all-girls school in Eau Claire, a suburb of Columbia.

"For the most part, Columbia is not a good-time city. We joked about going down on Main Street and watched, for excitement, the traffic signals change."

Dylan said, "That is a good one. I do not think I have ever seen Carolina listed as a party school."

I said, "Now you know why." We both had a good laugh.

"Albert and I both graduated with honors and were admitted into the Carolina Law School. Neither of us enjoyed the Law School experience. We learned about everything except what we were interested in. We were interested in politics and government. We had a couple of government classes, but they only dealt with the current government. We had a class on Constitutional Law, but we had read more and studied the Constitution and the fathers of the nation, so we knew more than we were taught.

"But Law School did change one thing. While I was in Law School, I met Jo Anne. During the summer between my first and second year, I went to a Youth Conference at Columbia

College. Jo Anne and a group of girls from St. George, South Carolina, were there. We had a great time with the girls, and I fell in love with Jo Anne the moment I saw her. She was three years younger than me and was a student at Converse College. This was another all-girls college. So that was the beginning of my ROTC career."

Dylan said, "I did not know you were in the ROTC program or any military program."

I said, "At Carolina, ROTC does not stand for Reserve Officer Training Corps. It stands for Run Over To Converse."

Dylan said, "You got me on that one." We had another good laugh.

Then I said, "During my second and third year of Law School, I spent a lot of time running over to Converse. I had Jo Anne come down to Columbia for the dances. During the summer between my second and third year, both Albert and I spent a lot of time at Edisto Beach. The girls from St. George all went to Edisto Beach. They had a bowling alley and a dance floor in a big building owned by a local family. Albert met Mary Brown, a good friend of Jo Anne, from St George. They became a couple. We had a great summer. They were building a new subdivision on Edisto Beach, and it had a good golf course. The subdivision had a Fairfield Inn, a resort that ran the golf course. This reminded Dad about the beginning of Wild Dunes, and he bought a house there. He figured it would be a good investment, and he traveled in and around Edisto Island and Edisto Beach. We used that house a lot. Dylan, maybe I should catch you up on Dad's pharmacy business. He opened one store after another all along the South Carolina coast and inland to Highway 17. He sold or closed the stores that were not doing well. He then began to open stores near

Interstate Highway 75. The stores all serviced the hospitals and the health-care homes in their area. This provided a large prescription business for the distribution center, and it grew like a wild weed. About the time I graduated from Law School, he had started opening stores up Interstate Highway 20 between Charleston and Columbia. Jo Anne's dad had a pharmacy in St George that did business with Dad's company. He and Dad were already good friends before I had met his daughter. Dad advised him to open stores in Branchville and Bamberg. He did, and they were a great success.

"Two weeks after I finished Law School, I went to St George and asked Jo Anne to go for a walk with me. We walked the short distance from her house to the County Court House. There was a very large old oak tree on the grounds of the Court House. It had those long branches that almost touched the ground. I sat Jo Anne on one of the branches and got down on one knee. I took a ring box from my pocket and opened it so she could see the ring I had bought. I then said, 'I do not deserve a beautiful and perfect girl like you for a wife, but I love you and want you for my wife.' She said, 'That is a long speech, but yes, I love you and have loved you since the first day I saw you. I will be happy to be your wife.' She then added, 'How is that for a long speech?' We both laughed before I enjoyed that long kiss."

Dylan said, "Well, after that I think we had better call it a day. Can we meet at the library next Wednesday in the late morning, say ten o'clock?"

I said, "That will be fine." We turned off the recorders and put them away. Dylan packed his briefcase, and we said our good-byes. The Secret Service man showed him out. Jo Anne and I had a great dinner at Marshall's. There were several

Island Boys there, and we looked at the old pictures around the walls and talked about the good times we had growing up. There was one picture of a camping trip we had taken, and Donnie was sitting on a tree with the rest of us looking up at him. There was one of the members of our basketball team in the old Sullivan's Island gym. After dinner, Jo Anne and I took a long ride. The Secret Service man was driving, and there was another one seated next to him in the front of the SUV. We asked for a ride around the Battery in Charleston. He took us down King to South Battery and to the end of the street. He turned and gave us a ride all the way around the Battery. We went up East Bay to Broad Street and then to Meeting Street on our way back to the bridge. When we got home, Jo Anne said that that was a nice ride and that she enjoyed it. I said that I enjoyed it too, but that if we would have stopped at that ice-cream store on Broad Street, I would have liked it better. She said, 'Not after that big meal at Marshall's.'

I enjoyed the ride to Columbia for my meeting with Dylan. Jo Anne and I had a nice breakfast, and she said she was going to St. George for a visit while I was in Columbia. When Dylan and I were together, I told him about our dinner at Marshall's and the pictures on the wall. I told him how much we enjoyed our ride around the Battery in Charleston. I said to him, "I always enjoy the ride around the Battery and a look at the park. There is a statue of William Jasper in the park. I first learned of Jasper's heroism at an early age. The National Park guides at Fort Moultrie tell the story. I read about him later in my life. Like many of our military heroes, he was killed when he was only twenty-nine. He was killed when the South Carolina militia attempted to take Savanna back from the British. When he was at Fort Sullivan as Fort Moultrie was called at the time of the Revolutionary War, he was a sergeant in the 2nd South Carolina Regiment. Jasper distinguished himself in the defense of Fort Sullivan on June 28, 1776. When a shell from a British warship shot away the flagstaff, he recovered the South Carolina flag. He stood on top of the Fort and waved the flag. When a new staff was ready, he installed the flag. His heroism inspired the troops, and they fought on until their victory. To honor his bravery, Governor Rutledge gave Jasper his sword."

Dylan said, "You do love history, don't you?"

I replied, "Growing up on the island and with the nearness of Charleston, most of the kids grow up with a love of history. I know that is why I majored in history when I was in college. As you know, Charleston is known as the historic city. That is enough of my history talk. It is time to get back to my life story. I had just told you about how I proposed to Jo Anne. We were married at the Methodist Church on Highway 15, just south of downtown St. George. I remember looking around the church during the ceremony, and all the Island Boys were sitting next to their St. George girlfriends. The reception was a big success, and Dad and Mom spent a lot of time talking with Jo Anne's parents. Jo Anne and I mingled among the Island Boys. There was a lot of tingling of the glasses, and Jo Anne and I enjoyed every kiss. We then left for our honeymoon. We went to Grove Park Inn in Ashville, North Carolina. Jo Anne and I both like to golf, and there are a lot of places to sightsee in Ashville. We returned to the island and lived with Mom and Dad for a time.

"My first elected office was to the Sullivan's Island city council. That job was very uneventful. Marshall's family pretty much controlled the jobs on the island. His dad was a local magistrate, and his brother was chief of the fire and police department. Albert had a much better job. He was elected to the Greenville City Council and was appointed to head the financial committee. He came down for a visit, and we discussed politics. He suggested that I move into Charleston and run for the City Council. After Albert left, Jo Anne and I were sitting on the porch with Mom and Dad, and I asked about Jo Anne and me moving into Charleston so I could run for office. Jo Anne said she could get a teaching job in the city school system. That sounded good to me. Dad said that everybody has to start somewhere and that a Charleston City Council job would be a good starting place. Mom said she did not know how she would like the empty nest. We found a nice apartment on the west Ashley River side of the city. It was not too far from the Battery and the downtown. It was very near Colonial Lake, and Jo Anne enjoyed a walk from the house and around the lake.

"I had resigned from the Sullivan's Island City Council. I got a job with a Law Firm on Broad Street. We joined every club that would have us. Jo Anne got a teaching job at Mitchell Grammar School. We tried to meet as many citizens of Charleston that we could. We had parties at the Fort Sumter apartment's activities room. We could rent it reasonably cheap. I remembered the success of our dance programs while I was in DeMolay, so we rented a few church activities halls and had dances. Jo Anne had gotten to dance the way Louise and I did when I was in high school and college. It took two years before there was a council election. One member was retiring, and all the rest were running for reelection. It did not look promising. Albert suggested I get a good campaign manager. I talked to several representatives at the State and Federal level. Several of them suggested Raymond Maul, a local boy about my age, who worked for the Post-Courier. He was an excellent writer and covered government and politics. I went to the library and read several of his articles and liked what I read. I called him and asked if he would manage my campaign. He said, 'I have managed a few campaigns for representatives, but not one for city council. It would be a new experience, and I would enjoy doing the job.' We discussed finance, and I told him his salary was not a problem and that we could discuss a campaign budget. He was on TV that night with a local commentator singing my praise. He got the newspaper to indorse me. I called those who had recommended him and thanked them and told them what a good job he was doing. Jo Anne and I kept up our efforts and had several parties and dances. I was invited to speak at service events. We had TV appearances and radio coverage. Bubs Cohen, known as the Mole, owned a local TV station and was a good friend. He lived in Mt Pleasant near the island. He was very helpful during the campaign. The election night came. We had rented a hall in a local hotel. Albert and his wife Mary were there. My mom and dad were there too. Raymond had everything set up with good TV and news coverage. I sure hoped to win as it might be embarrassing if I lost. It took almost a count of all the ballots, but I won. It was a small margin, but enough to win. Jo Anne said it best. She said that I was not that well known West of the Ashley, but I did well there. She thought my dad's business and the stores helped.

"That win and my first council meeting where I was welcomed by all the council members who had been elected several times made me think my political career was off to a good start. The win was not the only good news. Jo Anne told Mom, Dad, and me that she was pregnant. Now that was good news. Mom was so happy thinking about having a baby around again. I was appointed to the Financial Committee, and Albert was a big help. I was also appointed to the Hospitality and Tourism Committee. The Hospitality and Tourism Committee was a very important committee for the economy of Charleston. I served on the City Council for three terms. That was longer than it took Jo Anne to give us our first baby boy. We named him Thomas David and called him Dave. The Charleston County Council was going to have two opening at the time of its next election. I called Raymond and asked what he thought about me running for County Council. He said he thought I had a good chance to win. I had done a good job for the city and the county, serving on the Hospitality and Tourism Committee. I filed to run, and we were off with a new campaign. I had a lot of support from the East Cooper and the Island north of the city of Charleston. My childhood friends worked hard for me in those areas. Raymond set up a campaign office in every area. He staffed them with good people who knew how to get out the vote. We had a ballroom in a downtown hotel for the election night. The crowd was there. It did not take as long as it did in my first election before we knew I had won. Would you believe it? Jo Anne announced she was pregnant right after the election. She delivered her second boy. This one we named Donald and called him Don. We had the "d" going Dave and Don. The County Council work was stimulating. I was appointed to the Finance Committee again and also to the Hospitality and Tourism Committee. Albert had been elected to the Greenville County Council the year before I was elected to the Charleston County Council. He had been a big supporter and gave several speeches supporting me. He pointed out how he and I had been interested in government since high school and had worked together in college and law school to get a good background for a career in politics and government administration. He said we had several ideas that would reduce government cost. We did have those ideas, and we had discussed merger of city and county government. That would reduce the government overhead cost. We both began to work trying to merge the governments. But we were unsuccessful. We got support, but not enough. After a short time on the County Council, we both began to plan for a run for the South Carolina House of Representatives."

Dylan said, "I think I have enough. The recorder is full."

I said, "That is good with me. Can you come and stay a few days at the beach and bring Marlene? She and Jo Anne can have fun while we are busy."

He said, "That sounds good, and we get a lot of work done when we are together." We said our good-byes, and the Secret Service man showed Dylan to his car.

After telephone agreement, we decided he should arrive on Friday and that we could have some fun on the weekend as well as work. He liked golf, and we decided to go to Wild Dunes, and Jo Anne and Marlene could meet us there for dinner on Saturday. I planned to take Dylan to Charleston and for a drive around the Battery. He would enjoy all the historic sites. We could have dinner in Charleston on Friday night. I had my staff set up the golf, the trip to Charleston, and the two dinners. Dylan arrived with Marlene at about ten o'clock. They joined Jo Anne and me on the porch. I discussed the weekend plans with Dylan, and Jo Anne told Marlene about her plans for the two. They said they hoped they were not going to be a burden. Jo Anne and I assured them that they were not a burden but that we enjoyed their company and were happy for the chance to go to the places we planned to take them. It was a very warm day, and both Jo Anne and Marlene loved to swim. Jo Anne took Marlene to Wild Dunes for a swim in the ocean and in the pool. Dylan and I got down to work before we joined them on the pier at Wild Dunes for lunch.

We set up our recorders, and Dylan took out his yellow page pad. I said, "With the help of a lot of people, Albert and I were both elected to the House of Representatives. Jo Anne and I moved back to our house on the island. I wanted Dave and Don to enjoy growing up on the island like I had. Mom and Dad were only two doors down the street. That made it easy for Jo Anne to continue to teach. She got a job in Mt. Pleasant. I wondered why she kept working since we had more than an adequate income. She said she liked the medical insurance coverage and the retirement benefits. I said, 'They are good, but with what I am making, and my two trust funds, we do not have to worry about health insurance or retirement.' She said, 'Your mother taught school until she retired. So ask her why I want to continue to teach.' That shut me up. The legislative experience was good for Albert and me. We were not really rookies because we had spent so much time there while we were in college and law school. We were well aware of the organization and the workings of both the House and the Senate. We went right to work, trying to get cities to merge with county governments and county governments to merge with other nearby county governments. We pointed out the reduction in the cost of government and the tax dollar savings. We talked and spoke about other governments where the city and county governments were one. We pointed out the population size of counties in the State and the Nation. We talked a lot about California and the population and the number of counties. We pointed out the other states with too many county and city government. Once again, we got support and media coverage but not enough. I decided to point out that Nebraska had only one legislature body, a Senate. But Albert warned about getting ahead of the fight. We had enough on our plate trying to reduce the city and county governments. We were determined to have an effect on excessive government. We failed on every bill that we filed in an attempt to have State organization of local governments. We had a conference at Wild Dunes with a well-run golf tournament. We paid for the hotel rooms and the meals for those we invited. We spoke and had supports who spoke at the meeting. There was good agreement that money could be saved by reducing unneeded government. We filled another bill, and it was defeated. But this time, we had a lot more support. The upper part of the state seemed to be more receptive than the low country. Albert and I planned a porch secession. He would invite important leaders from Greenville and Spartanburg. There were city leaders and county leaders. After a lot of talk by Albert and me about being on the financial committee and seeing the excess spending, there was support for merger. Albert and I agreed that this was the way to go. Getting small groups together worked much better. The size of the state legislature was too large to get much done. Dylan, it is time we headed to Wild Dunes to meet the ladies for lunch." Dylan cut of the record, and I follow his move. He put the yellow pad in his briefcase. I then said, "We can leave everything right here. With the security this house has, nothing will disappear." Dylan laughed. We walked to the SUV and the security guards near the side steps from the porch.

Dylan commented on the SUV and the security it provided. He said, "This is different than any other former president I have worked with. No one is paying any attention to us."

We met the ladies as planned and had lunch at the end of the pier. The pier extended from the hotel to the beach. There were houses along each side of the pier. At the end of the pier, there was a cross pier with a pool on each side. The snack shop was always very good, and to my great enjoyment, there was an ice-cream shop. We each ordered a salad, and they were all very good. Both Jo Anne and Marlene commented on the excellent dressing that was served with the salad. A Secret Service guy, who was also named Paul, brought us ice cream sundaes from the ice-cream shop. They had driven the SUV out to the end of the pier. We were ready for our trip into Charleston. We took a slow ride through old Mt Pleasant, and I told them some of the history and the place names like Hungry Neck. As we approached the bridge across the Cooper River, Jo Anne said that Dylan and Marlene were in for a history tour. She said that I was an excellent guide and that I had knowledge of the history. She said that I often corrected the tour guides when we took guests on tours. I have to admit I do that. I asked the driver to take us down King Street to the Battery Park. I pointed out several points of interest as we passed down King Street. We had driven North on Meeting Street to Moultrie Street and turned down King Street. I pointed out Claire Rasher's Mormon Church to Dylan. That got me a good poke in the ribs from Jo Anne. When we were near Calhoun Street, I pointed out Calhoun's Statue high above the park. I told an old Charleston joke when I said that every time he heard thunder or saw lightning, he climbed down. That resulted in another poke in the ribs. I asked the driver to turn left onto Calhoun Street so they could get a better look at the statue. I pointed out the Knights of Columbus Hall across from the statue. The driver had stopped to give them a good look at the statue. I asked him to turn left at Meeting Street and circle the old Citadel. They got a good look at the old college buildings. I said that the early Citadel classes were for the young men from the plantations. There were so many slaves that there was fear of a revolt, so South Carolina formed a military unit in Charleston and in Columbia. They did not want the young men just sitting around, so they formed a college. The one in Charleston was called the Citadel and the one in Columbia was called the Arsenal. We turned left back onto King Street and made our way across Broad Street with a few comments from me. We reached South Battery Street and then turned left. The security driver knew I liked to stop at Sargent Jasper's statue. I pointed out the statue and reminded Dylan of his story. I talked more about the park and the part the White Point Gardens played in the protection of Charleston and the attack on Fort Sumter. I said that the Indians had advised the white settlers to move from their original landing three miles up the Ashley River to White Point Gardens. The Indians said the disease would be less. There was a good breeze most of the time and fewer musketeers. We turned and rode down the Battery to the north end and turned around and rode back to high Battery. We got out, and I pointed out the gun emplacements for the attacks on Fort Sumter, including Morris Island and Sullivan's Island. Dylan said they had it pretty much surrounded except for the seaside. I said that was true and that the guns on Sullivan's Island and Morris Island could prevent ships coming in from the sea. I pointed out that when Lincoln tried to resupply and add troops to the Fort, the Citadel Cadets housed on Castle Pinckney fired on the ships and returned to the ocean. They went onto supply forts along the Gulf shore. We then rode on up East Bay Street, and I pointed out the building that had

Black Beard as a prisoner in the basement. I also pointed out Rainbow Roe and the area of Charleston that was included in the Opera Porgy and Bess. I told them there was a walk that extended to Church through the area. We headed on up East Bay with my comments along the way until we reached the bridge back to Mt Pleasant and onto Sullivan's Island.

Dylan said, "I sure enjoyed that ride."

Marlene said, "I am not much of a history student, but it was good to see and hear about the attacks on Fort Sumter. I had heard about the start of the war."

Dylan said, "You and I are going to have to spend some time in Charleston. I love the history."

I said, "I thought you would, and we have not touched the surface yet. There are a lot of interesting historic places in Charleston. Especially, I want to show you the Citadel Library where they have murals of the battles the cadets fought."

Dylan said, "I hate to wait, but we have work to do. I think we are getting older every day." That brought a laugh from all of us, including the Secret Service men in the front seat.

When Dylan and I were seated on the porch, we got our recorders out and put them in their usual place. Dylan obtained his yellow pad. I said, "Albert and I decided it was time for a long secession on the porch. Jo Anne and I invited Albert and Mary to visit us at the beach for the weekend. Since Jo Anne and Mary were old friends from St George, they had a lot to do. That left Albert and me to our work. In the first secession on Friday afternoon, we decided to put together a budget and organization plan for Greenville County, if the county and the city merged. Albert had a lot of experience with the budget. We worked for about three hours on the budget, but we were hitting a dead end. I went into my office and retrieved a state highway map of the county that showed every building and every street or road. It was a large map. I laid it out on the coffee table and put weights at the corners. This was a big help. We found two areas that were underserved with both police protection and fire protection. It would have taken too long for fire trucks to reach the areas. We relocated two fire stations and improved the area service. We increased the police budget so they could hire additional officers to cover the areas. We reduced the County Council Budget and the overhead for the Council by reducing the number of Council members. We eliminated the City Council expense. We reduced the number of school boards and just had one for the entire county area. We divided the saved money so that each school had an increase in their budget. This would increase the teacher pay. With all our changes, we saved about eight hundred thousand dollars and improved services. At the end of the weekend, we were very happy with our product and could not wait to show it to the City and County Council. Raymond Maul showed up for a talk with me. We showed him the results of our work. He was very impressed and said he would write an article on our work for the paper. He said he would send a copy to the *Greenville News*. He knew a member of their staff that would eat that work up. We asked for time to show the plans to the city and county leader first. He agreed and asked that we let him know when he could release the article.

"We used our usual invitation to Wild Dunes for a weekend to get the leaders down. We included the usual golf tournament. Everyone accepted our invitation. We had obtained more of the Greenville County maps from the State and had them posted around the room at Wild Dunes we would use for our meeting. We had copies of the budget and the savings. We had highlighted the two underserved areas on the map. We showed the position of the two new fire stations and provided the cost for the change. We included the decrease in the fire insurance cost for each of the homes and businesses in the areas. The leaders were very impressed with our work and said they would support the changes. That was music to Albert and my ears. They said it would take the approval of the voters on a referendum. They said they would see to it that it was on the next ballot. We said we would start a campaign to inform the voters. They thought the voter education was a good idea.

Albert knew a lot of people in Greenville, and he set up a staff office for us in the downtown area. We paid Raymond to run the office. The office members worked at getting Albert and me speech times at various organizations. Raymond saw to it we got a lot of media coverage at each speech. The media was impressed with the savings and the better serves. We pointed out that there were a lot of much larger population areas that had a budget and organization similar to that proposed for Greenville. We found the Greenville population to be more receptive to change than the population of the low country. The referendum passed on the first ballot. The City Council voted to merge with the county, and the County Council voted to accept the city. The borders were moved to the county line. The County Council voted to accept our budget and the suggested changes in organization. The contracts for the two new fire stations were approved. We received telephone calls, e-mails, and letters from citizens, thanking us for our help with government problems. Albert gave me a great big hug that I returned. He said, 'Paul, we always knew we could improve government, and we have had our first success.' I said, 'We both need to thank our Civics Class teachers for that field trip to the South Carolina legislature.' Albert said, 'I will call mine tomorrow.' I said, 'I will do the same.' I did, and we had an enjoyable long talk.

"Something happened that we had not anticipated. The economy of Greenville County improved. The business had increased in sales and profits, and new businesses moved into the county. I was contacted by a leader from Spartanburg County. He wanted to come down and have a conversation with me. I agreed, and we met at the house. We went to the porch, and Jo Anne brought drinks and snacks. He said, 'This is very enjoyable. I have never had a meeting in better surroundings. The ocean and the sky are beautiful, and for South Carolina, the breeze sure helps the temperature.' I said, 'We have a lot of meetings here for those reasons.' He said, 'I am here to ask you to do for Spartanburg County what you have done for Greenville County.' I said, 'I would love to work with him toward getting a merger between the city and the county. I had a lot of help for Albert on the Greenville project.' He asked, 'Do you think you could get Albert to help us?' I said, 'Yes. Albert is as interested in improving governments as I am. Give us about two weeks, and we can have a meeting of the city and county leaders at Wild Dunes and present an organizational plan and a budget. You will see the savings.' He said, 'I will get back to Spartanburg and start getting the right people here in two weeks.' I said, 'Have them arrive at Wild Dunes on Friday after twelve, the check-in time. We will cover the cost for the people who attend.' He said, 'That is very generous of you.' I said, 'We have a staff that can help us arrange everything.' He then left with a big smile on his face. That is always good to see. Albert and I worked for the next two weeks."

Dylan said, "I think it is time for a break. I have never worked with a former president who wants to work as hard as you do. You do it with very little effort. That is good to see."

I said, "I am looking for the completed product. I take great pride in well-done, completed products."

Dylan said, "Once an achievement-motivated guy, always an achievement-motivated guy." We cut off the recorders, and Dylan placed his in his briefcase with the yellow pad. I left mine on the coffee table. Dylan joined Marlene and Jo Anne at the side of the porch. They talked for a while and then came over to where I was listening to my record replay what we had talked about.

I said to Dylan, "We covered a lot of ground today. Having you and Marlene here is going to work out well. We should get a lot done."

Dylan replied, "Yes, but remember, I have to go over all this again and again before the biography is finished. I will be working late into the night on all that we covered today."

I said, "Use my study. It is quiet and well equipped."

Dylan said, "Thanks, I will. I do not want to keep Marlene awake." We decided to go to the hotel at Wild Dunes to their dining room for dinner. We had an excellent seafood dinner with excellent wine. I was glad the security men would be driving home. I must admit that as much as I hated the symbols of power, it was good to have a driver. I could enjoy my drinks when we went out for dinner.

Elly and Julia were at the dining room. We invited them over to join us. They arrived just behind us. Elly and Julia enjoyed meeting Dylan and Marlene. Jo Anne told Julia how much fun they were having and invited Julia to join them. She said that she would enjoy going in to Charleston with them.

Elly said, "Dylan, I think Paul is the only Island Boy who has ever had a biography done. Maybe you should think about doing an Island Boy biography."

Dylan said, "It is funny you mention that. Since I met Paul, and the Island Boys that I have met, I have been thinking about writing about Island Boys." That brought a good laugh. Dylan continued, "I am not kidding. I am giving that a lot of thought. In fact, I have a lot of notes on my yellow pad right now."

I said, "Jo Anne, I think we will have to have an Island Boy party on the porch and let Dylan meet more Island Boys."

She said, "That is a great idea, and I will get to work on the party. We will have to arrange for a return visit by Marlene and Dylan, and I will set the thing in motion."

Elly said, "When you attend a party arranged by Jo Anne, you are in for a great treat."

Julia said, "I can say Amen to that." We all walked out together and said our good-byes. The Secret Service had our SUV at the door. The rows of seats in the back of the SUV were necessary for the four of us. There was a guard at the front of the car and one in the back.

I looked at Dylan and said, "I will never get used to the power symbols." Dylan and Jo Anne laughed, but Marlene and the Secret Services guys missed the joke.

Dylan said, "I never know what SUV I am riding in. The colors change so often."

When we got back to the house, Donnie and Tonya were there. Donnie was dropping off a lot of fish, shrimp, and crabs he had caught on a fishing trip that day. He had always brought us part of his catch. He started that shortly after Jo Anne and I moved back from Chicago. Donnie had married well. Tonya was about Donnie's height. She had a good figure and an olive complexion. She had long black hair with a little wave to it. Her eyes were brown and larger than most girls.' They had met while Donnie was on vacation in Mexico. When he got back, he told me he could not wait to get her to the island. They were married south of San Diego in Mexico. It was a lovely wedding. He married shortly after Jo Anne and I were married.

Dylan and I were on the porch early the next morning. Jo Anne and Marlene joined us and the house servants, and the security people served us breakfast. Jo Anne said, 'Paul, get that look off your face.' Dylan and Marlene laughed. I guess Dylan had told her how I hate the symbols of power.

Dylan said, "I told Marlene how you hated 'Hail to the Chief' when you were president. I also told her that it was a motivation thing."

Marlene said, "I know exactly how you feel. I had a friend when I was in school, who had to be dressed the very best of anyone in class. She had to have the most beautiful dress at the dances. She would not ride home with her mother because she did not like the looks of her car. She would only ride with her dad in his big Lincoln. She wanted to run everything in school and everywhere else, but she did not have the brains to run water."

I said, "That is a typical power-motivated person. They want power for the sake of power, but they do not know what to do with it."

Jo Anne said, "And Paul hates a person who cannot get things done."

I said, "If you put your mind to it, you can get it done, but when you put your mind to wanting symbols of power, you cannot get things done." We finished breakfast, and the girls went off to meet Julia and to head to Charleston for shopping.

They planned lunch in Charleston, so Dylan and I were on our own.

I started my recorder and so did Dylan. I said, "It turned out the Spartanburg deal was different than Greenville. There were no underserved areas. In fact, all areas were well served. The organization of the city and the county were excellent. The only thing was that there was too much overhead spending. We just had to merge the City and Count organizations. We were able to reduce the excessive spending on education overhead. We suggested one school superintendent and one board of education. We were able to organize the city and county police and get good coverage of all areas and reduce overhead spending on management of the single department. We did the same thing with the two fire departments. When we got our management plan together for the new single county government, we had saved just over one million dollars. When the leaders arrived at Wild Dunes, we presented our plan. There was one suggestion from a leader that Albert and I agreed with. It added about one hundred thousand dollars to the savings. The savings were larger than the savings in Greenville because Spartanburg had been giving good service but had a much larger overhead cost in their budget. When we eliminated the city government and reduced the number of members on the County Council, we made big savings. The merger of operations further reduced cost. We told them we would help sell the plan and with the education of the voters. They said they were behind us 100 percent. After they left, we called Raymond and said we were back at it. But this time, it was Spartanburg. He said he had wondered how long it would take them to wake up with the success in Greenville. He went to work on an office in Spartanburg with a staff that worked to turn out the vote. Albert and I made a lot of speeches around the city and county. The media was with us. In fact, Raymond had the media for the entire State behind us. I was surprised at what I heard on the Charleston media about what was going on in the upper part of the State and about the job Albert and I were doing. They said Albert had been a great representative for his part of the State and that my contributions to improving government were remarkable. This was not hurting our reputations around the State, and our names were becoming well known. This would be a great help when we ran for the Federal House of Representatives. The Spartanburg referendum passed on the first vote. The City and County Councils met together in order to adopt our plan. It passed on the first vote, and plans were put in place to implement the plan. We had Albert and Mary down for the weekend. Albert and I shared a big hug to celebrate the new victory. We went to Marshall's for a great dinner. The food was excellent, and the wine he had chosen was perfect. Albert said, 'This is the way to live.'

"The next day, Albert and I were sitting on the porch. Jo Anne and Mary were with other Island Boy wives at a ladies golf tournament. I said, 'I sure wish South Carolina would consider a unicameral legislature.' Albert said, 'Yes, that would put us out of a job, and we could live like this every day.' I said, 'You know the governments over the whole country are completely a mess. They are not organized properly. A lot of taxpayers' money is spent on unnecessary overhead costs. I had just looked at the data for Nebraska. They have always had a unicameral legislature. Their population is about 1.8 million, and they have ninety-three county governments. I would think that a state that was smart enough to have a unicameral legislature would know enough to reduce the number of county governments, especially since the population is located in and around a couple of cities. The state of South Carolina has a bicameral legislature. The population is about 4.5 million people, and there are about half the number of county governments. There were forty six counties. We have just seen the savings when Greenville and Spartanburg merged the city and county governments. We have areas of the state with low populations where county governments should be merged. California has a population of over thirty-eight million, but there are only fifty-five counties. That is fewer counties than North Dakota. With a population of less than seven hundred thousand, North Dakota has fifty-eight counties. It is easy to see that little thought has been given to government organization. This has resulted in a waste of tax dollars. You know how I hate inefficiency. Albert said, 'If we can get the voters of South Carolina to accept a unicameral legislature, we may be out of a job, but we will not be out of work. To set things straight, we have got a large platter for a plate, and the food is falling off the sides.'

"After the success in Greenville and Spartanburg, we arrived back in Columbia to our next legislative secession with a lot of praise and thanks. We were starting to get converts to the task. That made Albert and me very happy. I said, 'Well, Albert, it looks like we are making headway toward reducing the size of our platter to a plate.' He laughed and said, 'It sure makes you feel good.' I said, 'We have learned to work with smaller groups, and we have the perfect place to get them together.' He said, 'That type of arrangement worked with Greenville and Spartanburg.' I said that I would like to work on Charleston. They really needed to merge all the small towns in the county with the city into one government. I said, 'Charleston is too complicated to take on next. Let's work with Richland and Lexington county governments. We could work with Columbia and the Richland county governments. We could take on Lexington and the Lexington county government next.' Albert said, 'Most of Lexington County is just a suburb of Columbia. The two counties should merge. That is a large order, but I agree, and we should try it.' We began to visit offices and talk with leaders in both counties and the Columbia City government. We worked hard on these areas first. We knew we had to work with the smaller city and village governments, but they did not have the power that the large areas had. We got Raymond Maul to start working on the media in the Lexington and Richland county area. The articles and the TV coverage covered the success of the Greenville and Spartanburg merger. They pointed out the savings in tax dollars and the increase in economy in the Greenville area. They said the initial reports on the economy of Spartanburg were encouraging. We began to get calls from local leaders in Richland and Lexington counties. There were calls from two Columbia City Council leaders who said they would be interested in talking to us about government mergers. When we had enough calls to believe we could arrange a productive meeting at Wild Dunes, we invited several leaders down for a long weekend. We said it was at our expense. We included the Golf Tournament. The response was better than we had expected. We included a few people from the State Legislature. They were leaders and excellent budget committee members. We had the maps up and ready. We included a map of the City of Columbia and the suburbs. We had done our homework and had our budgets and organizational charts ready. I suggested we include two professors from University of South Carolina, School of Business. One was excellent on budgets and the other was good at organization charts. We talked to them about the project, and they were both interested in helping us. They said we were traveling the right road. Our invitation to Wild Dunes was accepted by all the leaders of the two counties and the cities involved. We found four small population areas in Lexington County that were underserved. There were two underserved areas in Richland County. One wide spot on a county highway in Richland County that had a name and a volunteer council did not have adequate fire protection, and they seldom saw a policeman. The largest savings were in the merger of the two County Councils. The merger of the City of Columbia with Richland County provided savings about 80 percent of the County merger. All the organization removals did not result in much in the way of savings. Education could benefit from a reduction in School Boards and School Superintendents. These funds could better be used to increase teacher salaries. With the combined tax base, it would be easier to have a balanced budget. The two professors from University of South Carolina were a great help with the budget structure and suggested changes in the method of tax collection. Raymond arranged to have them on several television shows and news programs.

"We held our breaths on election night. The referendum was defeated by a very small margin. The City was for the referendum, but the suburbs were not in favor, especially in Lexington. We were still fighting status quo and the love of the area where the people lived. They did not want change. We did not work hard enough on the fact that only the government would change. The voters did not realize that the zip codes, telephone numbers, addresses, and everything else except where they paid taxes and where the individuals who provided the services were located. The leaders decided we needed more education time and they would put the referendum on the ballot in two years.

"A lot of the smaller population county leaders began to call and write for assistants with mergers. Albert and I were getting tired of all the work and the possibility of failure. We thought we needed a few of our secession on where we were and where we were going. It was not going to be long before we were up for reelection to the House. We were wondering if we should run for the State Senate. We were very interested in the mergers of governments and the savings and improved efficiency. But we knew this was not the only thing that needed to be accomplished if we were going to have a method of government that was efficient and effective. I got an idea from a TV program I was watching one night when I could not sleep. We needed to use the Internet more, but we did not have the knowledge to set up interactive blogs and the time to be involved in Facebook or Twitter. I discussed this with Albert, and he thought I was onto something great. We decided to find us a couple of Geeks and see what could be done. We asked around and received a couple of names. One that I liked was Carolina Geek's Advertising. We invited the owner, and anyone he would like to bring along, for a porch secession with us. They were on time, and we went directly to the porch. Once we were settled in place, we got the comments that we had heard many times before. They helped each other describe the surrounds and said that this is a great place for a meeting.

"I asked about the business of Geek Advertising and how it worked. He told us they used the Internet to advertise products, events, and anything else. They said they used Web sites, blogs, Facebook, and Twitter. They said it was possible to buy a list of e-mail addresses. Many of these lists were put together to cover an area a subject or individuals with certain interest. They said they could make the blogs and the e-mails interactive so that they received feedback. The feedback provided data on how well they were reaching their audience. We told them what we were interested in doing. We wanted to educate voters. The owner said that if we knew what we wanted to teach, it would be a piece of cake. I told him Albert and I would write up a few White Papers, describing what we want the voters to know and send them to him. He said he would give us a quote on cost and time for results after he got the material.

"Jo Anne showed up right on time with the beer and the snacks. The owner said that this was the way to live. Albert asked if he realized that this type of life was why he had been my friend since high school. That brought a laugh even from Jo Anne. I said, 'We Island Boys adopted Albert a long time ago. We decided that he lived on the Island, but his house was just two hundred miles up Interstate 20.'

"The day after the meeting with the Carolina Geek's Advertising, Albert and I were back on the porch. I said I thought we should give them a chance, but I think I would like to have my own Geek organization. We could set up an office with cubicles and let them interact. We could feed them information and put them to work education the voters. Albert liked the idea but said we did not know whom to hire. I said we should go to the computer center at the University and talk to whoever is managing the place. Albert liked that idea.

"I called and made an appointment for the next day. Albert and I were on time for the appointment. We were shown into the manager's office. After a short get-acquainted discussion, we told him what we were interested in setting up. He said that he could give us some names, but he thought we would do better if we talked to a Professor Warren Anderson. He taught computer science and was the best geek he had ever met. We thanked him for his time and for the names he had given us, especially Professor Anderson. When we were outside, Albert laughed and said, 'That is just like us. We always seem to be in the right church but are always in the wrong pew.' I got on my cell phone and called the number given to us for Professor Anderson. A secretary answered the phone, and after I told her who I was, she put me on hold. Professor Anderson answered. I told him what we wanted to discuss and asked when he might have time to see Albert and me. He asked if three o'clock the next day would be right with us. I told him yes, and we were there the next day.

"Warren Anderson turned out to be a very friendly and likeable guy. He said he had heard great things about Albert and me. His home was originally Walterboro. He had spent time in the Spartanburg area. He liked the changes there and was saddened by the results in Columbia. We told him we would like to set up a Geek program at an office in Columbia. We said we thought we would like to have about four geeks working in the office. He liked the idea and said he had four graduates who had pretty good jobs, but they would be perfect. He said he could come down now and then and try to contribute. I asked if he would like to moonlight and work for us. We could make the time flexible. He said he would like that. He said he had always been interested in politics and government. That was why he knew us because we were interested in improving government. We asked about the budget for such an operation. He gave me a figure that was lower than I had thought, so I upped it and told him what he could make managing the operation for us. He was very pleased and said that he was happier about meeting us. He wanted to know how soon we wanted to get started. Albert answered and said, 'After we find a suitable place for the operation.' I said that we would be back in touch after a couple of days. He said he would be waiting. We said our good-byes and how much we enjoyed meeting him.

"The next day, I found the right place on Sumter Street near Elmwood Boulevard. Albert agreed, and we called Warren. He said he could come right down. We waited for his arrival in less time than I would have thought he could make the drive. He said his car was right behind his office building and that it did not take long to make the drive. He liked what he saw and said that with a little work, it would be fine. I got on the phone and called my dad's old friend, Al Kerry, and asked whom I could use in Columbia. He gave me a name and number off the top of his head. I knew he must have done business with this guy often.

"I called the number and got Dick Wallen. He said he could meet me the next day at eight-thirty or nine, whichever suited me. I suggested nine as I thought we might have a long night. Wallen showed up on time, and we discussed what we needed. He gave us a couple of great ideas. He had set up a lot of offices, and the traffic pattern had to be right. He gave us a coffee room where a small group of about twelve could meet. That sounded good. We asked when he could get started, and he said he would get the materials that day itself and have his men there the next morning. It would take about a week to complete. He said he was going by to pick up the necessary permit to repair the building that afternoon. We had already rented the building with the permission to alter the structure. I had made copies of the rental contract, and I gave him one. He said it would help.

"It was Wednesday, and Albert and I were ready for a long weekend at the beach. Mary and Jo Anne had been visiting St. George while we were in Columbia. They were to be back on Thursday morning, and we thought we should be there."

Dylan said, "I think it is about time I packed up and headed home. Your last statement has reminded me I promised Marlene I would get home early for a long weekend." He turned off the recorder and put it in his briefcase.

I said, "My last remarks and your remarks have reminded me that I am telling you the story of my life just like I lived it. I am leaving out my family just like I did when I was working. I was not home to be with the boys the way a father should be. I missed the ball games and the activities at school. But Jo Anne was always there and took wonderful care of the boys. She never missed a single event that a parent should attend."

Dylan said, "Do not be too hard on yourself. Every president I have interviewed has had the same complaint. They never had time for the family."

I replied, "At the next session, I guess I should talk about what was going on at home while I was working."

Dylan said, "That will be fine. Let me worry about the timing of events. When you put a biography together, you always have to be careful about the time at which something happened."

I said, "That is good because I have been worried I might have gotten something out of order." We said our good-byes and planned to meet in about a week.

Jo Anne and I had a lovely slow long weekend. We spent time on the porch talking about the boys and their families and with the boys and their families. I realized I had missed a lot of good times with the family. But they all said that they were very proud of me and what I had accomplished. They said their friends were amazed at the record of my career. Jo Anne and I played a couple of rounds of golf at Wild Dunes. I was glad I was out of office, or the media would say I was playing too much golf and not taking care of business. On Sunday, I played with the boys, and Jo Anne played with their wives. We had dinner at the clubhouse. There were several old friends there, and we enjoyed the conversation. Joe Davidson and his wife were there. He is a retired physician. He was in his constant complaining mode. He was fussing about: (1) the quality of the greens, (2) the bad condition of the course and how it was going to get worse, (3) the cart boys and how slow they were, (4) how bad the food was, and how slow the servers were. He was the only person there, or who had ever been there, that felt the way he did. We had gotten used to his complaining and did not pay attention to his raving. I do not think he had a friend at the club. He once told me about going back to a medical department where he had headed the department. He said they paid very little attention to his recommendations. He said he did not feel he was welcomed back. I wondered why. That gave me an internal laugh. Once we were home, Don said that there was a Joe Davidson in every club or business. Dave agreed. I said that I had run into a lot of them.

After the days at home, I was ready to get back to work with Dylan. He called and said he could be at the house on Tuesday. I asked him to bring Marlene. She and Jo Anne could have a good time while we worked. He said that would be good, and they arrived on Tuesday morning at about eleven o'clock. They were delayed in Atlanta. I have heard that story a lot of times. We sat on the porch until noon, and they served us lunch there. Marlene commented on the service, and Jo Anne said, "I will never get used to not having to do the housework." After lunch, they left us, and Dylan and I got ready for our secession.

I said, "I think I will talk about family. As you know, we had two boys. They grew up on the Island after we moved back to the house that Dad had bought after he returned from Chicago. We had continued to live for a short period in Charleston, but after I was elected to the statehouse of representatives, we were free to move back to the Island. The move was a sad one. My grandfather died, and Mom and Dad moved in with Grandma. They did not want her living alone. Dad knew I would want to move back to the Island, so we let the house stay vacant for about a year. Jo Anne and I were there often, and we stayed in that house. Jo Anne loved what Mom had done when she had furnished it. After I moved in, I enlarged the porch. Grandma only lived for about six months after Grandpa died. The boys went to the same schools I had gone to. Jo Anne got them dance lessons when they were in the seventh grade. The boys talked about playing on that same old gun emplacement that I had played on. Mrs. Purse was no longer at the school. She had become disabled and could not walk. We visited her regularly and made sure she had what she needed. She tutored the boys for a while. Jo Anne worked with the boys every day. They did well in grammar school. They played high-school sports and loved to dance. They belonged to the Gold Key Club. The DeMolay Chapter folded before they were old enough to join. They maintained good grades and finished high school at the top of their class. They went to the University of South Carolina and often told me they now understood what I meant when I said we went to Main Street to watch the traffic signals change.

"There were not the things to do in Columbia which they enjoyed in Charleston. They spent a lot of time on Folly Beach in the summer. Dave was a business major with a minor in economics. He went to work for Dad's company when he finished college. I wanted him to get a Masters Degree or a Ph.D., but he said he could learn more from working in Dad's business and being with him. I think he was right. Don took Pre-Law and finished college near the top of his class. He went to Law School and practiced law in Charleston. He got a job with a Broad Street Law Firm. Dylan, that reminds me of a funny story they tell about Charleston lawyers. They say the reason they have offices on Broad Street is because it is halfway between the post office and the banks. They rush to get the letters with checks from the post office and run to the bank to make a deposit that covers that check they just wrote."

Dylan said, "That story is too true to be funny." We both laughed.

I said, "Dad's distribution center was located near St George, so Dave moved into a house that he had bought in St. George. He met Gloria Meyers, and they got married. Cindy Meyer Gloria's mother was an old friend of Jo Anne. Don met and married Julia Abbott. After my dad and mom died, we moved into Grandpa's house. I liked it better because the kitchen was near the porch. Don and Julia moved into the house Don had grown up in. When Dad died, he left us all with a very large Trust fund and all the stock to his business. Dave took over and ran Dad's business. He continued to expand the number of stores and built additional distribution centers. It sure was good to have the money coming in. It made my career a lot easier when I did not have to worry about finances.

"Shortly after Dave moved to St. George, Jo Anne's mother died, and we were able to get her father into the Franke home. He enjoyed the home, and that was good. They took very good care of him. They made trips that he enjoyed, and he got to go shopping. They had group lunches at restaurants in the area and in Charleston. They went out for dinner once a month. Jo Anne said he was getting around more now than at any time in his life. I told Jo Anne to remember that we might need it. She asked, 'Do you think the Secret Service will let you live there?' I said, 'No.' We had a good laugh at that one. I asked Dylan if that was enough about the family. He said that it was for now.

Then I said, "The Geek program worked well, and the education of the voters in and around Columbia worked well too. At the next election, when they had the referendum on the ballot, it passed, and the two counties and the city merged their governments. After two years, everyone was amazed at the savings. While taxes were rising in other parts of the state, they were decreased in the areas where the mergers had occurred. They had little trouble having a balanced budget. Services improved in all areas. This made Albert and me to work harder at government improvement.

"We decided to run for the State Senate. We would be facing good competition. We knew we had the machine to run. We could use the Geeks and Raymond on the media. We set up offices around the state. Most of these were in the high voter turnout areas. We had a great name recognition and good government reparations. We visited and spoke in most areas of the state. Our message was on government approval. We wanted more efficient government that was very effective. Albert said he thought we need a chicken in every pot message. I said I thought we would do better if we stuck with the improvement in the economy in the areas of the state where we were successful with our merger program. He agreed that was a strong message.

"When election night came, we were in a hotel suite in Columbia. We had rented the ballroom of the hotel for our supporters. Raymond was with us in the suite. Warren Anderson had become a good friend, and he was in the suite with us. The early election returns were heavy in our direction. It did not change with later reporting areas. We got our congratulation calls from our opponents early. We went to the ballroom and gave our acceptance speeches. They were received well by the media. Warren made sure the Internet was full of praise for us.

"Once we were in the Senate, we could work on a unicameral legislature. We went to work with the educational programs. We pushed the fact that Nebraska had always had a unicameral legislature. We stressed the tax dollar savings. We also stressed the fact that we needed a better working government. We said, 'The size of the existing legislature and the two-house system make it too difficult to get anything done.' We said that the people of South Carolina deserved a government that was efficient and effective. Our voter education program was working well. They picked up on every speech and made sure most people knew what we said. We worked on the other senators. We visited offices and had parties in Columbia and at the beach. We had Wild

Dunes secessions. The senators from Greenville area and the Spartanburg area were supports. The Columbia area senators joined in. We had the votes in the Senate, but we knew we would not get anything passed in the House. We put voter pressure on the House members by pointing out that they were more interested in their jobs than in the welfare of the people of the state. We said that they were elected to serve the people and not to protect their jobs.

"We were not making many friends in the House. They were feeling the pressure. Their phones were ringing. The e-mails and regular mails were full. The media had picked up on our message. We tried to get a referendum on the ballots for the next statewide election. The leadership in the House sued us in the State Supreme Court for violation of the State Constitution. They won the suit. We went to work to write a new constitution for the state and getting it approved by the voters of the state. Albert did a wonderful job of taking the best out of the old constitution and putting new material that improved the constitution. The improvements included the unicameral legislature. But the conservative state voters were not in favor of a new constitution. Once again, Status Quo had defeated us. Every member of the House was in his district, calling in every favor. They went from door to door in the district. I do not think any of them had worked that hard to get elected. Naturally, they were well like individuals in the districts, and old friends worked hard for them. Albert put it best when he said, 'The people of South Carolina are more interested in helping a friend than saving tax dollars.' I said, 'We will have to remember that. It is most likely true of other states as well.'

"We knew it was back to the porch. We need to come up with a new plan. I invited Warren and Raymond down, and we added a few other politicians from the state. We included the governor and the two State United States Senators. They were invited for a weekend at Wild Dunes by us. We included a round of golf. They all accepted. The staff got the hotel rooms set up and left a schedule of events for the guests as they arrived. We included the wives, and Jo Anne had her usual plan for the ladies. They were invited to come in on Friday afternoon, and we had a dinner plan in the hotel activities room just off the kitchen. We had cocktails and about an hour getting to know each other. We had an excellent dinner with the right wine. I was glad none of them had to drive home, and that included Warren and Raymond. We had a limo coming for us. Albert and Mary were staying with us.

"We had breakfast in a side area of the Sea Biscuit. After breakfast, there was transportation to the house, and they were shown to their places on the porch. God was on our side. I could not have asked for a better-weather day at the beach. It turned out we were preaching to the choir. They were all on our side. They were interested in government improvement. They liked our efforts and encouraged us to keep up the good job. Warren suggested we just had to work on the voters. The governor said he would put as much pressure as possible on the House. He said he did not think he could put more pressure than we had with the amount of mail and calls they were getting to make the change. He said his office was very busy answering people who wanted the change. The two State United States Senators said we had the House members in the Federal Congress worried. Albert asked what they thought would happen if we ran for the Federal House. One of them said that we would be elected but that the House might reject seating you. That brought a good laugh.

Dylan, you know the old saying—'it is a small world'? Well, you will not believe this, but I had a boy in my high-school class who was from Maryland. He had his family in Walterboro, South Carolina, and his dad was from that area. He wanted his son to go to high school and to the Citadel in the Charleston area. He had a sister who lived in Mt. Pleasant. She agreed to have Jenkins Anderson to come and live with her. Jinks, as we called him, had a great personality. We became good friends. I soon found out that Jinks was a direct descendant of Major Anderson who was the Commander at Fort Sumter when the Civil War started. After our meeting at Wild Dunes, I told Warren Anderson that I had a friend named Jenkins Anderson. He surprised me by saying he was his first cousin. Jink's dad was the older brother of Warren's dad. They had a difference of fourteen years in age. Warren was the youngest child in his family. I got Jinks and Warren together on the porch, and we had a long talk. I found out Warren's family lived in Walterboro and that Warren grew up in Walterboro. He learned to fly at Anderson Field in Walterboro. The field was a form of air force training field. It was named after Major Anderson, the Commander who moved his troops from Fort Moultrie to Fort Sumter and withstood the bombardment of Fort Sumter without losing a man.

"Albert and I were spending a lazy Sunday on the porch. Jo Anne and Mary had just joined us when Albert came up with one of his attempts to be funny. He said, 'Ladies, do you know that old saying—'that's good enough for government work'? Well, that makes it obvious that the people do not think government work is very good. Paul and I are out to change that. The new saying is going to be—'You have to work hard to be as good as government work.' Mary said, 'Now that will be the day.' Jo Anne said, 'Amen to that.' While the girls laughed, I said, 'Albert, I agree with you. We are going to put efficiency into government work.' Albert picked up his beer bottle and said, 'I will drink to that.' We touched bottles and then touched them with the girls' lemonade glasses.

"Tom arrived and said that he had been talking with Jinks and found out we had met Warren Anderson. He said, 'I and Elly had met Warren years ago. We liked him from the beginning and made him an adopted Island Boy.' I said, 'They did not tell us that. I am glad to know Warren is an adopted Island Boy. He is a great guy and doing great work helping Albert and me.' Albert said that we were about to put him to real work. We were going to run for the United States House of Representatives. Tom said that was great and that we could count his favorable vote. Jo Anne came out with a beer for Tom. He thanked her and said, 'Another great beer on this porch.'

"Albert and I were off to Columbia. We had a lot of work to do before we announced our runs for the United States House of Representatives. We met Warren Anderson and Raymond Maul and discussed our advertising program. Warren said the Geeks would flood the Internet with talk about our success with the county and city mergers and about our interest in improving the government. I reminded him that more small counties near Spartanburg had merged their governments and the other governments within the counties into one government. I suggested he let the voters know we were meeting opposition from other politicians who were more interested in their jobs than in working for the improvement of the government.

"I also liked it when they pointed out that Albert and I could be considered as radical. We were thinking outside the box, and we wanted to change the Status Quo for a better method of government. I reminded them to push the idea that a reduction in government cost resulted in more spending in society. The more the money spent in society, the better the economy. Improvement in economy meant an increase in the size of the tax base, which helped both the government and the taxpayers. Warren and Albert both said they liked the suggestions. Raymond said he was going to take those ideas and get on a run. He said he and the staff would work to get us speaking engagements, especially TV appearances. I asked about campaign offices in the two districts. Albert would be running for the seat in the Greenville, Spartanburg area, and I would be running for the seat in the Charleston area. Raymond said, 'We have very good staffs in both areas. They know how to educate the voters, and they know how to get out the vote.' Albert and I were very satisfied to know that things were in place for a victory on election night.

"Warren and Raymond were as good as their word. We were very pleased with the progress before and after we filed for election. We were very happy with the reception on TV appearances and with the people and the comments that we received after our appearance. There were many kind remarks from people who attended our speeches. While both of our opponents were incumbent representatives, we were happy with the party support of our campaign we were getting. Both of our opponents were complaining to the party boss about this support. Both of them had offices in the areas they represented, but they were legislative support offices and not campaign support offices. They felt so secure they had lost touch with the voters. We had students and people who were unemployed knocking on doors in every neighborhood. They carried cards with talking points and handed out White Paper-type letters. We asked them to be sure to knock on as many doors as possible between six and eight in the evening but not to be out after eight.

"We had phone banks running, but ours were different from our opponents. We had people on the line to answer questions and to interact with the people who answered the phone. Our opponents had recorded messages and the rotor dialing. They called at dinnertime and after eight o'clock in the evening. We did not. We heard that many people were tired of the rotor calls and the recorded messages at these times. The staff and both Albert and I worked hard to make the voters happy with our message. We did not want them to be mad at us for something stupid that was done.

"The polls and the interactive Internet data showed we would win in a landslide. We both were very happy on the night of election. Albert was in Greenville. He had a suite, and Raymond was with him. We were in Charleston. We had a hotel suite, and Warren and several of the Island Boys were with us. Both Albert and I had the hotel ballroom at our hotels rented for our supports to watch the returns. We were in the lead by a large margin in every return. We received our congratulations from our opponents early in the evening. Both Albert and I waited until most of the returns were in, and we had been declared winners, before we went to the ballroom. Our acceptance speech was received well by the media. The governor called and congratulated us on our victory and assured us he was behind our ideas for government improvement 100 percent.

"The weekend after the election, Albert and Mary were our houseguests. We sat on the porch and planned how we would live in Washington. Neither Jo Anne nor Mary was at all interested in living in Washington. Albert and I were glad. We felt as though we had to maintain a residence in our district. We decided to rent a two-bedroom apartment in Washington and live together while we were in Washington. We decided to fly from Washington into Columbia, and each of us would drive from there to our home. It was about an equal distance drive for each of us, and we could discuss things on the plane, while going and coming from Washington. We rented a furnished apartment, but the girls came up and put their touch on the furniture, drapes, and a few decoration items. We stayed in a local hotel while the girls were in town. The hotel was near the shopping district, and they could shop while we were at our offices.

"We were not accepted with open arms by the House leadership. Neither party leader was happy with our unicameral government idea. There were a few House Members who came to the office and said they agreed with us. We had better support among our classmates in the House. I was impressed with a Rand McNally Road Atlas I had bought. When we looked at each state and the index and realized the number of villages, cities, and counties with governments we knew, we were overgoverned. I let Albert look through my copy.

"I went to three book stores before I got the necessary 434 copies I needed. I wrote a White Paper about the savings each state could make if they worked on government mergers. I pointed out our success in South Carolina. I was happy to report that three counties in the Florence area had just merged into one county and six district governments. My staff passed out the Atlas and the White Paper to each Representative Office. We received more support on the state county government mergers than on our change in the Federal government.

"This first effort showed the leadership in the House that we were serious and that we were going to be workers. I decided to add to their concerns. I invited twenty representatives to Wild Dunes for a long weekend. The invitation said they could bring their wives and that all expenses would be covered. There was the information about a golf tournament, and transportation would be provided. We include all our classmates and representatives who had told us they supported our ideas for government change. They began to arrive on Friday afternoon as planned. The staff had been in touch with their office and had their flight information. We had them picked up with limos and taken to the Wild Dunes hotel. There were weekend schedules in each room. Since we had a large group, the staff decided it would be easier to have cocktails and dinner at the hotel. The hotel suggested an area in the convention center for the cocktails and an adjourning room for dinner. We had one large room for cocktails and a room that had been a restaurant early in Wild Dunes history for the dining room. Both rooms had conversation pieces posted on the walls. They included posters of the counties in South Carolina that had merged and charts of the budget savings. With drinks in their hands, the representatives gathered around the charts and talked about the savings.

Breakfast was in the hotel dining room. After breakfast, Jo Anne and Mary took the wives to Charleston. We walked the representatives to the end of the boardwalk to an area near one pool where a meeting area had been set up. It was fun to watch the representatives look around at the environment. The ocean was on its best behavior. It almost looked like a lake. The sky was beautiful. The white sand and blue water made you want to go for a swim. The water was a little too cold for a swim.

I was afraid the breeze would be too strong, but it was just perfect. Albert was up first, and he talked about the success of the Greenville merger and the tax dollar savings. He gave them figures for the reduction in taxes. He pointed out the increase in the economy and gave figures. I watched the expressions on the representatives' faces. It was obvious they were very interested. He pointed out the data for the Spartanburg area and said that it was too early for economic data for the Florence area but that the early data showed economic improvement. He showed the tax savings and the reduction in taxes. He said that the most impressive thing for the voters was improved services with a reduction in taxes.

"I followed and said, 'It is my turn to give you the good news and the bad news. We intend to work hard to improve the Federal Government like South Carolina's government is changing. We want to reduce the Federal taxes like the county taxes have decreased.' I watched the faces, and there was interest. I then continued, 'The bad news is that we have to put each of them and ourselves out of a job. We wanted to make the Federal legislature a unicameral government. We wanted a legislature of one hundred senators elected from near-equal population districts. This removed the two senators from each state. It did what the original founders of the 1791 Constitution intended to do. That was to establish a one-man-one-vote legislature.' I asked if any of them wanted to speak. There were several hands raised. I invited them to the podium one at a time. The first one said he was very happy with the idea of reducing the number of governments within his state. He said it should be obvious to anyone there were too many governments in his state. He said setting up Senate districts would be a problem because they would cross state lines. He worried about gerrymandering the districts. He said gerrymandering was already a big problem for the House Districts. After he returned to his seat, I said that gerrymandering would be a problem. We now had 435 chances for gerrymandering. With the new government, there would only be one hundred. That was still a large number, but if the change in government included oversight on district formation, we could limit gerrymandering. I said that a new constitution that required Governors of States involved in the new Senate Districts were required to draw the districts, and the Supreme Court approved that the Senate Districts should be enough to decrease gerrymandering. The next speaker said he agreed with the first speaker. He felt changes in state governments were necessary, and reducing the number of governments in a state would reduce overhead cost. He was worried about the Status Quo when it came to changing Federal Government. He said it would take a lot of voter education before it could be accomplished. When he returned to his seat, I said I agreed it would take a lot of voter education. I pointed out we were going to cover that point in just a minute. This was the topic of the next speaker's presentation. The previous speaker stood at his seat and said, 'I should have known anyone who could set up a meeting like this would be thinking ahead of me.' That brought a needed laugh. I thanked him for his remark. The others who had raised their hands said they would like to move ahead to the next presentation.

"I introduced Warren Anderson, Professor of Computer Science at the University of South Carolina. I said that Warren had been a great help to us with the education of South Carolina's voters. Warren gave a great presentation about the use of the Internet and all the social media. He pointed out it was possible to get e-mail address and that they could be arranged in order to get the right information to the right voter. He pointed out this was better than mail-out contact because the voter was less likely to delete the e-mail but that they might throw the mail out in the trash can. He said they should just think about how many mail-out ads they had thrown into the trash. He said an office with four Geeks could be as effective at educating the voter as an office with fifty phone bank operations. He showed data from interactive Internet operations that indicated the individuals paid more attention to Internet information than they did to phone calls or mailed advertisements.

"The representatives were very impressed with his presentation. I asked if there were any questions for Professor Anderson. One member of the group stood up and said he now knew how Albert and I had won our election by such a large margin and how we were able to accomplish so much in South Carolina. I thanked him for his kind remarks. I next introduced Raymond Maul. He talked about direct contact with the voters. He talked about getting TV advertising and TV appearances. He talked about meeting with local newspaper reporters. I said that I thought we had covered voter education very well, that it was now time for a little individual discussion and that coffee and doughnuts would be served. I said I liked my mid-morning coffee, and I hoped they did too. It was great to see the individual discussion going on, and Warren and Raymond were at the center of their groups. Albert had his group, and mine had formed, and we were chatting. Two of my groups said they agreed with the need for morning coffee breaks.

"After a very successful morning, we had obtained four rooms in the conference center. Warren, Raymond, Albert, and I were in a room. The representatives who were attending the meet were divided into four groups. The staff was doing a great job in keeping everything moving smoothly. A group of representatives were guided to each of the four rooms. The rooms were typical of our meetings. The walls were covered with pictures, maps, and data related to the things we planned to discuss in that room. We were with each group for nearly an hour, and they changed rooms. There was a break between the second and third group. Drinks and snacks were available, and we engaged in small talk.

"Most of the representatives were interested in the talk about Wild Dunes and Charleston. I talked about the history of Sullivan's Island. After a busy afternoon, we had a party on the porch at the house. Jo Anne and the wives joined us. The party was catered. I talked about the number of secessions we had held on the porch. They agreed it was a great place for a meeting or a party. They liked the way we had made the porch large enough to have a crowd. We started the next day with everyone back on the porch for breakfast. The ladies left us for a trip back to Charleston and the West Ashley Mall. They planned to have lunch in Charleston. I was wishing I could join them.

"After the morning secession on the porch, we had lunch at the clubhouse at Wild Dunes, and we had our golf tournament after lunch. The Club Pros did their usual job of sitting up a fun tournament and a great time for the scoring and prizes. They had videotaped us during the round. They caught some funny situations. They had videos they had made that were funny. One video showed two of the pros showing up for a tournament in a BMW convertible. They were dressed in the worst golf attire. It was so loud you could almost hear it. They showed them playing the Harbor Course next to the inland waterway. Two girls showed up on water scooters. The boys jumped in to swim out to the girls in those laud outfits. After the scoring party, and the winners got their prizes, we had cocktails and dinner in the club dining room. I had the golf pros that could join us at the dinner. The Representatives enjoyed their conversations with the Pros. They were free for their breakfast at the hotel, and the staff had arranged pick-up times for their trip home.

"We received letters and phone calls, congratulating us on a great meeting. They said they had learned a lot and had an enjoyable time. Their wives were as pleased as the representatives were. They said they were going to work with their state leadership and try to get government mergers going in their states. We got a few comments about the job we would have getting a unicameral government. I felt we had won twenty friends in the House that would return favors. That was a long way from a majority, but with their help, we had a beginning.

"Our first year as House representatives from South Carolina was uneventful and a bore. We had poor committee assignments. We were not the House Leaders' favorite pair. Our interest in a unicameral legislature made us persona non grata. The Wild Dunes meeting was the highlight of the year. Jo Anne and I went to Greenville to visit Albert and Mary. Albert said his porch was not a good place for secession. 'So let us go to the golf course and discuss politics while we play golf,' he said. I replied, 'With me, that might beat the porch.' We shared a laugh and left the girls who were busy planning their day.

"Once we were on the course, I said, 'This has not been a very productive year. We have another one coming up.' Albert said, 'That was about the most boring year I have ever spent in my life.' I said, 'I feel the same way.' Albert then asked, 'What can we do to improve things?' I replied, 'I have been thinking about that. We are going to have to try to get elected to the Senate before we are going to make any headway with our unicameral Federal legislature. The chance of running a successful challenge to either of our incumbent senators is very unlikely. South Carolina has a long history of returning incumbent senators. The voters know that a senator has to serve for a long time before he gets the committee assignments that can help the State. I think the only thing we can do is go to the House Leaders and say that as long as we are members of the House, we will not mention unicameral Federal government. I hate to give in, but they hold the power.' Albert said, 'This is getting scary. I was thinking the same thing, but I hated the idea so much I did not want to bring it up. You are right. It is the only thing we can do and give the people of South Carolina the kind of representatives they deserve.' I said, 'Well, we are two politicians that are different than most politicians. We are willing to put the people first.' I suggested that Albert meet me in Columbia before we go back to Washington, and we can talk with the governor.

"We met in Columbia, and we had both called and got appointments at the same time. The governor was eager to see us. He loved what was going on in South Carolina with the county mergers. It appeared that large industries liked the idea of lowering tax rates and put plants in South Carolina. I told the governor about our problems in the House. He said that he could understand the problem. He was glad we had decided to serve the people, but he hated to see the lack of effort on a unicameral government. He was working to get a change in the South Carolina Constitution and have a unicameral legislature. He said, 'If we had a unicameral legislature, it would be much easier to get something done. The damn House is always a problem.' I said that 435 members of the Federal House was not a decision-making organization. The governor said, 'Neither are the 124 members I have to deal with.' Albert said we would be back to work on the unicameral legislature of both South Carolina and the Federal government when we are not in the House. The governor said he understood our problem and appreciated our solution to the problem and thanked us for coming. We had a good talk on our way to Charleston. We were not happy with our decision, but we were trapped for a while. Albert said, 'What the hell! We can work on our state and the rest of the states to improve their governments. We will have more time for merger talks.' I said, 'Albert, you can always put a good face on a mule's butt.'

"When the legislature was back in secession, Albert and I had our staff to set up an appointment with the Leadership. We both wanted to be in on the meeting. It took two days before we got our appointment. That showed us we were not in favor. When we were in the company of the Leadership, Albert asked me to speak first. I told them we would make a commitment to them that we would not mention the unicameral legislature anywhere while we were members of the House. In a voice that showed his dissatisfaction, he asked how long we planned to be members of the House. I said that was up to the voters in our districts. We were up for reelection for the next year. Albert said we would be around for a long time. We were elected by a large margin of the voters. I could have kissed him. The head of the House leadership said that he hoped we would live up to our commitment. I said that we always had lived up to our commitments and that we would live up to this one too. Albert said that we intended to continue our work on merger of governments within states. I had to say it. I said we hoped they would support mergers in their states. It helped the people. With that, we left.

"When we were back in the office, I said to Albert, 'Well, we made a big commitment, and I am not sure what we will get in return.' He agreed with me and said we were playing hardball. I said, 'And the pitcher has a hundred mile per hour fast ball.' We waited for the new committee appointments, and we were no better off. We were in for another boring year. I must admit that my time in the House of Representatives were the worst years of my life. I like to get things done. I want to be efficient in everything I do. I have heard of Do-Nothing Congresses, but in my opinion, the United States House of Representatives is a do-nothing government body. The leaders are a big part of the problem. The leaders are elected from a district of a state. Even when the population of the nation reaches 435 million, each member of the House will be elected from a district of just one million citizens. All the citizens are not voters. Some are not of voting age, and some are not eligible to vote. That means they only represent less than one million voters. That is not even enough of a sample of the population to give you a statically significant sample. But they are elected to an office of leadership in the House, and 435 million citizens are affected by their leadership. We need to get back to the one-man-one-vote rule. That is why we need a unicameral legislature composed of one hundred senators elected from one hundred near-equal population Senate Districts. The House Leadership has to look at themselves every morning in their mirror when they shave. I wonder what they see. It is not a person who is doing an effective and efficient job. They are the power-motivated individuals that always ruin everything.

"How is that for carrying coal to New Castle?"

Dylan answered, "I agree with you, but you were not preaching to the choir while you were in the House. Protection of their jobs motivates most of the members."

I said, "I do not know how it occurred, but I was appointed to the Ethics Committee. Albert said that he knew why they appointed me. They were hoping I would mess up on an important Ethics violation and get a lot of bad press. I told him that was most likely right. We did have one important case. A member of the House was accused of illegal use of campaign funds and illegal use of the Federal Mail. He was proven guilty and received a reprimand. He was tried in his state and sentenced to a jail term. While he was out of jail on bond waiting for an appeal, he was reelected to office. The House did refuse to seat him, and a second election was required. No wonder the ancient Greek philosophers said a democracy would never last."

Dylan said, "I have enough to work on for a while. Can the next meeting be in Columbia at the library next Tuesday?"

I said, "Tuesday at the library suits me fine. I have not been there for a while. It is time I get back there. How about ten o'clock?" He agreed and packed his briefcase. The security guards showed him out, and I remained seated on the porch. I saw Don walking up the path from the beach. He called out before he reached the porch.

He said, "Hello, it is a great day. I have enjoyed a good walk on the beach. I think I will go home and get my bathing suit and take a swim."

I said, "I hope you do not plan to swim alone."

He said, "I will not swim alone. I will call a couple of my friends." We had lived on the beach long enough to have a good respect for the power of tidal currents. Knowing how to swim in a tidal current had saved many Island Boys.

Even though it was late morning and too early for a beer and too late for a coffee, Jo Anne showed up with two beers and a glass of wine for herself. I laughed and said, "You are starting a little early, don't you think?"

She said, "I know the old saying—it is after five somewhere in the world."

Don said, "Mom, you are the smart one in this bunch."

I told her that I would have to go to the library next Monday morning and that I would be meeting Dylan there on Tuesday morning. Don said, "I thought you were a retired former president of the United States. Why do you have to go any place?"

I replied, "There is another old saying—while a woman's work is never done, a man works from sun to sun."

Don said, "Yeah, but six months' vacation twice a year isn't bad, especially when you have a house full of servants and a full force security service."

I said, "And you know how I feel about the lack of efficiency and what that has caused." Both Jo Anne and Don laughed.

I arrived at the library at about ten o'clock Monday morning. My secretary said, "Good morning, Mr. President."

I said, "They should make that good moaning. When you get to my age, you moan when you have to get out of bed."

She smiled and said, "You look great for your age. I am sure you are just making another joke."

My mail was piled neatly in an inbox. I went to work, and by noon, I had moved the mail from the inbox to the outbox.

I called John Camp who was working at the Foundation and asked what he was doing for lunch. He said he was free. I said I would pick him up in about ten minutes. The security guards drove to his office and took us to our favorite restaurant in Lexington. We had a good chat at lunch and asked the driver to take us on our old ride around the city on Interstate Highway 20. John and I had made that ride many times while we discussed everything from politics to religion.

Back at the library, I took a stroll around the library and spoke with the few guests that were there. There were two University students who were majoring in Pre-Law. They were writing a paper on the success of my administration. We had a good talk. I wished them well and said, "Remember, you will become the keeper of the flame. Please keep it lit." They promised to do their very best. Some people were saying the younger generation was going to let the nation go to the dogs. I did not believe that. I met a lot of young people, and I felt the nation was going to be in good hands.

Dylan was on time as usual. He joined me in the office. I had gone into the Rose Garden and picked a few roses. The secretary had found a vase, and I had placed them on the coffee table between Dylan and me. He said he thought that was a nice touch. With our recorders on and Dylan with his yellow pad, I felt at home. I was getting very used to these interviews. I said, "We have been on the subject of my time in the House, and you realize it was not a happy time for me."

Dylan said, "You have made that point, but as I understand it, you were making headway with the merger program in several states."

"Without those gains, I think Albert and I might have thrown in the towel. The northern Midwest seemed to be the area of the nation that was interested in efficient government. Minnesota, the Dakotas, and Nebraska took our message and ran with it. Nebraska, with their unicameral legislature, was very interested in what we had done in South Carolina. The State Representatives and the Senators were in our offices often. The reports on the Wild Dunes secession had impressed them. They invited us to be on programs with them on many occasions. We were on the Sunday talk shows in Nebraska. They took our advice to heart, cut their county governments to the bone, and moved the city limits to the county lines in three areas. Minnesota was slower in making the mergers, but they had merged several small counties with larger county neighbors. North and South Dakota reduced the number of county governments and produced a new state constitution that redrew the county lines. But they did not become unicameral legislature states. Albert and I were aware the members of the House in the States and in the Federal government were popular with the people of their states. We had to work harder to make the people know what that friendship was costing them in government overhead, and the cost of government was decreasing the societal economy.

"When I was appointed to the Ethics Committee, I called a meeting of all my staff people. I warned them about Ethics and money matters. I said to them, 'I want you to watch very carefully which accounts any checks are drawn. Make sure to error on the side of my personal account.' But do you know? We began to suspect someone was paying bills that were not part of our business. We thought we were losing office equipment and supplies. I called John Camp and told him about my problem and asked him to come up and run the finance side of the office. I asked him what it cost, and he gave me a very reasonable sum to do the work. I paid him almost twice what he asked for. He did an inventory of everything in the office. He went back years in the checking accounts and the books. He came into the office and confirmed my worst fear: someone was stealing office equipment and supplies. There were several false bills on the books with checks going to mailboxes. He said he had a private investigator he had used on many similar cases. The investigator had visited the mailboxes and come up with the name of the individual on the staff that was the problem. She was selling the office supplies, and she had stolen three laptop computers. She had also stolen other office equipment, but they were not very expensive items. She had not shown up for work since John's first day. She had called in sick twice but had missed more days. The investigator said she had checked out of her apartment and did not leave a forwarding address. He said, 'I can find her, and I will work on it.' I told him to do his best. I went to the House Leadership with my tail between my legs and told them about my problem. I said I would replace in money or item that were missing out of my own account. I said, 'I plan to call in the Attorney General's Office.' They said, 'That will bring in the media.' They asked how many people knew about this. I told them the people in the office had suspected that things were wrong. They thought John Camp was a new employee who was going to handle check writing and bill payments and the general finance of my campaigns. They said that was good. They said if the investigator found her, we would let the Washington police handle it. The Washington court case would not draw as much attention as a federal court case. The investigator found her, and he was a former Columbia, South Carolina, police officer. He made contact with a Washington detective and told him about our problem. The Washington detective took all the evidence and said he would turn it over to the local district attorney. I feared a big media story, but it never happened. She was arrested very quietly. She was charged, tried, and convicted and got a six-year sentence. The trial was not covered in *The Washington Post*. We all breathed a sigh of relief.

"I talked John Camp into giving up his office and business in Columbia and coming to work for me. I put him in charge of all our finances. This turned out to be a great move. John traveled about as much as Albert and me. He was great in working with counties and cities who were considering mergers. He studied their budget and developed an after-merger budget. The two budgets showed the savings in dollars that accompanied the merger.

"We served five terms in the House, and the fifth term was no better than the first. We were knocking heads with the Leadership, and they had rocks for heads. When we were up for our sixth term, we were sitting on the porch, trying to decide if we would run for a sixth term. I said to Albert, 'I do not think my constitution can stand up to another term in that Do-Nothing House of Representatives. I get sick when I think of all the wasted money and no results.' Albert replied, 'I feel the same way you do. I think we could be as effective improving governments if we work full time on the merger program. We will never accomplish anything in the House.'

"My phone rang, and I went to answer it. It was the head of the Republican Party in South Carolina. He told me the senior senator had died of a heart attack and that he was up for reelection. The party had decided to back me for the vacant seat. He said that the party leaders thought I was the best candidate and asked if I would run. I asked for time. I said it was a real surprise and not a pleasant one. I liked our senior senator very much. He said we all did. I asked if I could call him in the morning, and he said that would be fine. I then told Albert about the phone call. He was as surprised as I was. I asked him if he wanted to run for the office. He said he would love to be a United States Senator, but he too thought as the party thought that I was the best candidate. He would support me in the up-country. I said, 'As much as I would like to rub that under the noses of the House leadership, I thought he would be a good candidate.' He thanked me for my kind words and my support over the years. He said we could still work together, but I was the one who was to run. Jo Anne and Mary joined us. We told them what we were talking about. They were as surprised as we were. I asked Jo Anne what she thought about me running for the Senate. She said, 'You will win, and you will not have to campaign for six years. I love it.' We agreed I would call and accept the support and run for the United States Senate.

"I sat back in my chair and looked out over the ocean. I loved that view. Being able to see the sky and sea for about twelve miles in a half circle in front of you made many things seem small. I wonder what I could accomplish in the Senate. I knew the problems with the House and the plans for a unicameral legislature would not go away. I looked at Albert and said, 'We both know my being in the Senate will not help much with getting a unicameral legislature.' He said, 'We have both known for a long time that it will take a Constitutional Convention charged with providing an efficient and effective method of government to get a unicameral legislature. From your Senate office and my House office, we can work on the state governors to demand a Convention.' I said, 'You are right as usual. We will have to gear up our staffs and work on getting people to Wild Dunes and winning their support. We will have to find a way to get our Geeks, and most likely more Geeks, to working on voter education.' Albert said, 'We better get you elected first and then we can go to work.'

"We brought in both of our staffs from every office, and we had Raymond, Warren, and John at a meeting at Wild Dunes. I told them that I was going to run for the Senate. I had filled the papers the day before our meeting. Albert said, 'Our job, yours and mine, is going to be getting Paul elected. Once he is elected, we have to expand our efforts to get the voters informed on the savings we can get from a new constitution that provides a method of government that is efficient and effective.' John Camp said, 'Albert, do not forget that government savings increase spending and improve the economy.' I asked Raymond, Warren, and John if they were on board and ready to take on the task. They all agreed it was a good move, and they were ready to do their best. After the meeting adjournment, everyone lived up to their word and when to work. I was surprised at the efficiency and effective work that was done. I thought, *If only the government could work this way.*

"We had a large suite in Columbia Hotel rented for the day and night of the election. Both Albert and our families were there. The ballroom was rented for our supports. In addition to the leaders of our staffs, the governor was at the suite. He had been a great help. The polls closed, and the returns began to come in. The media was reporting the results of interviews they made at the exit from the voting places. It looked good for Albert and me from the first reports and only got better as more results came in. The call from my Democratic opponent came early with a very strong congratulation. The new senior senator was from Charleston, and my opponent assured me he would be a help to me. I was worried the state was not ready for two United States Senators from Charleston. We made our way to the ballroom. Albert gave his acceptance speech first. I followed with mine. They were both received by the South Carolina media. In fact, I got some good comments from the national media.

"Neither Jo Anne nor Mary wanted to move to Washington. It would be hard not having a wife in Washington while I was in the Senate. Albert and I agreed to keep our digs in Washington and to fly back and forth from Columbia. This had worked well for ten years, and we were very used to it. As the junior senator from South Carolina, I did not expect very good committee appointments. The Senate was under Democratic leadership.

"I was surprised when I was visited by the Democratic leader of the Senate in my office the first day. He was the senior senator from Minnesota. He told me he was very impressed with my work in the House that had the county and city mergers going in the states. He thought these were great improvements in governments. He said he was in favor of my interest in a unicameral Federal legislature but knew this would be a battle if we tried to bring it about. He then told me, 'Hold off on the effort for a time. We need to get the House to work with us if we want to get important programs approved.' I told him I would, but I told him my staff back in South Carolina was going to be working on voter education. He said, 'I have heard great praise about your Wild Dunes meetings and the great work of your excellent staff. I wish I had a staff as organized and as successful as yours.' He said that I should keep up the good work but that I should cool the unicameral legislature work for a while. I told him he could expect to see me across the aisle often. He thanked me for that. I agreed with him and told him I would. I told him about my commitment with the Leadership in the House. I also could not wait to go over and tell them that I was no longer a member of the House and that I was no longer bound by my commitment to not mention unicameral legislatures. He laughed and said, 'I heard you were a bulldog, and I am glad of it. We need a lot more congressmen with a reputation like yours. Go over and get it off your chest.'

"When he left the office, I was feeling good. I ask a member of the office staff to get me an appointment with the leader of the House. It took another two days, so I knew I was still not in good standing. When I arrived in his office, I told him I was no longer a member of the House and that I was released from my commitment to not mention the unicameral legislature and that I planned to do it often. He said, 'We all have our goals and objectives. You should not expect any help from me.' I told him I would not seek his assistance and thanked him for his time and then left the office.

"On the way back to my Senate office, I thought about how my dad had told about his leaving the Chicago Pharmaceutical Firm. The head of the leadership in the House was like his vice president for Research and Development. Like my dad had said, he needed a beer. I need to be on the porch with a beer."

Dylan said, "That last bit with the comparison with your dad is a nice stopping point for this secession. I like that very much." We went through our usual good-bye routine. We agreed to meet on Thursday of next week in the morning at the beach house.

When that day arrived, I was sitting on the porch and enjoying my time when the security guard showed up with Dylan. He took his usual seat, and I sat in such a way that I could still look out at the ocean. The security guards took their usual spots. Jo Anne, a security man, and two house servants showed up with coffee and sweet rolls. Jo Anne joined us long enough to ask about Marlene and the family. After she got her answer, she left. I said, "Well, I can start by telling you I felt a lot better being a senator than I did being a representative. I felt like I had a large load removed from my shoulders. I did not know how I was going to get things done, but I just felt like there would be accomplishments I could be proud of. I liked my classmates. They seemed eager to get to work on better governments. Most of them came by and said they had heard of my desire to improve governments and that they were on my side. They said governments really need a lot of improvement. I told a few of them about my desire to have the voters and the states to approve a Constitutional Convention to bring about a new constitution that provided an effective and efficient method of government. They were all for it and said they would go to their states with me and help me let the people know about our need for their support. I liked that very much. It made me think I could get the job done. Albert came over, and I told him how things were going. He said that was sure different from the House.

"I wrote a bill that would call for a Constitutional Convention charged with providing a constitution that provided a method of government that was effective and efficient. I took it to the Senate leadership and asked for their support. They said it could pass the Senate with their support, but it would never pass the House. I said that I knew that, but I wanted the voters to know who was against a method of government that was effective and efficient. They agreed that voter pressure would help the Senate on other programs as well. I told them my staff would work to get public support of all the Senate efforts. He said that he knew he was going to like me from the first meeting and that he was now sure of it.

"I said I would get the Geek program in South Carolina working on informing the voters about the House resistance to the Senate efforts for the benefit of the voters. The Democratic leader of the Senate said I was the first Republican he had liked. I said we all had to work together to get things done. He said that he wished more Republicans felt that way. He said he could broaden that statement and wished all senators felt that way. My bill passed committee review and was brought to the floor for a vote. It passed by a 58 percent of the vote. I failed in the House by an 82 percent of the vote. I had what I needed for our staff and the Geek program. The staff sent a write-up with the vote of the Senate and the House to every governor and asked for their support.

"Albert stopped by, and we left to have dinner and go to the apartment. He said, 'Just like I expected, you have hit the ground running.' We enjoyed a couple of beers in a local bar that had a great snack tray for happy hour. We finished the evening with a trip to our favorite restaurant. While we were having dinner, I talked to Albert about having a Wild Dunes meeting with the Senate leadership and some senators. I said, 'I think I will invite the two Republican leaders and the two Democratic leaders and let each leader bring three senators of their choice. We will include the wives. I will invite Raymond,

Warren, and John Camp. Naturally, you and I would attend. We will need nineteen rooms. You and Mary can stay with us.' Albert said, 'That sounds good, but what will you cover in the meeting?' I replied, 'I thought we would give them an overview of our staff setup. None of them has Geek programs. I could cover our goals and objectives. You would cover the success of our efforts. We would break up into four groups in the afternoon, and John would cover budgets and savings of the merger program. Warren would cover the Geek program. I understand he has been looking over the Internet contact efforts in the Senate. He thinks it could be greatly improved. But we are going to wait with that until he has the new software ready. Raymond will cover education of the voters. After the secession, we will run a general discussion. On Saturday, we will have the usual golf tournament in the morning, and they could leave on Saturday afternoon. Jo Anne and Mary will take care of the wives.'

"Albert said, 'That all sounds good. I think they will learn a lot. It will not hurt your standing in the Senate a bit.' We took a slow walk to our apartment, hoping we were burning off a few of the calories we had just ingested.

"I got my office staff together and had Raymond, Warren, and John there. I went over my plans for the meeting and told the staff to set up the transportation and make the hotel reservations. I said to include the airfare. When you know the timing for each person, please make the reservations and get the tickets. You can deliver the tickets. I put Cecil, my staff manager, in charge of the necessary actions for the conference. He was a past master at this after all the practice he had."

"Everyone who was invited agreed to attend the conference. We suggested they plan to arrive in the afternoon check-in time on Thursday, and their return would be after noon on Saturday. We sent an agenda for the meeting to each person who planned to attend. With this group, we had a crowd that Marshall could handle in his private dining area. Cecil had the transportation to Marshall's and the return to Wild Dunes planned. We had breakfast on Friday in the hotel's dining room. The wives joined in at the breakfast. Jo Anne and Mary had the transportation to Charleston and an all-day visit planned. Jo Anne and Mary had chosen their favorite restaurant in Charleston for lunch and had the private dining room reserved. It was the Magnolia Restaurant on East Bay. I was wishing I could be there for the meal.

"Our morning presentations and the discussions were well received. After lunch on the pier, the afternoon secessions were equally well received. Marshall never lets you down. The Friday-evening cocktail time and dinner went as I had expected. Once again, I was glad we were providing transportation back to Wild Dunes. The pros put on their usual great tournament, and the scoring was another good time. They had the usual videos. I was surprised by the long good-byes. Everyone had such a good time and felt like they had learned a lot. They took time to thank us and tell us about their experience.

"I was surprised by my appointments to committees in my first year even before the Wild Dunes meeting. I was appointed to the Armed Forces Committee and the Budget and Control Committee. I was not the senior Senate, but I had better committee assignments than he did. It was obvious the agenda Albert and I had worked so hard on was approved well by the leadership of both Parties. With our voter educational program and the fact that the Democrats were the majority in the House was working well for all Republican candidates. With some work, we could leave the Democratic Party in a shamble. I believe that is one reason the Democratic leadership was being good to me.

"Our big surprise came at the time of the reelection of the senior senator from South Carolina. He said he did not intend to run for reelection. He said that he was very shaken up by the death of his partner in the Senate for so many years. He was sixty-seven and did not think he could make the next six-year term. The party bosses were on Albert like flies on sugar. He was from the upper part of the State, and I was from the low country. That gave the State better representation. Albert said he would run and file the papers. I made several trips to the up-country and spoke on Albert's behalf. It was not needed as he was very likely an easy winner. We were all in our usual Hotel Suite in Columbia, and our supports were in the ballroom on election night. Albert was never behind, and his opposition called early and congratulated him. We all went to the ballroom, and I introduced Albert who needed no introduction. He gave his usual great acceptance speech. The State media and the major national media covered the speeches. He got glowing comments on the speech and our record of improving governments.

"It took a while to sink in, but I was now the senior senator from South Carolina—senior senator in my first term. I was not sure that had ever happened before. When we were back in Washington for the next legislative secession, Albert and I were in the apartment. He said, 'Mr. Senior Senator, what are we going to do in my first term in the Senate?' I said, 'We better do something, and it better be good, or I will be a one-term senator.' He laughed and said, 'That will never happen. You will be reelected without opposition.' I said, 'You now sound like Raymond with his wild predictions.' Albert said, 'You know Raymond is usually right with his predictions, and I believe mine will be right. The Democratic leadership, even with their majority, thinks you walk on water. They will most likely tell the State Party not to run anyone against you.' I said, 'I know Raymond and Warren are working hard to educate the voters.'

"Warren came to my office and said that he had the new software ready to try out. I asked what it did. He said that it improved the security of e-mails sent by one senator to another senator or to a group of senators. He said the sender could use, for your eyes only, an icon that would place the message in a secure file, and no one else could obtain the file. He said he had a new e-mail home page that the senators could obtain, and they would not lose anything they currently had on their e-mail. The home page was much easier to use. He said he had a different home page for staff, but they would have, for your eyes only, the feature. He said they could carry on conversations, and the data would be secure. We went to a desk in the office, and he showed me my new e-mail home page. I looked over the features, and I liked them. He then showed me the staff e-mail home page, and it was equally well done. I asked a few of the staff who had seen it, and they felt like I did. I got an appointment with the leadership of both parties and asked that they come to the office for a demonstration. They arrived that afternoon, and we demonstrated the new system with messages from my office to the staff in another room. The leadership was as impressed as I was. They asked how long it would take to get the new software installed. Warren said about ten minutes. He gave them instructions he had printed and told them all they had to do was go to one site and hit the setup icon. All one hundred senators had it up and running by noon the next day.

"Warren monitored the security of the software and found several hackers trying to get into the program, but they all failed. He showed the data to the leadership, and they were even more impressed. None of this was hurting my status in the Senate."

Dylan said, "You were having an easy time in the Senate than you had in the House."

I said, "You got that right. My committee work was interesting, and I helped South Carolina with my position on the Armed Forces Committee. The Budget and Control committee proved to be exciting, especially with John Camp's help."

Dylan said, "You have always had the talent to obtain good people to assist you."

I said, "Yes, like the guy who is writing my biography." That brought the big laugh that I suspected. We chatted for a few minutes more and then said our good-byes. I agreed to meet him on the porch the next Monday.

Jo Anne and I had an Island Boy party on Saturday night. Tom, Elly, Donnie, Jinks, and Warren and their wives were there. Dave and Don and their wives were there. Albert and Mary were also invited, and they came early. They were to spend the weekend with us. We had the porch decorated with gold and brown crape paper, and we had a lot of corn storks about the railing. We had a jukebox at one end of the porch. It was great to watch Tom, Elly, and Donnie's faces as they arrived on the porch. I had invited Evelyn Dalton and her husband and asked them to arrive a little early. They were waiting in the kitchen, and a security guard brought them out. Evelyn laughed heartily and said, "I sure wish my dad could be here. He would love this." The Island Boys who were with me when we had our visit with Mr. Dalton said this was not funny as it reminded us of a time I wanted to forget.

Jinks had heard the story, but Warren had not. He thought we had all gone nuts. I told him the story about the time we almost got arrested. He had his belated laugh. He asked if Mr. Dalton knew that I had become president of the United States. I said he had not as he had died a few years before I became president. The police officer attended my first presidential inaugural ceremony. When I heard he was coming, I had him and his wife a place on the podium. We had a good laugh after I was sworn in. I told Warren I had seen Mr. Dalton many times after the incident. I always thanked him for a great lesson I learned from that experience.

We got that jukebox going. Thank goodness, the volume was at the right level. We could still talk or we could dance. The old friends wanted Jo Anne and I to put on a show. I found a beach music song on the jukebox, and Jo Anne and I put on our Shag with our special moves. After that dance, I wished that Horace could be there, but he had died two years before. We Island Boys always had a good time when we could get together. We were lucky our wives all enjoyed each other's company as much as we enjoyed our good times.

Donnie said, "Who would have ever thought it when we were growing up? We have two presidents out of our old gang. Paul is a former president of the United States, and Tom is the president of the Medical University of South Carolina."

Elly laughed and said, "Both of them would always do everything to get out of work." We all had another good laugh.

Albert had been unusually quiet most of the night. I asked what was wrong. He said he always enjoyed these Island Boy get-together, but he never felt like an Island Boy, and he wished he was. Tom said, "How many times do I have to tell you that you are an Island Boy? You just live two hundred miles up the dual lane." The people in Charleston had always called the first part of Interstate 20 the dual lane. What was called the dual lane was an early dual lane road that extended from the place where King and Meeting Streets met to the North Charleston turnoff.

I said, "Albert, you have been a good friend and a great colleague for so many years. To me, you will always be an Island Boy."

When Dylan and I met the next Monday, I told him about the party. He said he was sorry he had a speaking engagement. He would love to have had time to talk with the Island Boys. He said he had been thinking a lot about the title for the biography. He said he had about decided to call it "Where Do Our Leaders Come From" with a subtitle of "Island Boy Leadership." I said that sounded great to me. I said that Jo Anne and I like to have parties with the Island Boys. We will set up another one when you and Marlene can be present. He said he did not want to put us to all that work. I said to him, "When you have fun, it is no work, and remember, we have servants and security to help us. Damn it! What ever happened to government efficiency?" He laughed.

I said, "We were talking about the time after Albert was elected to the Senate. Raymond came into the office and said we had a problem. I asked what the problem involved, and he told me it involved Albert and me. I said I should call Albert before we discussed it. Albert came over, and Raymond told us we had an image problem. The other party media were calling us antigovernment conservatives. We told him to get us all the media appearances he could and tell Warren and the Geeks to get on it. We would have a White Paper before the end of the day for the Geeks.

"Warren had the Geeks working on the congressional security of documents as well as e-mails. He reported to me that there were frequent attacks on the security system, from China mostly. He said that they had been successful on two occasions. He said he could improve the document security, and he thought we should have round-the-clock Geeks and software, looking for attacks and stopping them. I agreed and approached the leadership with the news. They were very disturbed. They approved a Federal Grant to the Geek program in South Carolina that put in place twenty-four hour Geek monitoring of the Congressional computer network. They paid me a great compliment. They said I had a great organization. They said what else could be expected from someone who had improved governments in so many states and wanted to improve the Federal government. I said, 'Thanks, you know my agenda very well.'

I suggested to Jo Anne that we have a party and invite Dylan and Marlene to meet the Island Boys. Dylan had met most of them, but he was not familiar with them. She agreed and went to work. We invited Dylan and Marlene to stay with us and to come to an Island Boy party. They arrived Saturday morning. Jo Anne and Marlene made a shopping trip to Charleston, and Dylan and I played golf. We planned to have the Island Boys on the porch when we brought Dylan and Marlene from the kitchen. Jo Anne welcome the guests to the porch, and when they were all present, she got us. When I stepped on the porch, I was really surprised. It was decorated in red, white, and blue. There were three American flags along the beachside rail. There were three South Carolina State flags along the house-side rail. The minute I was on the porch, the jukebox in the corner of the porch played "Hail To The Chief." I looked around, and there was a big smile on everyone's face, including the security guards, but there was no smile on my face. I asked who was responsible for that.

I thought it would be either Dave or Don, but Jo Anne said, "I am guilty as charged." I had received that record from the commander of the Marine Corp Band. Semper Fi was on the other side of the record. I walked to the jukebox and unplugged it. I changed the sides of the record so Semper Fi would play, and I turned the jukebox back on. That brought a laugh from everyone present.

I was glad to see the Island Boys taking every opportunity to talk with Dylan. The wives were with Marlene. They were having a great time. Marlene had been on Charleston trips with Jo Anne when some of the wives had come along. She was more familiar with the wives than Dylan was with the Island Boys. I heard them talking about the number of presidents Dylan had interviewed and the number of biographies he had done. Dylan said that he loved the presidential libraries. He said each one had its own particular architecture. He like the Ronald Reagan Library because it was on a hill and looked like it belonged there. He said the libraries were a great way to store the documents of the administration. He said that he thought they would need two libraries to store just the important documents from my administration. I then began to worry about how each couple would get home. The drinking seemed to be going too well. I soon found out each couple had a designated driver. I should have known the Island Boys would plan for everything.

When Dylan and I were together for our next secession, he was very complimentary about the party. He enjoyed the Island Boys and was surprised how well each one of them had made out in their career. He said that all the Island Boys seemed to be very successful. I agreed and said they never forgot a friend. Each one knew he could call on any of the others at any time. Dylan said that he liked it but that he would have expected it after meeting and talking with them at the party.

I asked if he was ready to go to work. He had his recorder on the coffee table next to mine. He turned his recorder on, and I turned on mine.

I then said, "After the summer recess, I was ready to go to work on my fifth year as a senator. I wanted to do something that would be memorable. I wanted to sponsor a bill to have a Constitutional Convention, but Albert talked me out of it. I had talked with the Island Boys, and they were concerned about college and university education. They had said what I knew, and that was, too many students were graduating from colleges and universities without being educated to obtain a job in the job market. The student loans were increasing every year, and tuitions were increasing, but the success of the program was not there. It was time for a Wild Dunes secession with some presidents of the major universities of the country. I put Raymond and Cecil to work on contacting the presidents and seeing if they would be interested in contributing to our knowledge about university education. When we had twelve who said they would attend a meeting at Wild Dunes, I had them set up the meeting. I called Warren and asked him to come over for a talk. He thought I was going to talk about the Geek program. When I told him I was concerned about the educational system, especially college and university education, he was very surprised. He said he had been wondering when someone in a leadership role would wake up and realize we had a mess. He pointed out that our high-school graduates were near the middle of a list of other countries of the world in math and science. That included third-world countries. He said that India and China were moving way out in front of us. I told him I had twelve university presidents who would attend a Wild Dunes program. I was going to ask each one of them to prepare a speech on the problems with our educational system. He said he hoped he could be there. I said that he would be with me. He asked me to remember Tom as he was president of MUSC. I told Raymond and Cecil to include Tom. The meeting was set up with the usual Friday-afternoon arrival and the Saturday working programs. The golf tournament was set for Sunday morning. They would leave on Sunday afternoon.

"The staff did its usual good job with the meeting arrangements, including the airline tickets and the transportation. Wild Dunes was ready for their arrival. We had the Friday-night cocktail party and dinner at the Wild Dunes hotel.

"Saturday morning after breakfast at the hotel, we had a conference room reserved in the Conference Center. We called on the university presidents in alphabetic order. The first one surprised us. He said that education was one thing people would pay for and not complain when they did not get it. He then went on to say something we knew, and that was how poorly our grammar and high schools were doing when they were compared to students in other nations. He said that Columbia University was the first university or college to have a School of Education. He said they were supposed to teach teachers how to teach. He said the current schools and colleges of education were teaching teachers how to teach, but they were either not teaching them or insisting their students are taught the subject they planned to teach. He said that recent data showed that the better the teacher knew their subject, the better the students scored on exams in the subject. He further said that we had a decrease in what the students learned and obtained since requirements had been put into place that required educational degrees for the teachers. That did not say much for the schools and colleges of education. He said the lack of proper education of the students who were entering colleges and universities was contributing to our problems with graduating students who could get jobs. I thought about that last remark. It appeared to me the curriculum in colleges and universities should be doing a better job.

"The next president was equally informing. He said that money was at the heart of the problem. He said governments had increased the funding of education because they wanted to have better-educated graduates, but they were not getting their money's worth. He said that tuitions were increasing because education was expanding. He said that student loans and increased tuition provided more money for higher education. He said that his job and the job of most presidents of educational institutions were to raise more money from gifts and grants. He said the more the money, the larger the faculty. The larger the faculty, the larger the number of departments and the larger the number of degree programs at the educational institutions. There was very little correlation between the degree a student could obtain and the availability of jobs. Professors were teaching what they wanted to teach. To improve their salary, they wanted to head departments that granted degrees. Therefore, the degree programs increased.

The degrees that the university granted was not at all related to the needs of the job market.

"I was looking around at the audience while these two people were talking, and I saw a lot of people nodding their heads yes. I was getting very anxious to hear the other presidents. The next speaker said he agreed with everything that had been said by the first two speakers. He said he hoped the audience would bear with him as he had to change his prepared speech. He said he was going to talk about why the presidents of the universities were not doing more about the problem and attempting to correct the problem. He said the president's job was controlled by a Board of Trustees who gave money to the university and who was interested in financing the university. The Board paid little attention to the academics. The president also served at the pleasure of the faculty. As long as he was financing their goals and objectives, the faculty was happy. The curriculum of the university was controlled by the faculty. One of the previous speakers had outlined that the goals and objectives of the faculty were to teach their personal interest. He said he recently attended a graduate school curriculum committee meeting. He said the professor had applied to teach a new subject and also wanted to expand the material being taught to a degree program. He outlined the material that he had planned to teach. He said one of the committee members from the Medical School basic science degree program asked what I wanted to ask. He asked who would employ the students who had taken the course. The professor who proposed the program said if he had had the material being taught, he would be a better teacher. The professor from the School of Medicine said, 'Well, I guess you are going to teach teachers to teach teachers. I do not see where society gains from your proposal. The president said I could have kissed him. I wish more of the members of the curriculum committees were interested in the value society gets from the courses and the degrees my university offers.' He added that the program was turned down by the committee."

Dylan said this was a good stopping spot. I agreed to this as a stopping spot. He needed to catch a plane, and I had plans with Jo Anne. We said our usual good-byes, and the security people took him to the airport.

Our next meeting was in Columbia at the library. Dylan arrived right on time, and we got to work quickly. Dylan said he wanted to hear the results of our Wild Dunes meeting. I said, "My friend Tom, an Island Boy, was the next speaker. We had discussed his speech, so I knew what to expect. He said he wanted to talk about getting business leaders, especially individuals who headed employment departments in industry, to talk with the university leadership and the faculty members. This would help the university to know the job market better. He said, "I am fortunate. My university has grown from a Medical School. We offer degrees in Medicine, Dentistry, Pharmacy, Nursing, and Allied Health Sciences. There are jobs waiting for our graduates. I can understand the problems that have been put forward this morning. We have faculty who are part-time members of the faculty. They are full-time professionals in their fields. This keeps our educational departments up-to-date on the problems our graduates will face when they would be working in their career field. I would suggest that colleges and universities think about hiring more part-time faculty members who are leaders in a career field. All my department heads and faculty teach and practice their in their field of expertise. My deans do the same thing. They teach and practice medicine or dentistry. The administration and faculty in all Pharmacy, Nursing, and the Allied Health Sciences has private careers. This combination of career and teaching has worked well. The research and the teaching are up-to-date with the problems that exist in their service to society."

"Every speaker said they agreed with what had been said by the earlier speakers. They mostly expanded on the problem of the lack of relationships between the job market and the educational programs. They also pointed out the administrative problems of a university president. I put on my thinking cap and tried to think what I could do to improve the situation. I could see the need for one of our secessions on the porch. I thought it might take more than one. It was lunchtime, so we adjourned the meeting and made our way to the end of the pier that extended from the hotel to the ocean.

Wild Dunes had arranged a wonderful seafood lunch for us. Several of the presidents made their way to our table and said how much they were enjoying the meeting. They also complimented us on the excellent meeting arrangements.

"In the afternoon, I spoke. I thanked them all for coming and thanked the morning speakers for excellent presentations. I then went through our organization. I pointed out we had developed a good program for educating on the Internet. I mentioned Warren Anderson's credentials and his Geek squad. I said we would be having additional small group meetings that I hoped they would attend when we set the meetings up. I said I wanted to get all the Federal government support to correct the problems that we could obtain. Warren spoke briefly about the Geek program and their success. Raymond spoke about the use of media for informing the people about problems and solutions. Albert talked about filing bills in the Senate and how he and I would welcome any suggestion where a bill might assist in helping solve the problems. The presidents were all very interested. They had good questions for each speaker, and the general discussions were informative.

We had an excellent cocktail party at the Wild Dunes hotel, and the dinner was superb. Once again, I was glad I had a ride home, and none of our guests had to drive home. The next day, we had our golf tournament, and the scoring secession and prizes were well received. The presidents all left, feeling the meeting was very informative and the arrangements were the best they had seen. Dylan, I am getting hungry. How about you?" He said he had actually eaten before he had left home but that it seemed like a long time ago. I suggested we go to a new restaurant I had learned about on Sumter Street. He said that sounded good. The security people were ready with the SUV, and we all went to the restaurant. Dylan and I engaged in small talk with the security guards at lunch. It was amazing how much they were aware of what was happening around the restaurant. The food was excellent. We took a little ride around town before we went back to the library. Once we were back, we turned on the recorders and got started.

I said, "When I was back in my Washington office, I got a phone call from one of the presidents who had attended our meeting. He said he was disturbed by the number of students who were applying to his university with credits from the so-called colleges and universities that were located in strip malls. He said he called them Strip Mall Colleges. They were largely Internet colleges. They were not accredited by the proper agencies, and their credits did not transfer. He said the students were getting ripped off by these Strip Mall Colleges.

This disturbed me as it had disturbed him. I told him I would get right on it and that I would keep him informed. I had the staff set up a meeting with Warren, Raymond, and Albert.

"When we were together in my office, I reported to them on my phone conversation with the university president. They were as shocked as I was. Warren said, 'We can set up an educational program on the Internet that will tell the students to make sure any college or university they attend is properly certified and accredited and that the credits transfer.' He said he could reach the group that we needed to reach. The social Internet sites and e-mail list would allow them to get the word out. Raymond said he would work the newspapers and the TV media. Albert said that he had not heard about this, and he understood why we needed to get the word out.

"After they left my office, I called the president and told him what we had planned to do. I also told him I would put up a bill that would not allow students at unaccredited Strip Mall Colleges to get student loans. He said he liked the bill idea. It worried him that the students were going into debt and not getting their money's worth. He also said he was working on reducing the number of degree programs at his university. He had gotten the approval of his board. He said he would deal with the faculty problem. He was inviting industrial leaders and company employee department people to the university to discuss the problems we had covered at Wild Dunes. He had talked with four other presidents, and they were following his lead.

"The Geek program and the media coverage got the word out about the unaccredited colleges. I filled my bill, and it was getting all the support I needed in the House and the Senate. I was just getting happy when the preverbal hit the fan.

"My bill passed, and the phone, e-mail, and mail pilled in. We were told many of the Strip Mall Colleges were accredited and were doing a great job in providing industry and companies with employees who had the education they needed. Most of the students at the Strip Mall Colleges were working while they were taking the Internet courses. They were usually promoted after they graduated. The employment numbers were very favorable, and the salaries were good for the graduates of the accredited Strip Mall Colleges. This caused me to think back to something I had learned at an early age and had been careful about until this time: I should always deeply investigate anything before I took any action.

"I had another meeting with Warren, Raymond, and Albert and told them what was happening. Warren said the data from the interactive Web sites indicated the educational program had been a success. A very large number of students said they had transferred to accredited Strip Mall Colleges. I was very happy my bill only dealt with unaccredited Strip Mall Colleges. Warren said he intended to stay after the unaccredited ones but that he would give good ratings to the accredited ones that were doing a good job. Raymond said that he would follow suit. After the meeting was over, I called the university president and told him about our response, and he said it sounded as if we were on the right track. I thanked him and asked if he was satisfied with our efforts or had additional suggestions. He said he was very satisfied.

"We stayed on the universities and colleges about the employment rate of their graduates. We got the presidents who were working to improve their employment rate to write and call the other presidents. The Geek program set up methods of measuring the employment rates for the educational institutes.

They listed the rates by the titles of the degrees. That was a big help. Albert took over this program and was doing a good job in getting things straightened out.

"I was still thinking about the nations standing in math and science as compared to other nations. I set up a secession on the porch to deal with this problem. I invited Warren, Albert, and the university president I had been talking with. His name was Vernon Strickland. I invited the South Carolina Superintendent of Education. I wanted representation from the midlands too, so I invited the Nebraska Superintendent of Education. Since Columbia University had the first School of Education, I invited the president of Columbia University. I invite Tom to come over before the others arrived. Tom arrived, and we sat on the porch with a beer. I told him about my concerns with our educational system. He said the Medical University of South Carolina dealt with the top of the graduates from mostly southern colleges and universities, and they were not having a problem getting qualified students. He said he had noticed that they frequently had to go at a little lower level in the lectures in order to bring the students up to a level where they could learn the material.

"We had our meeting, and Albert, Warren, and Tom remained after the others left. We were all very dissatisfied with the progress we made during the meeting. The State Superintendents of Education were all graduates of schools or colleges of education. They did not see anything wrong with our educational system. When we were seated on the porch, I said, 'I think we have seen the source of the problem.' Tom was the first to agree. Warren said he agreed too. Albert said we had another big problem that so many people did not see. I said that this would become a major economic problem.

With the increasing national and world population growth, having jobs for our citizens would become a bigger problem. When the other countries have better-educated populations, they will get the jobs. All the industries would move their production overseas. They all agreed. Warren said he would take that thought to the Geeks and get them to pointing out the possible economic problem and its connection to improving our educational system. I asked him to be sure to point out the population growth problem. I asked him to talk with Raymond and get him involved. He said he had thought of that."

I then said to Dylan, "That lunch was fine, but I need a beer."

Dylan said, "I have a plane to catch. Marlene has plans for me when I get home." We turned off the recorders and packed our briefcases. We said our usual good-byes, and he and I were shown out by the security people. The SUV was waiting for us. As hard as I try, the service still gets to me.

I arrived back on the Island, and Jo Anne had kept up with the trip home. She was on the porch with my beer, her wine, and a dish of nuts. The security guys had had lunch, but they would never take a beer with Jo Anne and I. That said that was family time, and they did not want to intrude. We had arrived home later than usual, so Jo Anne and I stayed on the porch, and we were served dinner there. Jo Anne told me she had arranged for cocktails on the porch the next night with Tom, Donnie, and Elly. Their wives too would be there. We were all going to Marshall's after cocktails. That sounded good to me.

I worked in my office the next morning. I had bruised my leg, and the dermatologist who was treating it said there were basil cells that had to be removed. I looked up basil cells on the Web site. I learned more about basil cell cancer than I cared to learn. I appeared to be in good hands with the dermatologist. After I was satisfied that I would live, I turned my attention to my favorite pastime on the computer. I started to use the search engines to find quotations on various subjects. As ideas always come, I got a sudden urge to write a book with the quotes to back up my data and comments about a subject. The first quote to come to mind was one by Albert Einstein who said, "Insanity is doing the same thing over and over and expecting a different result." This was what I thought voters did at the polls at each election. They vote for a candidate who promises a change in government, and they get the same do-nothing expensive government. I found another quote that backed up my impression of our method of government. It was a quotation by P. J. O'Rourke, an American political satirist. He said, "Fiscal conservatism is just an easy way to express something that is a bit more difficult, which is that the size and scope of politics in our lives has grown uncomfortable, unwieldy, intrusive, and inefficient." I sure agreed with him. I found one quote after another that agreed with my agenda and my goals and objectives. When I was done, I titled the book, *Expecting a Different Result*. This was my first attempt to write a book. I was sure my status as a former president would help. I just could not decide how to get it published. I had to think about that. I seemed to be having those turn-on-the-mental-light-bulb days. I remember something my grandpa had said to me over and over when I was staying with them as a small boy. He had said, "Before you do something in life, think about what you intend to accomplish." That few minutes of thinking about what I wanted to accomplish had helped me on many occasions. This was another one. I thought I did not need the money, so I was not interested in making money from a book I published. I was rather interested in having people think about their method of government. I needed to get an agent to help me publish the book and get it distributed. I had always gotten people who knew their fields to help, and it worked.

When Dylan and I were together on the porch, I told him about my plans to write a book. He said that was a great idea and that he had thought about asking me to coauthor a book or two with him. That sounded interesting. I said, "We could have a ball working on a book."

Dylan said, "I think so too."

I said, "I do not know what to do with the book I just finished."

Dylan said, "Send me a copy as an e-mail attachment, and I will send it to my publisher. My publisher is Simon & Schuster."

I said, "Thanks, Dylan, I appreciate your help. Well, I guess it is time for us to get to work in the salt mines. We have got to shovel a lot of salt over the next three days. I am glad you can stay with us for those days. Jo Anne said she misses Marlene and hopes she can come next time."

Dylan said, "Marlene enjoys Jo Anne's company. She is with the boys this week. The oldest bought a new house, and Marlene is helping in getting it furnished and set up for him."

I said, "Our wives are always there for our children while we seem to be always busy with our careers." Dylan placed his recorder on the coffee table, and I turned on mine. I then said, "The population increase both in this country and around the world worried me. Our poverty level had been increasing for a very long time. It looked like our poverty class would become the majority class of our population. We need to bring our educational level up to the top of the list of all the countries. The nation with the best educational system would have the largest percentage of their population employed and the lowest percentage of the population in the poverty class. Reagan economics had hurt the country for so many years. Trickle-down economics had not worked. The rich were not going to worry about the poor. Robin Hood did it right when he robbed the rich and gave to the poor. Warren and the Geek program and Raymond got this message out to the voters. Albert and I got the word out to the legislature. We both wrote White Papers on the subject and sent the White Papers to every member of the legislature. We visited every office where we had support and asked them to help get out the word.

"I had known since I was a small child that you could not reach a solution to a problem by talking it to death. We were doing a lot of talking, but we were not seeing much in the way of changes. The high-education institutions were doing a better job of graduating students who got jobs with adequate salaries. The Geeks had good data on this. But we were hearing that the colleges and universities were not getting better-educated students from the high schools. In fact, the data indicated the average students from the high schools were falling further behind the students in other countries and were not doing as well on entrance exams for college. I pointed out these facts to the State Superintendent of Education. We included all the data to support the conclusions. As far as we could tell, this was all falling on deaf ears. Albert and I were at the apartment, talking about our agenda. He said, 'Life is not a bed of roses. You try hard to help people have common sense, but they resist every effort.' I said, 'I think I remember being invited to common sense's funeral.'

"My second term in the Senate ended, and I was reelected without an opponent for the office from the other party. South Carolina was benefiting from Albert's work and mine on reducing the number of governments. It was paying off for the voters with lower taxes. The governor kept saying he thought he would get a one-House legislature, but it did not happen. More and more of the voters were falling in line according to the data from the Geek program. Albert had three years before he was up for reelection. There had been two bills passed that were designed to put pressure on the states to improve their students' educational performance. But we were not seeing any improvement, and the poverty level was increasing. There was a slight drop in the nation's rate of population growth, but the third-world nations still had rapid population increases. While we had grown and produced the most food, we were now losing family farms and replacing them with large corporation farms. They produced low-paying jobs. They used mostly immigrant labor. With the increase in immigrant labor and the loss of jobs to overseas plants, we had an increasing rate of unemployment. The congressional approval rate was at the lowest rate in the history of the nation. The president had a very low approval rating. It was obvious that voters were becoming more dissatisfied with the job government was doing. We were not collecting enough money to have a balanced budget. The deficit increased every year, and the national debt increased each year. I asked what he thought about another meeting with the leadership at the beach. He said it could not hurt. We discussed the plans for the meeting with the staff. We wanted to keep the number of people as small as possible. We wanted to have two legislature leaders from each party and from both the House and the Senate. That made ten, so we needed to be careful who else we invited. We did not want to look like we thought we were equal to the leadership. I thought we might invite the Secretary of Education and have him bring anyone he wanted to have come with him. I made an appointment and went to his office. I discussed the problem briefly and invited him to join us at the beach. He accepted and said he would bring two other people. Once we had that set, we invited the others. They all accepted. The staff set up the usual arrangements with Wild Dunes and the airlines. Transportation was arranged at the beach. We planned to have three meetings on the porch. One meeting would be held on Friday afternoon and two meetings on Saturday. The Saturday afternoon meeting would end early so that the attendees could make their flights.

"We had our Wild Dunes meeting on the problems with our educational method. It was like everything that we had done. There was a lot of talk and agreement that something had to be done. But something was not defined or agreed upon. There was a suggestion from the leader of the Senate Democratic Party. He suggested we should withhold all Federal Government money until the colleges and universities disbanded their education schools and colleges. The Secretary of Education said that he thought that was going too far. In general, we agreed with him. The Democratic leader said that was the kind of method the legislature usually used. They either gave more money or withheld money as a method for getting something done. Albert said that he agreed that was going too far. I just could not keep my mouth shut, so I said a major problem the Congress had was it had passed too many laws and regulations that reduced the ability of the society to run their lives. There was general agreement that we had removed social freedoms. I reminded them of Tom Paine's quote. 'Society is a blessing, but government in its best state is a necessary evil, and in its worst state, it is an intolerable evil.' One of the Republican leader said we could always leave it to old Tom. He let us know the way it was."

Dylan asked, "Are you ready to stop for the morning?"

I said, "No, I was on a roll and wanted to go a little further."

I said, "That meeting pretty much summed it up for my third term in the Senate. We worked every day, but we did not get much done. The country was in its doldrums. The economy was not doing well, and the unemployment rate was increasing every month. We were making headway around the country with more mergers of governments, and three more states had unicameral legislatures. This had proved to decrease the cost of government and put some money back into the hands of the taxpayers. Without this stimulus, we would have been bankrupt. Albert and I decided we had been working with the wrong group. Our efforts to work with the Superintendents of Education were a total failure. We decided to work with the governors and see if we could get something done. I thought we might try the Party Leaders in both parties. But we decided that fifty governors were a large enough group. The Party Leaders would involve too many people. We did get the Geek Program to contact the Party Leaders and give them the data and the pitch for improving education as a way to improve the job market and the economy. Albert and I sat down and started a White Paper that included the data and the conclusions from our Geek program and asked what could be done to improve our educational system. We did not include the ExxonMobil data and conclusion that our teachers needed to be better educated in the field they intended to teach. The teachers with the best knowledge of their subject had the best student results on test and examinations, including the college entrance exams. We wanted to see what they had to say before we gave them that data. Every governor that answered our White Paper agreed with us that our educational system was at the heart of our employment problem and our economic problem, but there was not one suggestion for a solution.

"Now that I have gotten that off my chest, I am ready for lunch."

Dylan said, "God does answer some of my prayers." He turned off his recorder, and I turned off mine. With the security, we had gotten used to leaving them on the coffee table.

Jo Anne appeared and asked how many beers we could drink for lunch. She knew we would have one at lunch, and but she wanted to know if we needed one before we left for lunch. We smiled, and I said, "Where is the one we need right now?" She turned and motioned to the kitchen, and two beers were brought to the porch. We discussed lunch while we were drinking a much-needed beer. I had been thinking about my third term in the Senate, and there was not much that could make me proud.

Jo Anne said, "You two like Dunleavy's, but I like the end of the pier at Wild Dunes."

I said, "The ice-cream shop makes that an interesting place."

Dylan said, "I like the ice cream to finish off the lunch."

The security brought the SUV to the side steps from the porch, and we entered the car. Dylan asked, "How are your boys doing?"

Jo Anne answered, "They are doing fine. Dave is living in St. George, which is near the distribution center where he works. Don is living in the house we bought when we moved back to the island. He bought it from us two years ago."

Dylan said, "As I remember it, they are both married, and each one has one child—a boy."

I said, "Yes, you have a good memory. Dave and Don had a joint wedding. They said they always did things together, so they decided to get married at the same service. Dave married Gloria Meyers. Her mother was an old friend of mine. Don married Jewel Abbott. I knew her father. It turns out to be a small world."

Dylan said, "Disney got that right. It is a small, small world."

As we approached the end of the pier at Wild Dunes, I saw Elly and Tom with their wives. We joined them and had a great lunch. The company exceeded the food. The ice cream at the end of the meal could not be beat.

When we were back on the porch, Dylan and I looked at each other for about a minute. He was first to say, "I am really enjoying this job more than I have any other biography I have ever produced."

I said, "It has been an enjoyable experience. You are a great friend, and I have enjoyed the memory of parts of the things I have told you."

When the recorders were on, I remembered my thoughts as we were riding to lunch—*Much of the third term should be forgotten.* I said, "The Do-Nothing Congress of my third term was not something that one can look upon with pride. I was still on the budget committee, and I was the Republican chairman of the Armed Forces committee. I was able to save both Fort Jackson in Columbia and the Air Force Base in Charleston. I worked with the Armed Forces Chiefs to improve our drone capability. I loved the drone program because it kept our service people out of danger. We were making good progress on the land-based drones, and we had developed a drone helicopter. Several of the helicopters were under construction. Albert and I continued to work on our agenda to reduce the number and cost of governments. We were having just enough success to make us proud, but nothing like what we really wanted. It was good to be able to show some progress in a government with a very low approval rating. The economy remained a problem, and the congress was spending more money than they were collecting in taxes. At the same time, we had, and deserved, the Do-Nothing Congress title.

"Two years before the end of my third term, while we were seated on the porch, I got a call from the Republican leadership. They wanted me to run for the post of president of the United States. I can't say I had not thought about it, but I was thinking about not running for a fourth term in the Senate and running for president in the election following the next one. I asked for a few days before I gave them an answer. Albert, Mary, Jo Anne, and I were sitting on the porch. I told them about the call. They were very interested. I told them I had thought about running in the election following this one. I wanted to finish out my commitment to the people of South Carolina. I did not want to resign from the Senate.

"Albert pointed out, 'If a Republican was elected in the upcoming election, he would be an incumbent president, and I would not want to run against an incumbent president in a primary.' He was right as that would mean I would have to wait another four years before I could run. That would make it ten years from now before I could run, and if elected, I would have to serve eight years. At my age, eighteen years seemed like a long time. We called the boys and asked them to come over. They arrived in time for dinner. We all went to Marshall's and had a good time. When we were back on the porch, I told them about my call. Everyone there said they would work hard in support of my election. They agreed it looked like the best time for me to run. The next day, I called the state governor and told him about my call and that I was considering running. I asked what he thought. He said it was up to me and that I would have his total support in whatever I decided. I thanked him for his support.

"When I was back in my Washington office, I called and invited the Republican leadership to the office at two that afternoon. They said the time was good with them and that they would be there. They arrived on time, and we had a good discussion of the things we had covered on the porch. They promised 100 percent support from the party. They said I would have one opponent in the primary. There was one person they could not convince not to run. His name was Martin White, a former governor of California. I knew him well. He was a power-motivated individual who saw the president of the United States as the most powerful office in the world, and he could not wait to be president. I was sure he did not know what he would do if he was elected, but the power motivation was at the heart of his desire to run. He had made money in the stock market, and many of his gains were ill-gotten. He had bought well-operated industries and borrowed money from the industry and bankrupted the company. Many people had lost good-paying jobs and their retirement. One of the plants was a steel mill in Georgetown, South Carolina. Georgetown was a small town with two industries. When one went bankrupt, it hurt the whole area's economy. It would be a great pleasure for me to kick his ass.

"While no one was sure, it appeared that there would be at least three democratic candidates for their primary election. I hoped there would be more, and they would tear each other up by comments made in the primary. Albert and I talked about the primary and the general election campaign. I asked him to run as my vice president candidate. He said he was not sure how two people from one state would work out. He said, 'Two people from one state are bad enough, but South Carolina is a small southern state, and it is known for its conservatism.' He reminded me of the name the media from the other party tried to stick on us. They called us antigovernment southern conservatives. I said, 'For this election, I would love that name. We had a reputation for lowering government cost and lowering taxes. We would pitch our agenda right from the get-go.' He said, 'If you want me and are not making the decision based on friendship, I will be proud to run with you.' I replied, 'Much of my decision was made on a longtime friendship that included many good successes, and we were together on the agenda. We would pursue if elected.'"

Dylan said this was a good place for a break. We turned off the recorders, sat back, and looked at the beautiful sky over the ocean. Dylan said, "I have never worked in such a wonder environment." Before we parted, we planned to get back together in about two hours. Dylan said this would give time to arrange some of the things we had covered.

When we were back together, with the recorders going, I said, "Albert and I got our team together and started planning our attack. We met on the porch, and I told the members of the team to expect many meetings on the porch in the coming months. I had asked the Republican leadership why they were approaching me so early, and they reminded me that the primary elections were being moved up near the first of January, so we had to begin campaigning very soon.

"We had our team working on the election at the beginning of the next month. The first thing they did was put up a program to draft me for a presidential candidate. The program worked well, and the media joined in on the draft. The data from the interactive blogs and other sites showed that a large part of the population were in favor of drafting me as their candidate. This was especially true among Republicans. As soon as the office was open, I filled my papers to run for president. This was met with very favorable reviews by the media. I announced my vice presidential choice very early. This was met by more support. Our record was very much in our favor. Albert and I made trips together to the states with early primary elections. We traveled the state of South Carolina because it was going to be a state where the primary election was to be held early. We visited Florida together and at different times. California seemed to be a problem, so we went to work there. We needed those electoral votes. We made media appearances with our wives and, on several occasions, our families. Raymond had the boys and Jo Anne making appearances around the nation and on media programs. With the Geek program and the offices we opened all over the nation, it was obvious we had the best-organized campaign.

"I kept hoping we were not going to skew up somewhere. One wrong remark could do a lot of harm. Everyone remained on message. We used our longtime record on reduced number of governments and the reduced cost of governments. I came up with a new phrase that made me very proud. The new phrase was, 'Peace and Prosperity for All.' I wanted this phrase to replace the old phrase, 'the American Dream.' Albert and

I began to point out that Peace could lead to Prosperity. We made visits to nations where there was no peace and pointed out that peace could bring prosperity for all. When we were in the United States, we pointed out that working for peace in the world could mean peace and prosperity for all. The Geeks picked up on the phrase and had it on the Internet all over the world. I saw where the Geek program was going to be as it was an important part of my administration if I was elected.

"The one thing both Albert and I wanted the voters to know was we were not remaining silent about the extremely large and expensive government. It was not only large and expensive but also ineffective and inefficient. We included this message in every speech. The voters were paying for a Do-Nothing oversized congress and an Executive Government that was spending money which the Federal Government did not have. The tax base could not fund the budget. There was a yearly deficit that added to the national debt. It was time to have an administration that would work to produce a method of government that was efficient and effective. The nation needed an administration that would work toward Peace and Prosperity for All. This message was received well by the voters, according to the Geek data. In fact, I was called by a leader in the Democratic Party who told me their data showed a large number of Paul Harvey Collins Democrats. Our data supported this conclusion.

"The nearer we got to the primary elections, the more the Democratic Challengers were fighting each other. They were attacking each other's character. The media was having a ball pointing out the division in the Democratic Party. We got a big break just over two weeks before the primary elections. My opponent dropped out of the race. He endorsed my campaign.

I thought Albert and I needed more contact with the world population. We made overseas trips during the early part of the campaign after the primary elections. Our message, Peace and Prosperity for All, was well received in each nation we visited. The efforts I had spent supporting the land-based drone program and the increase in fire power without putting our military in the path of danger was seen as important by the military of each nation. I was approached about buying this type of equipment by the military leaders of each nation.

"Albert and I had a secession on the porch with our team leaders. We were assured by all that we would win by a landslide. Raymond was the one who was most sure. Warren believed the landslide was going to happen. Cecil Dempsey, a campaign manager we had hired from California, supported the conclusion of the others. He said our support in California was the best he had ever seen. He was known by politicians in California as the best campaign manager in the state. He cautioned us that we needed to have every office in every state working to get out the vote. He said we were so popular that many voters, thinking we were such a sure winner, might not get out and vote. We took his warning to heart and got letters and phone calls off to every office to be sure to work to get out the vote. Warren worked on the offices around the country by way of the Internet.

"Albert and I talked a lot about where we should be on the election night and who should be with us. We wanted our supports in a large ballroom somewhere. Naturally, I preferred Charleston. We thought about Columbia, but our campaign managers wanted Washington. They thought we could get the best of the media there. We agreed with them, and the staff got just the kind of place we had wanted in a well-known Washington hotel. We were in a very large suite with our best friends from among our workers. The ballroom was running over, and the best of the media was there. It was obvious from the very first returns that we would have the landslide that had been predicted would occur. We received our congratulations from the Democratic candidate before the polls closed in the west.

"We had our acceptance speeches written and rehearsed. We would stay on message. We wanted everyone to know what our agenda would look like. After I was introduced, I started my talk by saying loudly, 'Peace and Prosperity for All.' This brought cheers from the crowd that lasted for at least a minute. I had to calm them down. I said that peace and prosperity for all was possible. That was followed by another long response from the crowd. After they settled down, I said, 'It would take work, but Albert and I have never been afraid of work. We want accomplishments. We are against a do-nothing government. One voice can be heard, and our voice would be heard. We would not remain silent while the people of the nation suffer. When we say all, we mean all. No one or no group would be left out. To have prosperity, the world needs peace. It would be ALL FOR ONE and ONE FOR ALL. We would work to get all the people of all the nations of the world to be working for every other person in the world. We will then achieve Peace and Prosperity for All.' I thought the walls would cave in as the noise from the crowd was so high."

Dylan said, "Let's break for the day."

I said, "I thought I was on a roll."

Dylan said, "You were, and that is the problem. I have now got a lot on the recorder to transpose. I will be up for quite a while."

I said, "I guess it is much easier trying to remember one's career than it is to write about it." He agreed, and we said our good nights.

The next morning, we were back on the porch with coffee and sweet rolls. I loved the coffee rolls with their glaze. After a period of small talk, we were back with the recorders. I said, "The media carried our speeches over and over. They said our speeches rivaled JFK speech and Martin Luther Jr. speech. We went back to the beach, feeling very good as we waited for January 20 to come. I wanted to hit the ground running fast. Albert agreed. We had waited a very long time for a position where we could accomplish our goal. I had planned to announce I would contribute the salary of the president of the United States to the budget of the nation. I wanted the people to know I was serious about lowering the cost of government. I said I wanted the people to know I would cover many of my expenses while I was president. Albert agreed and said he would do the same.

"I said I wanted to cut an Executive Order the first thing that did away with the following government departments. I wanted to remove education. I wanted the states to be responsible for their education programs. I wanted to return power and sovereignty to the people. The money saved by removing the Department of Education was to be given to the states. The amount each state was to receive depended upon the student population of the state. I decided to remove the Department of Energy. They had done nothing to reduce our dependence on foreign oil. We were not making the progress on renewable energy that we should have been making. The money saved from this change was to be given to research agencies that were working on renewable energy. Another department I wanted to remove was the Department of Housing and Urban Development. The state's new problems were related to development, and not all development was urban.

"We needed to give the states and the people the freedom to act on their problems. The nearer the decision-making to the people affected by the decision, the better the decision. The money saved from this change was to be used to reduce the deficit in the budget. Albert and I had been talking about these changes for a long time.

"Albert and I had discussed the problem of unemployment that the people would face during our administration. We hoped to move the people from depending on the government funds for their livelihood to people who were contributing taxes to the budget. My second Executive Order was to create an agency that would assist the people who would become unemployed. We needed an outplacement agency. We wanted everyone affected to know about this agency and to receive their help. They would be looking for placement of the individual in good jobs in society. I hired Carl Walters as head of the outplacement agency. He had been a professor of business and taught class and had run employment programs for students. He had a good knowledge of the needs of the industry, and I had used him to aid us on the curriculum program of colleges and universities that provided graduates with the best chance of getting good-paying jobs. He impressed me with his first move. He had his staff contact every government department and agency to find out what jobs were currently available and what jobs were to become available due to retirements.

"I called John Camp and asked him to put together a staff to help him audit the various departments and agencies of the government. I wanted to know which ones were doing a good, efficient, and effective job and which ones were not worth their salt. He agreed to take on the task. In fact, he said he was looking forward to helping improve the efficiency of the government.

"I got a call from Tom. He said that after I would be sworn in to office, he wanted to talk to me about a problem. He did not say what the problem was. I said he could come to Washington on the twenty-first or he could see me at the beach. He preferred a porch secession. He said he was more familiar with the porch secessions. I told him I would call as soon as I was back at the house on the beach.

"The wait for the inauguration was worth the time. I gave the speech I had planned for a long time. I pushed for a unicameral government. I pushed for efficiency in government. I said I would do everything I could to see to it that the people got the effective government they deserved. I pitched 'Peace and Prosperity for All' as our motto for the administration. I said that I wanted Peace and Prosperity for All to be something that everyone worked for. I said it was time for our efforts to be one for all and all for the American people. I announced to the people my intent to serve without pay. I said this was part of our effort to reduce the cost of government. I told the people I would cover as many of my expenses as I could. The administration would be one of efficiency. The address was very well received by the media, and I got compliments from the opposition.

"Albert's swearing in went equally well. His speech showed we were joined in our efforts. He would serve without pay and cover as many of the expenses as he could. He stressed the need for an efficient Federal government if we wanted Peace and Prosperity for All. He said when we worked together without individual greed, everyone had an opportunity to be prosperous. He pointed out we had struggled with Reagan economics long enough. Trickle-down economics did not work. It was time for everyone, including the president and the vice president, to pull his or her load. We hugged each other after our speeches. The media loved the speeches and played them over and over so everyone could hear them."

Dylan said, "Aren't you hungry?"

I said, "Dylan, I have never been hungry. I eat to keep from getting that way."

He gave me one of his big smiles and said, "I'll have to remember that one."

I said, "That should not be hard as we have not turned off our recorders."

He reached over, turned them both off, and said, "Mr. President, it is time you learned to relax."

I laughed and said, "Now you sound like Jo Anne."

The security men gathered around and wanted to know what we wanted to do for lunch. I asked if Jo Anne was at home. They said yes, and one went to get her. When she got there, I asked if we could have lunch on the porch. She said, "Yes, you can. In fact, there is a very good lunch for everyone ready in the kitchen."

I said, "That is good, and I hope it includes a beer."

She said, "Yes, beer for the two of you and wine for me."

We ate our lunch with a lot of small talk about the families. Dylan reminded me I would have to bring the family side of my life up-to-date. I said, "Maybe you should interview Jo Anne for that. She is more up-to-date than I have ever been."

Dylan said, "I have been thinking about asking you and her if she would mind."

Jo Anne said, "I do not know what I can contribute, but I would enjoy working with you."

He thanked her and said, "As soon as we get to a good stopping spot, I will arrange a time with you."

After lunch, we were back to work. I said, "When I got home, I called Tom, and we set up an appointment for Saturday night. He arrived, and we went to our favorite spot on the porch. There was a windbreak at one end of the porch, and it made a quiet corner for us to talk. The view was good from there, and the sky was full of stars.

"He said, 'I want to talk about paperwork. Common senses had died, and we are burdened with do-nothing work. The government has burdened everyone with unnecessary paperwork that fills the files but is never used.' He said he knew I was interested in efficiency and wanted to reduce cost. He said a good place to start was to look at how rules and regulations had removed common sense and good judgment from many things people do. He had a good ear, and I was very interested in what he was telling me. He said that paperwork had assured the bosses that the workers were doing their job and had become a way of life in most industries.

"I remember a story I had heard, and I related it to Tom. I said, 'I heard about an industry in Germany during World War II that had been destroyed by bombs. There was an office building next door. The employees showed up every day and shoved paperwork from one to another even when the plant was destroyed.' Tom said, 'We have reached that point.' He said that he had a story for me.

"He said one of his retired professors was a good friend of his. He said, in fact, the professor had taught him when he was a student in medicine. He said that the professor and his wife lived in an assisted-living facility. They were both somewhat disabled. But his friend got around well. He still was a good driver and did not have the senility that many people of his age had. His wife had a bout of low blood pressure caused by a mix-up in dose at the Facility. The people at the Facility insisted that she go to the hospital. When she was in the emergency room, her pressure was low, and her heart rate was slow. They moved her to the cardiac floor. Within a few hours, her blood pressure became normal, and her heart rate also became normal. Tom's professor friend who was a Distinguished Professor Emeritus of the School of Medicine knew all the cardiology staff. He told them he had always given his wife her medications when they were living in their home. He would check her blood pressure before he gave her the meds. He said she had a very labile blood pressure—sometimes it was high and sometimes it was normal or low. He would only give her the prescribed dose when her pressure was elevated. When they moved to the assisted-living facility, they took over all the medications and gave her the dose on a regular schedule. She had gotten an overdose of her medications. The medications needed to be adjusted to the new method of administration. The cardiologist agreed with him and made a change in medication and dose. She was released from the hospital, and his friend was ready to take his wife back to the Facility. The nursing staff said she had to see a social worker before she could be released. The social worker told his friend there was paperwork that was required before he could take his wife out of the hospital. He told the social worker he was totally qualified to take his wife. The social worker said she had to contact the Facility and see if they would let her come back and stay there. My friend used his cell phone and called the director of the Facility and asked him if there would be any problem with them returning to the Facility. He said there was no problem, and he did not understand what the holdup was. My friend put him on the phone with the social worker, and the director told her that the Facility did not have a problem with having the Kinnards' return. The social worker said she had to fax paperwork to the Facility, and the Facility would have to return the necessary paperwork to her by fax. My friend and his wife waited at the hospital in the room for another four hours while the paperwork was being done. My friend asked why they needed the paperwork. She said, 'It shows the hospital and my boss I am doing my job.'

"I said, 'Tom, I can see in this case and a lot of others that our Federal Rules and Regulations are interfering with people's rights and freedoms. That is wrong. We are a nation of free people. I will do everything I can when I get back to Washington to put a stop to this paperwork problem.' Tom thanked me and said he knew I would do what I could. Jo Anne brought us two beers and a plate of snacks. She said, 'It is great to see you two old friends together.' I said, 'A couple of Island Boys working on a problem. We will correct this paperwork situation.'

"When I was back in the Oval Office, I asked John Camp to join me. It was not long until he was there. I asked how things were going, and he said, 'Well.' He said he had data for me. I took the data and said I had something I wanted to add to his task. I told him about the meeting with Tom and the story Tom had told me. He said, 'A part of my data indicates how I have dealt with this problem of loss of freedoms of people caused by government rules and regulations.' He said that the paperwork problem was a major cause of inefficiency. He showed the data to me and suggested an Executive Order to correct part of the problem. I said I would include in the Executive Order a requirement that every department and agency take every effort to reduce the paperwork caused by the rules and regulations. I said the Order would require the heads of the departments and agencies to limit their effects on the freedoms of the citizens. John loved it. When he left, I drew up the Executive Order. I had Albert look it over, and he made a couple of suggestions that improved the Order. I made the changes and called in my secretary and asked her to have the Executive Order executed."

Dylan said, "The sun goes down very late when we are on daylight saving time. That will give us some time tonight to work. I could use a beer before dinner."

I said, "With the longer day, I dry out early myself. I could use at least one before dinner." The security guard overheard out conversation and used his radio to get things moving. Jo Anne and two security guards came out of the kitchen, carrying a tray. Dylan and I got our beers, and Jo Anne had her glass of wine. I said, "Dylan and I plan to work for a while tonight after dinner."

Jo Anne said, "We have everything arranged. We can have dinner right here."

Dylan said, "She never fails to amaze me. I think she is reading our minds from the house."

I said, "I have always feared she had that property."

Jo Anne said, "If I could read minds, you and I would not have remained married." That brought a laugh from everyone on the porch. We had a good dinner and got back to work.

I started the evening secession by saying, "I called Tom and told him I had issued an Executive Order. I said I would send him an e-mail with the Executive Order as an attachment. He said he would appreciate that. When I hung up the phone, I sent Tom the e-mail and attachment. He confirmed he had received the e-mail and read the attachment. He thanked me for getting right to work on the problem. I wished that all problems were that easy to start a procedure that should help to solve.

"A funny thing happened. I was thinking back to our problem with education. I was wishing we could solve our problem with the degree programs not providing the education the student needed to get a good-paying job. Albert turned up at the door and asked if he could come in and discuss something that would be very interesting to me. I said, 'You can come in anytime.' He said that he had just learned about Kahn Academy, a free educational program, that was run by a young man as a not-for-profit institution. He said that the Kahn Academy was gaining students all over the world. Bill Gates used it to help his children. The program was being used by more and more schools. It was changing the method of education. It was putting the homework in the classroom and the schoolwork at home. The students worked at a rate that their ability allowed them to learn. The program helped the teachers see who was doing well with their learning and the ones who needed more individual help.

"I asked Warren to look into the Kahn Academy and, if possible, find out if the schools using the program had better results than those that were not. He said he had heard of the Kahn Academy, and he had learned a little about it. He had heard that he started by helping a young member of his family on the Internet. She was having trouble with algebra, and he helped her. He soon found out that a lot of other students were looking at the material and using it as a learning method. That got him started. He said he would look into it and report to me. I thanked him and turned my attention to another problem.

"I was less than a week into the new administration, and we had made good progress on improving government efficiency and effectiveness. Letters and phone calls were coming in at such a rate that the staff could not keep up with replies. The Internet and e-mails were coming at a rate that was causing problems, and we had to increase staff. Most of the mess was caused by individuals and organizations as well as governments wanting one of us to come to some event as a speaker. Poor Albert was on the road 24 7. I was very selective since I wanted to be in the office working on problems. I decided to have Warren, Raymond, Cecil, and John Camp to come in to the White House and teach a group of speakers who could fill in for Albert and me at many of these events. We had them very familiar with our agenda and our goals and objectives. This worried me that they might say something that would get us in trouble since they were speaking for the president. But that was a risk I had to take. Raymond Maul was doing a very good job as my Press Secretary. He had been with me for a long time, and I knew he would not get me in trouble. In fact, he had covered my butt on many occasions.

"The economy and my motto were on my mind every minute of the day. Peace and Prosperity for All was no easy task. The data indicated we had made progress with improving the number of college graduates who were getting paying jobs. We had been able to reduce tuition at many of the colleges and universities, and the student loan program required less money. It was good our young people were not getting into such high debt levels. Our efforts proved that throwing money at a problem did not solve the problem. It takes thought and work to solve a problem. It was time all governments learned this. More work for the Geeks.

"I did not know what I could do to improve the economy and lower the poverty rate. This was a constant worry. I decided I need a secession on the porch. We had a record in the first week that exceeded the one hundred days record of most presidents. That made me happy, but something was missing, and I could not put my finger on it. I asked Albert what he thought about a three-day visit to the beach and him and me discussing things. He said he thought we needed that. He felt the way I felt. We both thought we were missing something.

"We told our staffs we would be available at my place on Sullivan's Island for the next three days. We asked not to be disturbed unless it was necessary. Travel to Charleston was a lot different as president than it was when we were in congress. A motorcade met Air Force One on the tarmac. We made it to the house without a single stop. Jo Anne and Mary were already there and had a day planned for a visit to Charleston. Jo Anne was speaking at a meeting of the Garden Club at noon. She planned to visit the school where she had taught in the afternoon. She would show Mary her old room.

"I was amazed as we approached the house. The place looked like a construction camp. The security measures were under way. They had put a fence all the way around the property. There was a large house being built next to the street on the side of the yard. There was a gate at the driveway with a guardhouse.

"I got in touch with the head of the Secret Service and requested that the fence across the beachside of the property be removed. He said he was concerned about doing that. An attack on the house would most likely come from the ocean side. I said that was my favorite view and the fence across the beach side of the property was unsightly. He agreed to take it down and replace it with motion detectors and cameras. I thanked him for his consideration. The fence came down while we were there, and there were so many people stringing wire and placing devices that it looked like a crowd on the sidelines at a football game. Even a seagull could not land there without alerting the security guards."

I then asked Dylan if this was a good place to stop. I could tell him about Albert's and my meeting in the next secession. He agreed and turned off both recorders. We went into the house, and Dylan said good night and went to his room. Jo Anne and I sat in the family room and chatted about the boys and their families for a while. She had a glass of wine, and I had my beer. I needed to go to the bathroom, and she followed me into the bedroom. We were ready for a good rest.

Morning came a lot sooner than I wanted it to come. We got out of bed and went through our morning shower and my monotonous shaving and dressing for the day. I headed for the porch, and Dylan was there. After a trip to the kitchen, Jo Anne joined us. She said, "I will never get used to not having to go to the kitchen to get things started."

Dylan said, "You and Paul amaze me. You have lived in the White House for eight years and have been former President and First Lady for a few years now and you still cannot get used to servants and security." We laughed and said it would never become a favorite way of life for us.

After a good breakfast on the porch, Dylan and I were ready to go to work. Jo Anne said she was meeting the girls at Wild Dunes and left us. I turned on our recorders, and we were ready. I wondered why Dylan had not carried his recorder to his room. He generally wanted to listen to the recording and do some writing. I asked why he did not take the recorder to the room, and he said he was tired and decided not to do any writing previous night. I could understand that.

I said, "Well, I was about to tell you about Albert and my meeting on the porch. We had set aside three planning days. I told him I was looking forward to John Camp's report and reducing the government further before the end of the first one hundred days. He suggested we have a Wild Dunes-type meeting with some organization and budget people and review John's report. I said I thought we should do that at the White House. We would need to have Raymond fully in touch with what we were doing. It was hard for him to be away from the White House.

"Albert agreed and said, 'We need to get in touch with some of the better universities and have their business faculty members who are familiar with organization and budget to come and review the data and make suggestions for improvement.' I liked the idea, and I said, 'I think I will use the Delphi method after the meeting to get agreement on government organizational and budget changes.' Albert said he had not thought of the Delphi method in a long time, but that was an interesting method to get the thinking of a lot of people and a good decision-making tool."

Dylan said: "I do not think I am familiar with the Delphi method."

I said, "I learned about the Delphi method from a friend who worked at UCLA and for the Rand Corporation. The Rand Corporation was a think tank in Los Angeles."

Dylan said, "I am familiar with some of the work the Rand Corporation had done. It was always a very impressive work."

I said, "They developed this method where their people with different backgrounds could be quizzed on a problem while they were in their offices. They used the computer network. They presented a question and asked for an answer and the reason for the answer. They would take the answers and the reasons from both ends of the distribution curve and send them to individuals and see if the information changed their answers. They repeated the procedure until they got the vast majority to agree with a decision. They called the method the Delphi method.

"I got Warren to get in touch with business school and colleges and put together a group of about thirty people who were known as good organizers or good budget professors. When we had the list, we asked for dates when they could come to Washington at our expense for a meeting. We got the best date and invited them to the White House. That would not look too bad on their resume. We had John Camp give his findings on one department or agency at a time. We then asked for suggestions for better organization or method of management for the department or agency.

"There were several that had not made a significant contribution to improving life for the people or providing them with a service. It was easy just to close these operations and add the employees to the outplacements offices of people who needed a job. I was beginning to feel like these investment entrepreneurs bought plans and closed them and shipped the jobs overseas." In my case, I was not benefiting personally. Society and the taxpayers were the people who benefited.

"We worked on John's reports for two days with great results. I then asked how many were familiar with the Delphi method. The majority were very familiar with the method. We informed those who were not familiar with the method. We said we were going to set up an Internet program where we could use the method to make improvements in government. This was very well received. Warren said he was near completion of a security system we could use with the Delphi method. He said he would be in touch with each member of this new team. I looked at Albert, and he was all smiles. It was good to be achieving our goal of improving government and reducing the cost of government. We were getting very near a balanced budget with no deficit.

"Using the Delphi method on the secure Internet network Warren had set up, we were able to have a national balanced budget, and apply about a billion dollars to reduce the national debt by the end of our first one hundred days in office. The media was going wild with praise of our administration and its accomplishments. The Geeks were letting everyone know about out record. I decided to go to congress and request more money for the Geek program and move it to Washington. I had the head of the Senate and House budget committee visit the Geek program in Columbia with me. They were very impressed and filed a bill to increase the funding and to move the operation to Washington.

"I selected a small building on the government property where the first government computers were built. The building was small but large enough for the Geek program, and it was prefect when we rebuilt the inside, so it served the program well. We had room for growth if we needed it in the old computer construction building."

Dylan said, "This has been a very productive morning. Your first one hundred days will make great reading. Maybe it will cause other presidents to hit the ground running and trying to beat your new record of accomplishments."

I said, "I sure do hope so. Nothing pleases me more than accomplishments. They make me proud."

Dylan said, "I think I live to eat. Nothing pleases me more than a good lunch."

I said, "We should be off to Dunleavy's Bar and Grill."

Dylan said, "I guess we will see some of the Island Boys there."

I said, "You can count on it." As usual, the guards heard the conversations and had radioed for the SUV. We went down the side steeps and got into it. It was a short drive to Dunleavy's. Both Elly and Donnie were there. It was not long before Jinks showed up. We joined Elly and Donnie, and Jinks joined all of us.

Dunleavy came over to the table and said, "I never thought I would have a former president of the United States eating in my joint, especially with the riffraff that eats here like these guys."

Donnie said, "It is the poor food we get to eat that causes us to be riffraff."

Elly said, "But the beer is good."

Just then, Magritte the cook showed up. She said, "Did I hear someone criticize my food? The one that did will be eating poison soon."

Donnie said, "It is not your fault, Magritte, it is Dunleavy's fault. He does not buy good ingredients for you to cook."

She said, "Now that is better. I will not have to kill you today." Dylan was about to roll on the floor as he was laughing so hard. He was not used to these Island Boy ways.

Dunleavy's sister was half owner of the Bar and Grill. She said, "I am very glad to see all of you. You keep us from going broke. My brother is the only person in the world who would buy a bar without a bathroom." It was true he had bought a bar that joined another building that had contained a restaurant. The owner of the restaurant boarded up the door to a hall where the bathrooms were for both properties. She said,

"With a partner like that, I have to break my back to keep us in business."

Dunleavy looked at Dylan and said, "Dylan, I apologize to you. She is my loving sister. These others are familiar with her humor."

Donnie would not let it go. He said, "Dylan, I feel very sorry for his sister. Last Saint Patrick's Day, I was here, and the floor gave in at the middle of this place. Her brother never keeps up the property. He leaves everything for her to do."

She leaned over and kissed Donnie. Dunleavy threw his towel at the bar and walked out the door. We all had a good laugh. We had another good lunch and lots of fun at Dunleavy's.

When we were back on the porch, Dylan said, "You Island Boys sure have fun picking on each other and laughing at yourselves."

I said, "We have always enjoyed each other's company. I think we pick up the idea of teasing each other from our parents. I remember Dad and, in fact, Grandpa teasing their friends and their friends teasing them. Who knows how it got started, but it is great fun now."

Dylan asked, "How about Dave and Don and their friends? Do they tease their friends like you Island Boys?"

I said, "Yes, they do, but the Island Boys respect their elders, and it never happens with them when they are with us. Their friends all behave well when they are around their elders. It is a generation thing, I guess."

When we were ready, I started by telling Dylan about the movement of the Geek program. I said, "Warren and the Geeks moved to their new quarters at the old computer manufacturing building. They were very pleased with the new arrangement of space and organization of the work space. Albert and I paid for their move and the increase in the cost of living. They worked on the Delphi method and improved the manner in which the questions were asked. This weighted answer gave us a better answer distribution. When the information and the questions were sent out three or four times, the data from the returns was much better. We used this Delphi-method program with all the security Warren had added to assist in most decision-making that was needed.

"We were able to reorganize the Executive Branch of government. The savings amazed us. We knew we would reduce the cost of government, but we never thought we would not only balance the budget but also have a sum large enough to get the national debt paid off in ten years. That was to be two years after I got out of office, if I could be reelected. The leaders of congress said they never thought we could accomplish what we had, much less in the first one hundred days we were in office. Naturally, both Albert and I bugged them about the excessive cost of congress. We pushed every button to get a unicameral legislature. The House would not budge. We knew it would happen, and everyone could see the handwriting on the wall. Three more states had adopted a constitution that produced a unicameral legislature. We still had things we wanted to do with the Executive Branch, so we were willing to put the fight off to get a unicameral legislature.

"It did not make me happy to realize we had the largest White House staff of any president. But the Geek program and our staff stayed in constant touch with the people, especially the voters. Our phones, mail handlers, and Internet staff were working round-the-clock. It was obvious no other White House had been in contact with the citizens the way we were.

Raymond was doing a great job with the press and the TV media people. The citizens realized we were doing a good job running the government. Our approval rating was the highest any administration had had at the end of our first one hundred days in office. The congress, especially the House, had the lowest rating any congress had ever had. We were making sure the congressional leaders were aware of these facts.

"Albert and I decided it was time we got out of the White House and were on the road. If we were going to get a new constitution that gave us a method of government that was efficient and effective, we needed the people's support. John, Warren, and the Geeks could continue to improve the organization of the Executive Branch. I had three staff members who were working with them, and when an Executive Order was needed, the staff produced the Order, and I signed it while I was in Washington.

"There was no shortage of invitations to speak. The problem was deciding which invitation we would accept. We wanted to cover the nation. At the same time, we wanted to work on the areas that had the greatest effect on the election returns. While we still had almost four years in office, it did not hurt to have Electoral College votes in our pockets. We wanted the people to know that the cost of government could be greatly reduced if we had a unicameral legislature. We needed a new constitution to give us a government that was efficient and effective. We would stress the fact that the freedoms granted by the 1791 Constitution were timeless and must be preserved, but the method of government was time-dependent and needed to be brought up-to-date.

"I hated the expense of traveling as a president of the United States of America. I did all I could to hold the expense of the traveling at a minimum. I must admit that traveling on Air Force One was a pleasure. Unlike commercial flying, it was easy to work, and I was intact with the White House all the time. Whenever possible, Albert and I paid the price of our trips. We were not able to pay for the security. We did make contributions to cities for their expenses. It did not take long for the media to pick up on these payments and to bring them to the attention of the citizens. Our lack of pay for our service in office and our contribution to our expenses earned us the title of the Efficiency Administration. I realized we were giving the House leader a talking point when I saw him at a weekend interview program. He said, "The work and the accomplishments of the president proved that the government could be operated effectively and efficiently under the present constitution. The nation did not need a new constitution. The nation had been governed by the current constitution for over two hundred years." I jumped on the phone and called Warren first and Raymond next and got them working to show how wrong the House leadership had become.

"When we were asked about our lack of pay for our services, we always said it was a pleasure to serve the citizens of the United States. We wished that everyone who had the ability to help their fellow citizens would exert every effort to do so. We pushed our motto—Peace and Prosperity for All. We said that Prosperity for All meant everyone benefited from a thriving economy. Robin Hood had it right when he robbed the rich and gave to the poor. When the poor had money, the economy benefited. It was not the top of the income that gave us a good economy. It was the middle class. We need to have the middle class keep as much of their income as possible. That meant lowering the taxes of the middle class.

"We also pointed out that the inefficiency of the previous governments had caused a national debt that needed to be paid. We no longer had a budget deficit. Our calculations indicated the national debt could be paid in ten years with the savings in government spending that had been produced during our administration. We now needed a congress that wanted to work to lower the cost of government. The waste in congressional spending would help pay off the national debt in a much shorter time. Everyone would benefit from a unicameral legislature.

"Our speeches brought down the House. I had never heard such cheering. When we left a group, they always promised to support our agenda and usually did. Albert and I needed a few days' rest and some fun. All work and no play made Jack a dull boy. I like that quote. My grandpa told me that hundreds of times. He also said that everyone needed to stop and smell the roses."

Mary was visiting Jo Anne, so it was easy for us to make it back to the beach. We let our staff know that we needed a break and to call us only if they needed us. We enjoyed the porch without a phone ringing.

There was a flag that was flown on a poll in the street side yard when I was in my residence. I asked that the flag not be flown. We did not need company on this visit. It was hard to keep it a secret with Air Force One sitting at the airport. We had it put away in an Air Force hanger as soon as possible. I asked security to be as discreet as possible. We did not want everyone to know we were on the island. They thought that was a good idea and helped the security. We had landed and taxied to the Air Force base hanger area. That kept us away from the commercial terminal. We had only three cars. One was a lead car, the second was a chase car, and the third was the one I was in. They did not want us in the same car, but they broke the rules this once. Albert's vice president's plane had landed just after mine. The lead car was well in front of us, and the chase car was well behind. They did not go onto Sullivan's Island, so only one car went through the gate at the house. Since security always used these cars, a single car going and coming did not look as if I was in residence. The security at the house said we should use this secrecy more often. If no one knew I was there, an attack was unlikely. I liked it because it saved money."

Dylan said, "The lunch and beer was good, but I like a snack in the afternoon. How about you? Do you like a snack in the afternoon?"

I said, "I usually have a snack in the afternoon when I am on this porch." The security was right on the ball, and they radioed the kitchen. Very quickly, there were trays and beers on the way. We had nuts, sandwich-making meat and cheese, chips, and trail mix. I stayed with the trail mix and the nuts, and chips. Dylan made himself a sandwich. We were about through with our first beer when Jo Anne and Mary showed up. They were offered wine, and they each accepted a glass. They joined us eating the snacks. By the time we ran out of small talk and snacks, it was approaching four o'clock. I said, "Don't you think we should work a little longer?" Dylan agreed. Jo Anne and Mary left us.

I listened to the recording just before we stopped for lunch. I said, "We had a quiet weekend. I remember it well because it was a quiet weekend, and I had not had many of them in a long time. We did not leave the house. Albert and I spent a lot of time talking on the porch. Jo Anne and Mary joined us often.

We were both very happy with the results of our efforts to reduce the cost of government. As we talked about our travels and speeches, we were happy with the way the citizens had accepted our message. I said, 'I hope nothing goes wrong. I hope no one says or does the wrong thing.'

"The minute that left my mouth, I thought of something I had to do right then. I stood up and started for the secure phone in the house. Albert asked where I was going. I stopped and took the two or three steps back to where he was seated. I said, 'I did not get that last sentence out of my mouth before I knew something I had forgotten.' Albert asked what I had forgotten. I told him I had forgotten to warn everyone at the White House about ethics and the need to be very careful in money matters. He said that everyone knew about the ethics necessary at the White House.

"I said that I was going to remind them with a presidential memo. I was going to have my secretary to mark my calendar so I would be reminded to send this memo frequently. Albert said it could not hurt and might help us avoid a nasty situation. I got my secretary on the phone and told her I was faxing a memo that I wanted circulated right away. I asked her to mark my calendar, and she said she would. I prepared the memo and faxed it to her. She called back and said copies of the memo were given to every White House employee. She said she thought that was a good move."

Dylan said, "I have to remind you always when it is time to take a rest. What about the advice your grandpa gave you about Jack and smelling the roses?"

Jo Anne was on the porch and heard what Dylan said. She said, "Dylan, I have been preaching that message for years. But I think he needs a hearing aid."

I said, "Sticks and stones may break my bones, but words will never change me."

Dylan laughed and said, "I should have known you would have a quote, even if you had to make one up."

I said, "Dylan is rapidly become my psychiatrist. I have not been laying on a cough, but he is now analyzing me. I knew I was talking too much."

Dylan said, "You are not talking too much—we still have a long way to go. But you do deserve a break."

I said, "I generally have a beer before dinner, but the snack we had is still with me. I do not need a beer now. It might hurt my dinner appetite."

Dylan said, "I am sure you are right. A beer now would ruin my appetite too." We sat around and enjoyed the environment and a lot of small talk about our families. Jo Anne joined us and entered the conversation. At about 6:30 p.m., I called for the SUV, and we left for Marshall's.

We had a good time because a lot of old friends were dining at Marshall's. Donnie and his wife and Tom and his wife joined us. We had a lot of the table hoppers stop by during dinner. It would be nice to have a quiet dinner out, but when you are a former president, I guess everyone wants to talk to you. This is doubly true when they have known you all your life. Marshall dropped by the table. He had watched all the people stopping at the table. He said, "Paul, just call me and let me know you are coming, and I will have a place set up in the private dining room." I thanked him and said I would always call after this time. That worked fine every time we called.

The next morning, Dylan and I had breakfast on the porch with Jo Anne. Dylan said, "You sure had a lot of friends visit the table last night."

Jo Anne said, "It happens everywhere we go. We have lived here for all our married life, and Paul grew up here and has held office for so long that everybody thinks of him as a friend."

Dylan said, "I noticed that you were as popular as Paul."

I said, "It goes with being the first lady. But a lot of the people who stopped at the table were students of Jo Anne. I guess if we wanted our privacy, we should have moved from the White House to an uninhabited island."

A security officer brought me a secure phone and said I had a call. I asked who was calling, and he said, "John Camp."

I took the phone and said, "Hello, John."

He said, "Good morning. I apologize for calling so early, but have you seen the new budget?" I said that I had not seen it. He said, "It is a disaster. It is not balanced and added a lot of unnecessary expenses to the size of the government."

I said, "I will sue. That is unconstitutional." He said that the media was all over the fact the budget proposed by the president was unconstitutional. I asked him if he would please stay on the problem and let me know how things were working out. He said he intended to make sure this budget never saw the light of day. I called Raymond and asked him to call a news conference. I returned to Washington and was present at the news conference. I said, "Anyone who is here knows that the new constitution realizes the president submits a budget, the Senate develops the budget, and the constitution requires a balanced budget and a surplus fund."

Dylan said, "You have been out of office for several years, and you are still having to keep up and work to keep the government efficient."

Jo Anne said, "He sure does. He gets calls like that all the time."

I said, "It goes with the territory. Let's get to work on our problem." Jo Anne said she was meeting friends for a shopping trip to Charleston. I said, "There goes the national budget." We laughed and turned on our recorders. I said, "The remainder of our first two years in office was much like the first hundred, but the reduction in government gradually slowed down, and the savings in tax dollars were at a slower rate. There were changes in the governments within states, and four more states became states with unicameral legislatures.

"In the last two years of our first term, Albert and I decided to work on foreign affairs. We would not have Peace and Prosperity for All until there was peace in the world. We decided we needed a TV station in the Eastern world like we had broadcasting into the Soviet Union during the cold war years. We got network people, and they said it would be easy to set up TV stations that could cover the area, but we would need permission from the nation where we wanted to put in the stations. We had little problem getting good coverage and the permission to put in the stations. The nations with democratic governments wanted to cooperate.

"For years, Albert and I had agreed that the Eastern world was left out of the Age of Enlightenment. The invention of the printing press had brought the Western world together, and with the writing of Locke, Paine, and other philosophers, the population soon threw off the yolk of tyrannical governments. The kings like George III who lost the American Colonies used their tyranny to control the people. France beheaded the members of their tyrannical government. We got the approval of congress and the funding to put in the stations. We turned the Geek program onto the needs of educating the Islamic world about tyranny and the need for a democratic government. The two programs worked well together.

"Soon our message of Peace and Prosperity for All was known all over the whole world. The interactive blogs and social network data indicated we were making a headway with the education of the Islamic world. I decided that I needed to visit the more friendly nations in that part of the world and to preach our message. The staff made the contacts and got the invitations for my visits. I prepared my speech carefully. I had a translator work with me to make sure everything could be translated and gave the message I wanted to deliver. When we were satisfied, I memorized the speech. The speech stressed the need for Peace and Prosperity for All. I pointed out how the Colonies had thrown off the tyrannical governments of the kings. I took passages from the works of Thomas Paine and John Locke. I had three quotes from Aristotle. I had a meeting and invited over one hundred members of the Islamic religion that were citizens of the United States. I delivered the speech, and it was translated into several dialects of the Eastern world. It was very well received, and I was assured it would be understood by the audiences in the Eastern world.

"I visited three Eastern world nations and delivered my speech. The TV and Geek program had copies of the speech and pushed the message. We were sure that a large portion of the Eastern world heard the message. The data generated by the Geek program indicated the speech was heard by a major portion of the population, and the women in the Arab world were the most impressed. The young people who used the social Internet were also impressed.

"A few nights after I returned to the White House, Jo Anne and I were watching TV. There was an inspirational program on. The singers had beautiful voices, and the old hymns they sang were very inspirational. In fact, if it had been one of those come-down-the-aisle-and-be-saved programs, I would have been running down the aisle. The next day, I had Raymond in the office, and I told him about the program. He said he could get copies of the program. I told him I wanted to get the hymns translated into every dialect of the Arab world, and I wanted singers with beautiful voices singing the hymns. I said the words needed to be changed so they would not sound so Christian and would suit the Islamic nations. When we were ready, I wanted similar programs for all the TV stations in that part of the world. Within four days, the programs were airing on the TV station network we had set up.

"I knew what I wanted. I wanted to single out the tyrant religious leaders and have the Arab world turn against them. I wrote another speech. I pointed out that since the time of the Crusades, the tyrants preached war and terror. I said that God, the Almighty leader of religions, did not want people to kill people. He wanted people to love people and work to help each other the way he loved the people and helped the people. The leaders who preached war from the time of the Crusades until today were power-hungry tyrants and not true leaders of the religions. As long as the people allowed them to rule and followed their leadership, they were supporting power-hungry tyrants. The power-hungry tyrants were false prophets. God had warned about false prophets. Once again, I worked with the translators and gave the finished speech to a smaller Islamic religious leader group at the White House. It was well received, and I was told it was what was needed to be said in the Eastern world. I delivered the speech on the TV network first and then made trips to several nations and repeated the speech. The Geek program data showed we were making friends in the Eastern world.

"Next, I wrote a speech that said the United States of America was not the Great Devil. In fact, we were freedom-loving people who wanted Peace and Prosperity for All. Our constitution gave freedom to all to practice the religion of their choice. We were God-loving people who wanted to obey the teaching of the true followers of God. God had pointed out that there would be false prophets, and the tyrannical leaders of the religions who called for jihad and terrorism were false prophets. God did not support bombing synagogues and killing people who loved him. Anyone who was teaching terrorism and the killing of God-loving people was a false prophet. The people and the government of the United States wanted Peace and Prosperity for All. The Geek program had a ball with this speech, and the data showed it was loved by most people of the Arab world.

"What was called the Arab Spring began in Egypt. Our Secretary of State did what he could to get the power-hungry leaders to step down, but that did not work. It was obvious that freedom in the Arab world would come as it had in the United States and France. It would take killing and civil war. I did not want to support war, and I pushed every button to try to avoid war. I said that revolution brought chaos and evolution brought about order and change. I also said that power motivation was behind the killing of innocent individuals.

"I went to the United Nations and gave a speech, trying to get the nations of the world to support peaceful change in governments. I asked the members of the United Nations to support the trial of leadership that resulted in killing of the citizens of any nation. I said I was very disturbed to learn that leaders of any nation would kill protestors among their own citizens. The International Court in Den Hagan should be used to bring killers to justice."

Dylan said, "Do I need to remind you it is near time for lunch?"

I said, "No, in fact, I was about to tell you I would stop here and start on the rest of the story after lunch." Jo Anne joined us and said she wished Marlene had come with Dylan. He said as usual she was helping the boys. This time it was the one in New York. He said he was not so sure if it was her love of New York and the shopping that had her there or if it was helping her son. I said, "That analysis has a familiar ring to it. I wonder about Jo Anne's motives often." That got me a teasing slap on the cheek. I said, "Be careful, dear, there are armed guards near to protect me."

One of the guards said in a joking manner, "In a case like this, I have been known to shoot at the hen and kill the rooster." We all had a big laugh. We had lunch on the porch; it was all ready.

After lunch, I said, "This will not surprise you, but I was against boots on the ground anywhere to put down the conflicts. Americans had suffered too much to continue putting boots on the ground. I did intend to help any fight for freedom. We would use our Drone capability to support the side of our choice. We dropped ground-base Drones in several of the conflicts. They were very successful. We placed ground-based Drones to protect our Foreign Service and citizens in each nation. We had 24 7 Drone coverage in the most dangerous areas.

"Randy Woods was our Secretary of State, and he was doing a great job as usual. He was a former well-respected senator from Texas who had served on the Foreign Service Committee and the Intelligence Committee. We had served together on the Armed Services Committee. Our intelligence people were in touch with both sides in every uprising. We were watching for power-motivated individuals that would use every avenue to get to power. There were several splinter terrorist groups who would love to take advantage of the chaos of war. I gave the order to locate and kill the heads of those terrorist groups. I indicated to the Chief of Staff of the Armed Forces that I was not necessarily limiting my order to the leaders. They could wipe out terrorist groups.

"I talked with Warren about the religious program we had going on TV. He said it was a good idea when we advised against using Christian signs such as the Cross. He said the favorite song seemed to be 'When The Saints Come Marching In.' I said I was glad many of our hymns had references to the places of the Arab world like the angels coming over Jordan. The people we had working in that program understood the purpose of the program. When there was a problem with a hymn, they rewrote the hymn so it presented its message in Islamic format. The Geek program was backing up the TV program with messages about the program on the social Internet sites. Their blogs were getting a lot of hits.

"I got a lot of help with a White Paper I prepared on religious freedom. The paper stressed the need for governments that gave as much freedom to the people as possible. It condemned the tyrant leaders and the so-called religious leaders who were dictators in Islamic nations. We stressed the fact that the Almighty God had warned against false prophets. We pointed out that the Western world had more than their share of false prophets who waged war against other religions. We gave examples of Protestant and Catholic wars in the United States and other countries. We mentioned Northern Ireland. We put the blame on false prophets. We said we knew God did not want his believers involved in war. He was a God of love. We said we did not believe Mohammad would want Sunnis killing Shiites and Shiites killing Sunnis. The wars in the Middle East between the Jews and the Palestinians were maintained by individuals with power-motivations and were not supported by individuals who truly believed in a loving God. The White Paper was read over and over on the TV stations we had set up. The Geek program had a ball with the White Paper. The data showed we were making progress in the Islamic world. Many individuals who had studied in the United States were helping us in their countries. We had the Geek program contact as many of them as possible and offer them any assistance they needed.

"Even the hard core in congress who were against any program we wanted to institute came around when they saw our progress in making friends in the Islamic world. I was contacted by an American citizen who was a member of an Islamic religious group. He was concerned about a trial involving bribes. He said that in Persian, there was no word for our concept of 'no.' 'No' in Persian meant 'maybe.' The Arabs and members of Islam believed in barter. They negotiated for everything. He reminded me of the fact that Saddam Hussein had said when he was found in that hole. He had said, 'I am the president of Iraq, and I want to negotiate.' He said in his mind and the mind of many Arabs that the war was a mistake because we did not know about the need for negotiation in the Arab world. Saddam want to negotiate oil prices and the right to sell oil for information about Weapons of Mass Destruction. We could have gotten anything we wanted if we had given something of equal or better value to Saddam.

"I contacted several members of the Islamic community that had helped us and asked about this problem with our understanding negotiation. They said this had been a long-term problem. Americans and people from the Western world did not know how to negotiate and did not understand the Eastern world's commitment to negotiation. I looked into the trial in our court and found out the accused had negotiated with an Arab official for a right to build a store and paid the official for a permit. He said he was following the rules of the country where they were working. The official had something they wanted, and they had to negotiate to obtain it. There was no given price for the permit. He was found guilty in our court, but I gave him a presidential pardon.

"The media went wild crying foul. They said I did not have any respect for the Criminal Justice System. I went on every program I could and pointed out we had to learn to do business with the Arab world and that we would have to live by their country's rules when we were in their country. There is the old saying, 'When in Rome, do as the Romans do.' If the United States is a world leader, the citizens and the corporations have to learn to do business with every nation in the world. The culture and the business practices cannot be unknown to us. I said I was an attorney and a member of the bar, and I had total respect for the Criminal Justice System. I said that no one believed the Court System results were always correct. We had put innocent people to death. In this case, it was a misunderstanding of the business practices of other nations. The White House received calls from international business leaders praising the administration for its support of international business.

"Dylan, I think I will beat you to the punch and call it enough for this secession." Dylan reached over and turned off his recorder and mine. I asked if he was interested in working that night. He said he did not think we needed to work that night as we had the entire day for us the next day. Jo Anne and the beers and snacks arrived, and they placed the tray on the coffee table next to the two recorders. Jo Anne was carrying her glass of wine. She surprised me when she asked Dylan if he thought Marlene would fly down. He said he missed her and would go in and make a telephone call. When he returned, he said Marlene was very pleased by the invitation and would fly down the next day. We had dinner on the porch. Jo Anne was looking forward to having Marlene as a houseguest for a few days. After dinner, we had the Secret Service give us a ride into Charleston and around the Battery. We stopped at the ice-cream store on Broad Street. The security guard riding with the shotgun went in and came out with ice-cream cones for everyone. When we got home, we each went our own way.

We were back in our usual positions with the recorders turned on. I said, "Albert and I were having a talk on the porch just before the first midterm elections. We had supported congressional candidates around the nation who were our supporters. We felt like this was a bell weather test of the popularity of our administration. We were not disappointed. Candidates who promised that they would support a constitutional convention charged with producing a new method of government that was efficient and effective and won their elections. In fifteen cases, they defeated incumbent congressmen who had held their seats for many years. We viewed this new support in the House as a blessing. After the midterm elections, we were back on the porch. We were discussing our plans for the next two years. We agreed it was time to start playing hardball. I said, 'I am going to issue an Executive Order that requires a constitutional convention charged with our desire to have a method of government that is efficient and effective.' Albert agreed that was a good idea. If the congress voted down the Executive Order, each voter would be showing his hand. Everyone would know who supported an efficient and effective government and who was supporting an expensive legislature that was unnecessary and ineffective.

"When the congress was back in secession, I issued my Executive Order. The House cried foul. They said the Order was unconstitutional. I was trying to become a dictator and not a president. We loved the debate because we were winning. The media and the Geek program had a ball battling the speeches that were coming out of members of the House. Our approval ratings hit the top of the charts. The congress had the lowest approval rating that the congress had ever received. The leaders knew they were losing the fight, but there were still a majority in the House that wanted to maintain a House of Representatives. The Executive Order was repealed by the Congressional vote. We almost won in the Senate, but we lost by a big margin in the House. We found out that the Senate had three bills pending that they wanted the House's approval, and they got it. The unconstitutional charge for the Order was never tested in the Supreme Court. I think we would have lost in the Supreme Court. They read the constitution as literal, and it did not allow changes in the constitution by Executive Orders.

"Our administration got nothing through the House. Every bill we supported was voted down in the House. This made the congress another Do-Nothing Congress. The media was on our side, but several members of the House and the two leaders in the other party said they would do everything they could to make us a one-term administration.

"I called every state governor and asked that he get his legislature to approve a Constitutional Convention. I told them we would need the governor's support as well. We received the support of more than the two-thirds of the states for a Constitutional Convention. We issued a call for the Convention. The House went through the roof—they said Article 1 of the Constitution applied only to amendments to the current constitution. It did not give the States, the Congress, or the President the right to call for a new constitution. We called the Attorney General and asked him to take it to the Supreme Court. He followed our instructions and the Supreme Court agreed to hear the case. We claimed the States had the rights to call for a new constitution. The court ruled against us five to four. There was a strong dissent to the ruling written by one of the four who voted in our favor."

Dylan and I then took a midmorning break, and Jo Anne joined us and said that Marlene had arrived at the airport and was on her way to the island. Security had picked her up. By the time we had finished a cup of coffee and a couple of doughnuts, Marlene arrived. After a few minutes with Dylan, she and Jo Anne headed for the kitchen.

I was glad Dylan had remembered the recorders and turned them off. After he had turned them on again, I said, "The ruling of the court was a big blow, but we were ready for it. We said this was another reason to have a new constitution that provided a method of government that was controlled by one branch of the government. We believed the Senate in a unicameral legislature should have the power to run the government. The president should be appointed by the Senate, and he should serve at the pleasure of the Senate. His duties were to manage and enforce the laws and regulations passed by the Senate. The nation may have needed a three-branch government at the time the 1791 Constitution was adopted, but as everyone knows today, it is difficult to serve two masters, more so three. We preferred a government similar to the administration of corporations. We wanted a Senate that was like a Board of Directors and a president like the Chief Executive Officer. The people were like the stockholders of the corporation. They elected the Board of Directors. This was the first time Albert and I had outlined our method of organization of the government of the United States. We got a divided response after we made our opinion known. But it did not take long for the Geek program to greatly support our plans. Our initial problem had been the same old thing. The Status Quo was well known and understood, but we were a couple of radicals who thought outside the box.

"After our loss in the Supreme Court, we got even less support from a majority of the House. They were really after our hide now. The leaders from both parties were hitting us at every chance they got. They condemned everything we did— even going to the bathroom. Well, maybe not that bad, but it sure seemed like it was that bad. But the majority of the Senate stayed on our side. We had good support from the members in the Senate who belonged to the other party. The Senate was in favor of our proposed method of government origination. We worked hard for the last two years of our administration. We traveled and spoke all over the world. We visited the States that had not supported our efforts to have a new constitution. As the end of our term appeared on the horizon, we had a government with a balanced budget, and the government was making major size payments on the national debt. A few more states had changed their constitutions and had legislatures that were unicameral. The Rand McNally Road Atlas looked very different from the one I passed out when I was in congress. The number of county governments was reduced to such a point that the index was much shorter. The number of city governments and villages with governments was greatly reduced. The savings had been remarkable. The economy was doing very well, but we still had too many people who were unemployed or working part-time. The number of two-family incomes had increased, but that meant the children were missing their parents' teachings.

"I decided I would take on the House in another battle before I might not be elected for a second term. I issued an Executive Order that removed all taxes from corporations and businesses. The order pointed out that corporations and businesses hired people who paid taxes. The stockholders paid taxes on the dividends they earned. The order allowed corporations and businesses to retain earning until they reached two years' operating capital. Once their reserved reached two years' operating capital, the corporation or business had to pay the remaining in salary or dividends. Dividends were taxed as all salary income. As expected, the House cried foul, but the measure was very effective, and unemployment decreased. Not a single member of the House wanted to challenge us on the Executive Order." I turned off the recorder and asked the security guard as to where Jo Anne and Marlene were. He said they had gone to Charleston and were now having lunch at Magnolia's. I said, "Well, Dylan, I guess it is Dunleavy's for us."

He said, "That sounds like fun and another great lunch." The SUV arrived, and we were off. There were the usual crowd and a few I did not know. It turned out that a group from Wild Dunes Men's Golf Club was there. They played a golf tournament on this day every week, and after the tournament, several of the men came to Dunleavy's for lunch.

Dylan and I joined Elly, Jinks, and Dick Hair. I had not seen Dick for sometime. He said that Claire Risher had died recently. I had not read or heard that news. She had married and had three children who were grown and married. Dick asked if I ever saw Louise Peden. I said I had not seen her for sometime. He then said to Dylan, "Paul and Louise were great dancers." Dylan said that I had covered that early in the meetings we were having. After a good lunch and lots of fun with the Island Boys and Dunleavy, we were back on the porch, ready to start the afternoon secession.

I said, "I finally got my chance to appoint a Supreme Court Justice. One of the members of the court who voted with the five votes that defeated our attempt to have a new constitution was resigning because of bad health. He was considered a conservative Justice. My party wanted me to appoint another conservative Justice. I decided to appoint the most qualified constitutional Justice I could find. While I had never heard of her, I soon had my candidate for the court. Her name was Charlene Jefferson. She was a direct descendant of a slave who served Thomas Jefferson. According to reports, she might have been a direct descendant of Thomas Jefferson. She was a graduate of the University of Virginia and of the Law School at the University of Virginia. She was on the faculty of the University of Virginia, School of Law, for nine years. She taught Constitutional Law. She was recruited by Harvard Law School to teach Constitutional Law. I called ten Law School deans, and they all were familiar with her and supported her appointment to the Supreme Court. I called the dean of the Law School at Harvard, and he was excited by the possibility that Charlene Jefferson might be appointed to the Supreme Court. He said she was the most qualified person that he knew. He sent me a copy of her curriculum vitae and copies of her publications in law journals.

"I read her papers and was very impressed by her knowledge and her original concept of the law. Her publications pointed out that governments and law began early on the coastal towns and villages along the Italian Coast. They needed to join forces to protect the lives and property of the citizens from raids by bands from the north. She felt that the protection of the lives and property of the citizens was a major component of the criminal justice system. She quoted the Declaration of Independence. 'We hold these truths to be [sacred and undeniable] self-evident, that all men are created equal and independent; that from that equal creation they derive rights inherent and inalienable, among which are the preservation of life, and liberty and the pursuit of happiness; that to secure these ends, governments are instituted among men, deriving their just powers from the consent of the governed.' Her paper said that if the Declaration of Independence were written today, it would read as follows—'We hold these truths to be self-evident that all *persons* are created equal in the eyes of the law and the Justice System. All persons should be free of oppression, and all governments should be with the consent of the persons. The United States of America is first a Democracy and then a Democratic Republic. As a Democracy, only after the approval of the majority of the people to be governed can the people be governed.' She said that Democracy was defined as 'a government in which the supreme power is vested in the people and exercised by them directly or indirectly by individuals duly elected by a majority of the people.' When the majority of the people decide to be governed indirectly, the government becomes a Democratic-Republic. Thus, the government gets its power to govern from the people, and the majority of the people should have the freedom to change the representatives or the method of government."

I said, "Dylan, to me that is a powerful paragraph she had written. I am very much in agreement with the last sentence where she says the people have the right to change the method of government."

Dylan said, "I am sure you and I agree with her completely."

I said, "Wait until I tell you about all her papers. I will give you copies before you leave. She said that all citizens should be considered innocent of crime or cause of harm until they are approved guilty of the crime or harm in a duly organized court of law. No police officer or a group of police officers or departments of police are a duly organized court of Justice. The Justice system is authorized to find individuals guilty or innocent of a crime that involves the loss of life or property. Individuals have a system of Justice that allows them to address any grievance. Therefore, no individual or group of individuals has the right to deny the rights of the court system. The court system, which involves the state or federal court, the court of appeals, and the Supreme Court, receives its power from the people. The people are governed by a constitution that defines and establishes the method of government, including the system of justice for loss of life or property. Since the constitutional powers are granted by the people when they adopt the constitution, the people have the right and freedom to alter or totally change the constitution. The Second Amendment of the constitution, a part of the bill or rights, is often seen as a right to bear arms. An armed militia necessary to defend the rights of the people is different from individual gun ownership. A militia is not necessary when there is a court system approved by the people. Gun ownership should depend upon the need and use and be a right granted by a state government and not the national government.

"I was sure Charlene Jefferson would have many members of congress who would not agree with her outspoken views of government and the court system. But I planned to use her last article to support the candidacy. The article said that the people were the source of power. The people had adopted the constitution of the present government. Until the people voted in a majority to change the constitution or adopted a new constitution, the present constitution should be in force and defended by the courts, including the Supreme Court. We would fight heard against any member of congress who did not believe in the power of the people."

Dylan said, "I sure am glad that Charlene Jefferson became a Justice of the Supreme Court."

I said, "You are getting ahead of my story. But that is OK. We do not have to go into the fight we had getting her confirmed. But that fight sure helped me in the upcoming election for a second term."

Dylan and I turned off our recorders and sat back in our chairs. Dylan said, "I sure like these chairs. They are very comfortable."

I said, "They are another invention by an Island Boy. They are called Sullivan's Island chairs and are made and sold right here on the island." I called Don and asked if he and Jewel could have dinner with us at Marshall's. He said they could be there. I called Marshall and told him we would have a party of six in about one half hour. He said that would be fine. Jo Anne and Marlene joined us on the porch. Dylan and I were just finishing a beer. They brought the SUV around, and as we were pulling out of the gate, I saw Don's car coming out of his driveway. We had a lot of good small talk, and I had a few exchanges with Marshall the way my dad had his running feud over our college backgrounds. Like he had told my dad, he told Jo Anne he would be glad to have her at the restaurant anytime, but the former president would be placed out the back near the garbage cans. Since I was a former president, he would place a clean white napkin on top of the garbage where I would sit. I said, "Just like a Clemson graduate—no respect for the former leadership of the nation. You must remember I now have armed guards that protect me at all times." Jo Anne joined in and said she heard one of those armed guards say he might shoot at the hen and kill the rooster. Marshall loved that one.

Don asked Dylan, "Dylan, you should bring your boys down with their wives. We have two extra bedrooms and would be happy to have them." Dylan thanked Don and said he would ask them if they would like to come down. When we were back at the house, we called it an evening and went our different ways.

The next morning, we were back on the porch for breakfast, but the weather was not cooperating. It was raining, and the wind had come too bad to stay on the porch, so we moved into the kitchen for breakfast. We went to my study for our secession. We were about to get started when Dylan got a phone call from one of his sons. He said that he and his wife would like to come down. He said he had talked to his brother, and he and his wife would like to come down too. I gave Dylan Don's phone number and asked him to have his sons call Don. He gave his son the number to call. I said that would be nice. He, Marlene, and their two sons and their wives and Jo Anne and I with our two sons and their wives: that made for an enjoyable weekend.

We turned on our recorders, and I was ready to start. I said, "After Charlene Jefferson was confirmed and was seated on the Supreme Court, we were ready for our campaign for a second term. We had an excellent record of achievements for our campaign. The economy was doing well. The unemployment rate was at the lowest level that had been seen in many years. Our TV stations and the Geek program were showing wonderful results, especially with the Arab population below thirty years old. They were very impressed by our Peace and Prosperity for All efforts. The international business communities were doing more business in the Arab world and were hiring young Arabs for their assistance. We had used our Drones to assist the young fighters who wanted freedom and a Democratic-Republic. With our help, they had defeated the tyrants who were dictators in their nations.

"For the first time in a long time, there was peace in the world, and all the nations were beginning to see prosperity. Albert and I decided to push the writing of Charlene Jefferson during our campaign. We intended to make this a worldwide push for freedom of every population and support the fact that the power to govern came from the people. Raymond and Warren said the data showed another landslide victory for us. Our approval ratings were excellent. The changes in the governments within the states had increased the economy in every state—well, almost every state. I received a call from a County Council Chairman who said they had merged with another county and had merged with four cities in the new county, but their budget was slightly larger. I called John Camp and asked him to go have a look. After about a week and a half, he came into my office with a big smile on his face. He said I would not believe this one. He said they merged, but they kept every office holder and every employee. He said they increased the County Council to have seats for both County Council Members and the City Councils. He had gotten their organization changed and their budget in place. They saved over six hundred thousand dollars. He said it was not an easy sell, but when they saw the savings, they bought the budget.

"Our educational efforts had paid off. Colleges and universities had joined the effort to have efficient operations. Tom praised me every time I saw him for the reduction in paperwork. He said that the savings in administrative cost was increasing the bottom line of every business he had contact with.

"The first day the paperwork was available for individuals who planned to run for president, we signed up. The Republican leadership assured us that no other Republican would run against us. They would put their total effort behind our campaign. Since we were not running in any primary elections, we could get ready for the Republican Convention. We were called by the Democratic Party leadership and told there would be three candidates running on the Democratic ticket. One of them said it was a terrible waste of money and time.

"I was surprised by the manner in which the Democratic Party was coming apart. Our polls showed that about 50 percent of the Democratic voters were Paul Harvey Collins supporters. Warren said that estimate was not correct. He said the data showed that about 68 percent of the voters who were members of the Democratic Party were Paul Harvey Collins supporters and would vote for him. Albert and I were riding on cloud nine.

"I suggested a week's vacation at the beach, and Albert said he needed it. Albert and Mary came and stayed with Jo Anne and me for the week."

Dylan sat forward and turned off the recorders. He said, "I want to take a few weeks off too. I need to spend time in your presidential library and catch up on the documents I need. I want to get the first term up-to-date before we start on the second term."

I agreed and said, "When you are ready, give me a call. Remember to bring Marlene and your boys, and we can have some fun times while we are working." He said that sounded good, and he would call.

It was longer than I thought it would be before I heard from Dylan. I had been at the library in Columbia several times, catching up on the mail, and I saw him working. He always had a large pile of paper around him when I saw him. That yellow pad looked like it was filling up. I did not see a recorder, so I guess he was writing down everything he wanted to remember. Jo Anne and I enjoyed the free time. We had a party for the Island Boys and their wives. We visited St George and stayed at Dave's house. Jo Anne always enjoyed being back in her hometown. She and Gloria, Dave's wife, and her mother Cindy were constant companions. I spent a lot of time viewing the changes in the Distribution Center. There were now twelve Distribution Centers that covered the area, mostly east of the Mississippi river. Dad would be proud of the job Dave and the other managers were doing. I was very happy with my stock dividends and the contributions to the Trust Fund. Since I had become a former president, my expenses had decreased. The foundation Albert and I had set up after we were out of office was covering a lot of the expenses of the staff we had retained. I had very little travel cost. The Secret Service covered most of that.

I received a call from Dylan. He said he would be ready to start next Friday morning. He and Marlene would arrive around ten. The boys were coming in later on Friday, and they were in touch with Don. I called Don, and he said the Johnson boys were arriving at the airport at 3:15 p.m. He said he would use Jewel's SUV to pick them up. It was a big job and had three seats and plenty of trunk room. I asked him if Jewel would let him drive her car. He said no; she would not let him drive, but she would go with him to pick up the Johnson boys and their wives. I told him I would set up cocktails and dinner at Marshall's Friday night, starting about 6:30 p.m. He said that would be fine. I suggested I will have a limo pick them up and return them home. That way he would have a designated driver for the trip home. He laughed and said that sounded like a good plan.

Dylan and Marlene arrived on time and were picked up by the security service. They arrived at the house at about 10:20 a.m., and we gave them a little time to get settled into the room for their stay. Dylan and Marlene had agreed to stay for about ten days. We sat in the family room and chatted until noon. The weather was not cooperating for us to sit on the porch. We had lunch in the dining room. We had not used it much; we ate either on the porch or in the kitchen. My grandpa had insisted on a big kitchen when he had remodeled the house.

That afternoon, Jo Anne and Marlene were off to a garden club meeting at the Island Club. Dylan and I went to my study. Once we were ready, I said, "Before the Republican Party Convention, Albert and I decided to take a weeks' vacation. It was not all vacation. Albert and I could never leave business for a week. We were in secessions on the porch almost every day. On the days we missed being on the porch, we were in my study. It was the second week in August, and the next week was the Republican Party Convention. It was to be held in Los Angeles, California. I thought that was kind of rubbing it into the Democratic Party. Southern California had supported the Democratic Party for years. I gave a copy of my proposed Convention speech to Albert, and he told me the next day that he had made changes in his Convention speech so we would not be covering the same material. He made two suggestions to me, and I accepted both of them. They improved the speech.

"We did have some fun over that week of vacation. We played golf at Wild Dunes three times. We had fun at lunch at Dunleavy's on two occasions. We were at Marshall's twice. We were in Charleston and ate at Magnolia's once and Just South of Broad once. I took Albert fishing and shrimping behind the Isle of Palms. I wanted to take him graining on the beach, but there was just no time. I still had three gigs from my high school years. I am sure he would have liked to see those two shining eyes of the flounder lying still under the waves in the shallow water.

"Albert and I felt we were ready for the convention, the election, and another four years in the White House. We talked about this being our last four years of our political careers. Albert said that he would not run for president at the end of my term. I tried to change his mind, but he was ready to retire.

I don't think I will be ready to retire when my term ends. Albert said we would not have to stop our efforts to improve governments. He and I could form a Foundation for Good Government. The funds that were donated to the Foundation would help us keep our Geek program and our speaking travel working. We could write articles, White Papers, and books. I said, 'You are way ahead of me. I had not thought about retirement. You seem to have retirement planned.' He said, 'Yes, Mary and I have talked about it. We plan to buy a home in Wild Dunes. We do not think we want to retire to Greenville. That will keep us near each other.' I said, 'Albert, you have always been a great planner, and I love every bit of your plan. I especially like the idea of you and Mary living in Wild Dunes.'"

Dylan and I did not get much done that afternoon before we decided we had enough for the day. Jo Anne and Marlene had returned, and we prepared for our trip to Marshall's. I had called and reserved the private dining room for cocktails and dinner.

Marshall had done a good job for us. He had flowers around the room. He had put in Red, White, and Blue curtains. There was a large American Flag painted on one wall. At the head of the table for thirteen were an American Flag and a South Carolina Flag. The backs of the thirteen chairs were the names and colors of the thirteen original colonies. The remaining walls of the room were in a light blue. Marshall knew that was Jo Anne's favorite color. Around the double door where you entered the room was our motto in very large letters: Peace and Prosperity for All. This was not where his former private dining room had been. When you entered this room, you had to go down eight steps. He said the steps represented my years in office. Then he got in his first shot. He said I should notice there was an elevator on the right side so I could get into the room when I got a few years older. I said I noticed the elevator, but I thought it was so he could get into the room now. He said he started to get the wall in the back of the elevator painted to say, "This elevator is a courtesy of the regulations of the Federal Government." I said, "Be careful how you talk about the Federal Government. There are Secret Service guys present."

Marshall said, "They are my friends. They eat here more than you do. If you notice near the door, there is a table marked for Secret Service use only. There is another one across the room, out of direct sight from the entrance, that is also marked for Secret Service use only. I know how they like to sit so they can provide the security they provide for you."

Both Jo Anne and I said, "All kidding aside, we love what you have done."

Jo Anne added what I was thinking. "When did you have time to get all this work done? It has not been that long since we were here last."

Marshall said, "I bought this building next door to the restaurant to put in this private dining area. You will remember there is one you used before on the other side of the restaurant. They worked on this during the day, and the door to the restaurant and the steps were the last thing they did. I wanted to call this the Paul Harvey Collins Presidential Dining room, but I wanted to ask you first."

I said, "I would be honored, but I do not deserve the honor coming from you after all my teasing you over the years."

Marshall said, "I think I got my share of the teasing."

Jo Anne said, "You did. You got him good many times. I can remember. I have used many of your good ones in order to get him myself." That brought a good laugh from everyone. He said that he would put the name on the doors. He said he did not want to change the motto around the door.

Cocktails were being served while the conversation was going on. He had a new cocktail that he served in a small glass with a handle he called the Collins cocktail. It was vodka and prune juice. He had gotten the glasses made at a glass factory in West Virginia. When he served me the first one and totaled us, it was vodka and prune juice.

Jo Anne said, "You got him again."

I tried it and said, "It is not bad. I think I need a few of these each day." Then I asked, "Marshall, when did you get your pharmacy license?" That brought the second good laugh of the night. I changed drinks for the Collins to my favorite beer. I did not see anyone drinking Collins cocktails. Dinner was as good as or maybe better than the cocktail time. Good food and good conversation with friends: I do think there is a better way to live. It was good the boys had a stretch limo to take them home. We had the security to drive us. We visited a little long in the family room when we got home. I think the boys and their wives took off for a taste of Charleston nightlife.

The next morning was a good day. Dylan and I had breakfast with Jo Anne and Marlene on the porch. The ladies talked a lot about the dinner at Marshall's and the new private dining room. After breakfast, the girls took off for a day of shopping in Charleston. Dylan and I turned on our recorders and were ready for our work. I reminded Dylan that Albert and I were on what we called a vacation before the Republican Party Convention. I told him that "I said to

Albert, 'It appears we were lucky during our first term. We did not have a crisis every morning when we walked into our office. I have talked to other presidents, and that was their main compliant about being president. It appears we were out in front of most catastrophes during our first term. I hope we can stay ahead of them during the second term.' Albert said, 'Paul, you and I were always guys who planned ahead. Your efforts in the Eastern world and with the Islamic population helped reduce the number of major problems that have faced other presidents.' I said, 'I want to put even more emphasis on Peace and Prosperity for All during our second term. This time we will not have to be worried about another term. The midterm elections will require a lot of work. We want to increase the number of members of the House who are in favor of a unicameral legislature. We will have to wait until we are out of office before we start working on our Foundation to support better government. We do not want people thinking they need to give money to get favors.' Albert said, 'Yes, when gifts are involved, there are always chances of ethics violations or apparent ethics violations.' I said, 'Lord knows we have worked to prevent ethics violation charges.' I walked over to the porch railing and knocked on wood.

"The Republican Convention was a big success in Los Angeles. We had worked hard on our acceptance speeches. I stressed Peace and Prosperity for All in my speech. I included an agenda that would put a major effort on foreign policy. Foreign Policy was a major part of the operations of an efficient and effective presidential administration. I stressed the need for population reduction in the United States and in all the nations of the world. I said the world cannot support an unlimited population growth. I said that because of the population's rate of growth and the improvement in student education in the world, the administration and society would have to continue to work on improving our educational system. Albert stressed improvement in governments. He pointed out our efforts to have a unicameral legislature in every state and the Federal government. He said while we were not able to accomplish this in the first administration, we would try harder in a second administration. He expressed our happiness with the reduction in number and cost of governments within states.

"The media was very kind to us and reran our speeches over and over. Everyone in the nation and in most of the world heard what we said. We had great support from the media for our election to a second term. The media pointed out our major accomplishment in the first term. They stressed that with a second term, we could continue our efforts for a constitution that provided an efficient and effective method of government. After the convention, Albert and I decided to stay in Washington for the returns on election night. We wanted the local Washington coverage of our acceptance speeches. While many of the members of congress would be at home in the states they represented, there were members of their staff who lived in the Washington area. As you know, we won by another landslide. We were amazed by the number of votes we obtained from members of the Democratic Party. Their Party Convention got very bad media reviews. They did not have a good platform or a good agenda for leadership. They were supporting the current constitution and methods of government. Our vote totals showed the voter population was not buying the Status Quo agenda. We were very happy our efforts to support Members of the House who supported our agenda paid off with elections of individuals who supported us. The Republican Party now had control in both the House and the Senate."

I reached over and turned both recorders off and said, "I think that is enough for this secession."

Dylan agreed, and we sat back and relaxed. We had a second cup of coffee while we relaxed. Neither of us wanted anything to eat as we were still full from the night before. The weather and the ocean were cooperating today. There was a nice cool breeze. The sky had just the right amount of white clouds. It was almost high tide, and it was going to change soon. The breeze seemed it might die down a little when the tide changed.

After our coffee, we were ready to work again. I said, "It did not seem as long between the election and the January 20, inauguration. We spent the Christmas and New Year time at the beach. Albert and Mary were with us. Many old friends came by to congratulate us and wish us good luck in the next four years. We played golf twice between Christmas and New Year. Albert and I talked a lot about what we would face and what we might accomplish in the next four years. I said, 'I have never been afraid of a task, and I think I will start with trying to get the mess in Palestine and Israel straightened out.' I was aware we had better relationships than we had ever had with the Arab world. Albert said, 'That is a lot to put on your plate, but you can handle it. If you succeed, the world will never forget you.'

"The inauguration came, and we were sworn in for our second term. Our speeches were the best we had ever given. We both talked about the need to maintain peace in the world. We talked about the need for business all over the world to work together for prosperity in the world. I said we needed this—One for All and All for One. We were approaching Peace and Prosperity for All. There had not been one member of the Armed Forces killed in action during our first administration, and I did not intend to allow one to be killed in the next four years. The media gave us their usual support, and our inauguration was a great success.

"I had not used Camp David in Maryland during my first term. In fact, I had not visited Camp David. Albert and I made a visit to Camp David on my second day in office. I had a grand plan in my mind, and I thought I might need Camp David. I was surprised by the limited living space and the small conference rooms. I thought we needed to build a building with a resort atmosphere. I wanted it to have well-furnished hotel-like rooms, a large conference room, and a smaller round-table conference room. When we were back at the White House, I called a contractor I had known for some time and asked him to come by. When he showed up, I took him to Camp David and showed him the area that would suit my plan. I outlined the plan for my building and its purpose. He agreed it would be easy to do the work, and he would get the plans drawn up for me to see. I told him to include the cost.

"When the contractor had left, I wished I had started this project during my first term. I must admit I did not think about trying to establish peace in the Middle East until we were on vacation. I did not want the hotel resort at Camp David to be called Paul's folly, so I was going to keep it under my hat as long as I could. The plans arrived in my office, and the price was something I could cover from my own money. When Albert saw the plans, he wanted to pay his share. I said I would not need it as the business my dad had built would take care of it, and it would not put a stress on my budget. I wanted to begin to have meeting with Arab leaders and with the leaders from Israel at Camp David. I hoped that after meetings with both sides, I could have an agenda that each side could agree to discuss.

"I got word from the contractor on the cost and the time required for construction. He assured me that the hotel would be ready for occupation in one year from the start date. I asked about the furniture and decorations. He said it was all included in the cost he had given me. I gave him permission to get started. He said he would start on next Monday. That was January 31. I had a year to work on the leaders before we made our major effort. I thought about by plan of action. I did not want to sound like a Pentecostal minister preaching hell and damnation. I wanted to preach peace and love of one's neighbor."

Dylan said, "Paul, I must admit you were never afraid of a major challenge."

I turned off the recorders and said, "We can continue after lunch." We decided to have lunch on the porch and then get back to work. We had a very good cold soup and a sandwich for lunch. We both preferred beer to drink. I was surprised when they brought out apple pie and ice cream when we finished our sandwich.

Dylan said, "That pie and ice cream was an excellent ending for a good lunch." I agreed with him and sat back to let my meal digest. We were quiet for about three minutes, and Dylan said, "I must admit your biography has become the most interesting piece I have ever written. You were very successful in office, and you have been a great host to work with." I thanked him and turned on the recorders.

I said, "I had a lot on my plate that first year of the second term. Albert and I decided to visit every state governor and speak to every state legislature. We would divide the states, and he would work on half while I worked on the other half and then we would change halves. We were going to try to get every state governor and every state legislature to support a constitution convention that would provide a constitution that provided a unicameral government that would be governed by an efficient and effective method of government. We wanted each state to put a referendum on their ballots that allowed the electorate to confirm or deny a constitution convention, and we wanted to know if they would support a unicameral legislature. I took twenty-five states that included Alaska, and Albert took twenty-five states that included Hawaii. We had our staff working on a schedule of meeting and speeches.

"I went to work on my efforts to bring peace to the Middle East. I arranged a schedule of meeting with the leaders of the major Islamic nations. I was listening to TV one night, and I heard a girl with a beautiful voice sing 'How Great Thou Art.' I decided to have the reference to Christ taken out of the hymn and replaced with angels. I received the recordings I wanted—'When the Saints Come Marching In' and 'How Great Thou Art.' I got a speaker system with a recorder such that the hymns could be heard in a very large auditorium. I planned to play 'When the Saints Come Marching In' before I started to speak. I planned to play 'How Great Thou Art' at the end of my speech.

"I worked on my speech for several days. I planned to start my speech with Peace and Prosperity for All. I planned to say there could not be prosperity without peace in the world. I wanted my audience to know that I was an American and a citizen of the United States, who believed in freedom of religion for all. The Almighty God did not want his children killing each other in the name of religion. It was the false prophets God had warned us about that were power-hungry and were not satisfied until they controlled the minds and bodies of all their citizens. This had been true at the time of the first Crusades, it has been true ever since the Crusades, and it is true today. God wants his children to be free in body, mind, and soul.

"Governments received their power to govern from the people, and the representatives of the people who governed should answer to the people. There had been great effort over the world, including the Islamic world in the previous years, to rid the people of false governments. These governments were tyrannical and existed for the pleasure of the people who governed. The United States was born after the people had fought a tyrannical king and won. Most of the nations in the Western world had won their freedom by defeating tyrannical people who governed without allowing the people to enjoy their God-given right to freedom. I finished my speech by pointing out how the governments in the United States had merged governments to reduce the cost of government. I showed charts of mergers and the reduction in the budgets. I said the Islamic world needed to consider mergers. With dually constituted governments, which were efficient and effective, there could be Peace and Prosperity for All. I then played 'How Great Thou Art.'

"Albert, Warren, and Raymond said they loved the speech. Albert said he thought I should reverse the order of my hymns. I thought about it and realized he was right. I wanted the audience thinking about an Almighty God in the beginning, and I wanted them to think about marching into a new world of religious freedom with Peace and Prosperity for All.

"I would be dividing my time between in-country travel and foreign travel. We wanted to have a new constitution with a unicameral legislature before our term was up. I suggested to Albert that we each begin to write a new constitution. We could compare notes. I thought if we had a draft constitution, we could show states that were not in favor of a new constitution that it could change their minds. When we had a draft constitution, I hoped we could work out a budget and show everyone how much money the nation would save. I was very glad I would be able to work and stay in touch with the White House while I was on Air Force One. Both Albert and I were going to be spending a lot of time in the air during this second term. We could stay in touch with our office and each other while we were in the air. I think it is time for an afternoon break."

Dylan agreed and turned off the recorders. As we stopped talking and sat back, the security guards were on the ball. They radioed the kitchen, and out came a tray of snacks and two beers. The tide had changed, and by afternoon, the breeze had died down. It was not hot on the porch, but it was warm. I asked Dylan if he was comfortable or adjourn to my study rather. He said he was comfortable on the porch.

After we finished our snack and beer, I reached over and turned on both recorders. "After getting the Camp David project started, I went to work on my version of a new constitution. I decided to follow the preamble with the Bill of Rights. So I began my constitution with the preamble. I used a lot of the points what Charlene Jefferson had said in her publications. Basically, my preamble gave the power to the citizens. They had the right to delegate their power to a dually elected representative. I pointed out that the primary purpose of government was and always had been to protect the life and the property of the citizens.

"As far as the power of the Federal government was concerned, the delegated power went to a Senate that was composed of one hundred members who were elected from one hundred Senate districts of near-equal population. This turned the power back to a one-man-one-vote system of government. I wrote my constitution so that the Senate was like a Corporate Board of Directors. The Senate appointed a president who served as Chief Executive Officer for the nation. The citizens who were allowed to vote would elect the senators the way stockholders elected a Board of Directors.

"The president served at the pleasure of the Senate. His duties were to reinforce and carry out the laws and regulations approved by the Senate. The president had the right to create regulations in order to carry out his task of maintaining operations passed by the Senate. Otherwise, my constitution was very similar to the 1791 Constitution. I did insist that laws, regulations, and decisions should be made as near as possible to the citizens who would be affected by this process. This gave the State governments and their internal governments more power. Notably, I gave the right to bear arms question to the States. The opinions and the need to bear arms were different from state to state, and therefore, regulations involving the bearing of arms belonged to the states.

"As you know, copies of the original draft constitutions and the constitution that was finally adopted are on file in the presidential library. When I went to the library after it was finished and all the documents had been moved there, I was surprised at what a wonderful job they had done. It looked like every scrap of paper used in drafting the adopted constitution had been saved.

"I had my speech and the recorded hymns ready and then made my first trip to Palestine and Israel. In my talks with the leaders, I wanted to plant the seeds of mergers. I felt the answer to the Arab and Israeli problem could be handled through proper mergers. There would have to be borders that were moved, but there was a lot of unused land in the Middle East, including Lebanon, Syria, Jordan, and Iraq. I wanted to include Iran because citizens and government there would have to be satisfied if we were going to have peace. When one would read the history of the Middle East, peace would seem like an unheard-of word. From at least a thousand years before the birth of Christ, there had been one war after another in the Fertile Crescent. The area was given this name by James Breasted, a University of Chicago archaeologist. The crescent-shaped region is moist, and like most people in early history, the inhabitants were successful farmers and raised cattle and sheep. This part of the Middle East has been ruled by one conqueror after the next. Thus, the area has always been a seat of geopolitics and diplomatic efforts to secure peace.

"I knew that the Fertile Crescent would be extremely important to my efforts to secure peace in the area. As I studied the area, I noticed that during World War I and after the Western nations, especially Britain and France had divided up the old Ottoman Empire. They formed new nation borders. Part of the area was controlled by France, and the British controlled other areas. The British were unable to bring peace to the area known as Iraq. The Shiites and the Sunnis fought each other over an argument that started after the death of Mohammad. They could not agree on who was to become the primary leader of their fate. The British finally pulled out and left only a small air force to help stabilize the area. They continued to fight until Saddam Hussein became dictator. He had the third-largest army in the world and an excellent internal intelligence system. He was a very ruthless dictator and killed people who did not follow his directions. He wiped out the population of several villages that were against his rule.

"When we captured Hussein, and he was hanged, we hoped there would be democracy in Iraq, but the old battle between the Shiites and Sunnis still existed. I thought that the efforts of the Western world had failed. It was time the people of the Middle East and the Fertile Crescent had an opportunity to control their own destiny. They should decide where the borders should be and who should rule. Naturally, I wanted a Democratic-Republic method of government. I hoped that I could bring the various population divisions together, and with diplomacy, I could establish Peace and Prosperity for All in the area.

"I was still most worried about Israel. This was another case where the Western world had moved the Jews into their historic area of existence without the approval of the nations of the Middle East. It appeared to me that despite the history of one conqueror after another, when people were given the opportunity to self-govern, they can live in peace. After a period of attempts to educate the population and to get them to believe in themselves, I planned to bring them together and let diplomacy work. I was going to keep the United States government out of the process as well as the other

Western nation's governments. I only tried to keep the process operating.

"Albert and I discussed this idea, and he was in agreement with my plan. We needed the Camp David facility. In the meantime, we planned to go to the area and visit leaders and give speeches. I wanted the Geek program to be totally involved in the educational procedure. I had maps of the area produced in large numbers. I knew that with the leadership, there would be the Status Quo devil at work. People were always afraid of change even when things were not working well. They feared the unknown of change. The Geek program began to fill the Middle Eastern world and the Islamic world with the philosophers writings during the Age of Enlightenment and the beginning of the Industrial Age. We would be returning to this period for their world. Like the Western world at that time, the Eastern world still depended on agriculture and raising animals. Israel had become an industrialized nation and gave jobs to many workers who were Muslims."

I then said to Dylan, "If we keep going like this, we will miss dinner."

Dylan said, "I was so interested in the history of the Eastern world that I lost track of time." He turned off the recorders, and we were joined by Jo Anne and Mary. The security had let them know we were calling it a day. We had beers, and the ladies had wine. We discussed where we should go for dinner. God bless Jo Anne—she suggested Charleston. I wanted Magnolia's, but Jo Anne suggested the Queen Street Inn. We had not been there for a while, and that sounded good. We would sit on the patio. The patio is protected by the surrounding buildings and that keeps it comfortable. It is always quieter than the inside of a restaurant.

Security brought around the SUV. I asked if we could keep the security at a level that would not raise too much attention. They assured me they would. They said they would send guards to the restaurant as customers before we arrived. The SUV would not draw attention. We arrived, and our table was ready on the patio. The security was well placed and did not draw attention. They looked like any other customers. Their cars had all gone from in front of the restaurant. I found out later they had used the other SUV. We were lucky there were not very many diners on the patio. There were two floors inside the restaurant, and we did not know how many were there. It seemed the owners had kept most people inside. The people on the patio had been advised not to bother us. That made for a dinner of excellent food and good conversation. It sure was a pain in the butt being a former president. We had excellent service from the staff of the restaurant. That was just like it was before I became president. The better Charleston restaurants had become acquainted with occasional calls from security about our arrival for dinner or lunch.

We took our usual ride around the Battery after dinner and stopped on Broad Street at the ice-cream parlor. I suggested we park and all go in. At that hour of the night, there were parking places on Broad Street. Everyone thought that was a great idea, even the security men. They had small tables inside. We put in our orders, and Jo Anne and Marlene sat at one table, and Dylan and I sat at another table. The security guys did not sit down; they took their places at different spots in the ice-cream parlor. They had their ice-cream cones, but they kept vigil. The SUV we were riding in sure made it different from the past when there were at least three cars on each trip. It did not take long to finish the ice-cream cones, and we were back in the SUV. We turned at Meeting Street and continued in the direction of the bridge to Mt Pleasant. I heard John the guard in the front seat talking with security. He suggested a turn at Columbus Street and then onto East Bay to get to the bridge. I would have continued on Meeting to Huger Street, but they never took the obvious route. Security at the house and any other security that was sent out knew where we were at all times.

Once we were back at the house, no one was ready to call it a night. We were having good conversations and enjoying each other's company. Marlene said their boys had enjoyed their trip to the beach. They were very impressed with what Marshall had done with the Paul Harvey Collins private dining room. I told her how my dad and Marshall always teased each other about their colleges. She was surprised when I told her my mother was on Marshall's side. I told her it was a state reverie thing. Mom was from the up-country in the state, and that was Clemson territory. Marlene said her father was a military officer, and they moved around the world. She had spent time in Japan, Korea, and Germany. She had attended military base schools. They never stayed in one place for long. She said she would liked to have grow up on the island like I did or in a small town like Jo Anne did. She would have loved to have known most people in the town. Jo Anne said it was fun, but the different age groups where cliquish. I had noticed that when I was dating Jo Anne. I was older than Jo Anne, and the older girls appeared to be jealous when I dated Jo Anne. After a couple of hours, we were ready for bed.

After breakfast, Jo Anne and Marlene said they were going shopping. Jo Anne wanted to take Marlene to the Citadel Mall, which was in the West Ashley area. Dylan and I went into my study. The porch was chilly, and the ocean breeze was too high to sit on the porch and try to work. A cold front had gone through the area during the night. There were very dark clouds over the ocean.

I turned on the TV, and we listened to the morning news. We were in for a rainy day. I said to Dylan, "Welcome to the sunny south."

He said, "Just blame the Yankees. That cold front came from the north." We had a good laugh.

I said, "After all these years since the War Between the States and we are still talking about north and south. I still cannot believe we were able to bring about peace in the Middle East." Dylan turned on the recorders and said that sounded like a good place to start. I said, "Albert was working hard on the states and their governments to get support for our new constitution.

"The Geek program was telling me that my program was doing well with a large portion of the Islamic population. They wanted to govern themselves and wanted the freedom the United States citizens had. We had informed them about the Revolutionary War and how that had freed the people from tyrant government. We had reminded them about the French Revolution and Bastille Day. The Islamic Spring that had taken place during 2010 and until about 2025 had freed most of the nations from tyrant rule. We needed to get the governments organized and working for the peace and prosperity of the people. They needed to have a greater industrial society. They needed to become more self-sufficient. They had relied on oil too long, and the world was rapidly moving to renewable energy. The women were joining the educated population, but the educational system was still behind the Western world. We had gotten the religion in the educational system to become almost nonexistent.

"I had the Geek program push the Kahn Academy and Internet learning throughout the United States. We had finally got most school districts to believe in Internet learning. The classroom teachers had become more like individual tutors. In addition to the Kahn Academy, other Internet sites were providing Internet learning. Some had become income-producing sites, but there were other sites like Kahn Academy that remained as nonprofit sites. Since the Internet sites were available 24 7, they were available at homework time. Most of the sites were interactive sites. At any time, they knew which students were doing well and which students needed help. The interactive sites provided special tutor support to the students who were having trouble with any subject. For the students who were not motivated and were not working at their best level, there was counseling on the Internet, and the schools were notified. The schools also gave counseling. The student population was doing much better. They were moving through the lessons at their own pace. We had moved up to near the top of the list of nations in math and science. The reading level for both content and understanding had improved remarkably.

"We now had the Geek program working with the Islamic schools. They were quick to accept the Kahn program and the other programs the Geek program made available. We had seen to it they had the computers in the classroom. Microsoft and the Bill Gates Foundation were helpful in getting laptops for the students. The ExxonMobil Foundation was a big help in the United States and the Islamic world. We knew that the education of the Islamic society would help both the Peace movement and the Prosperity movement.

"The work on the facility at Camp David was near completion. We had made remarkable progress in the Arab and Islamic world. There was much to be done. We had known for a long time that on a one-on-one basis, there was acceptance on both sides. The affluent members of their society attended either a college or a university in the United States. They had become good friends of American students. They visited them in this country, and the American friends visited their Muslim friends in their country. But when it came to society or government issues, they still saw the American society as sinister. America was the great Devil. This was because of the presentations in movies and TV programs. They knew about strip clubs and pornographic material at adult theaters. We viewed as wrong the way they treated women. They could not drive, and they had to be covered—even their faces—when they were on the streets. The men married more than one woman. They would not allow women to become educated, and they wanted them to remain home and provide for the men. We were two very different worlds. Our government was seen as imperial, in that, the American and Western world wanted to rule everything.

"Our Geek program and the programs from our TV stations had done a lot to lessen the differences. The citizens of the Eastern world, especially the women and the young population, wanted more of the kind of freedom the citizens in the United States have had for generation.

"I was working very hard not to be seen as imperialistic. I believed the citizens should be free and should decide on their government and their national borders. The Western world had not done a good job of bringing peace and prosperity to the Eastern world. There were pockets of overcrowding and place where there was open, fertile land. The oil was a major source of money. But with effort, their share of the market would support more industry. Like Iraq, before Saddam was removed, the Eastern world could be a place where living was cheap. Gasoline was very cheap, and the electricity was free under Saddam. The Arabs and the Muslims needed to find their entrepreneurs. It was time for an Industrial Age in the Eastern world.

"In my travels, I had met most of their leaders. They liked the things I said. Syria and an area on both sides of the border between Iran and Afghanistan were hotbeds of terrorism. The old Al Qaeda fighters hated the United States and Israel. They wanted to destroy both nations. They wanted the Islamic Religious Rule of the people. They were not big in the use of the Internet, and the Al Qaeda fighters along the Iran-Afghanistan border were in a fringe area for our TV network. They attempted to block or prevent any of our material from reaching the citizens. There were similar attempts in Syria, but they were less successful. This pocket of Al Qaeda fighters was left over from the Syrian conflicts that occurred earlier in Syria. They had killed the dictator and established Islamic Religious Rule similar to the rule that remained in Iran. Our attempts to point out the tyranny of the rule and the false prophets who ruled were only minimally successful in these areas. It would take a majority of the Islamic world in our favor before we would have success in these areas.

"Our State Department was doing a wonderful job of supporting our agenda. Each of our ambassadors and their staffs were well received in the nation in which they were stationed. They kept up with the Geek Program and the TV efforts and gave excellent feedback on the success of each effort. They could provide me with the names of the leaders in each nation who would work well with our agenda. I took a trip to Camp David and looked over the new facility. It was everything I had hoped it would be. It was elegant without being overdecorated. The meeting rooms were just what the doctor ordered. We had headsets with plug-ins at each desk or seat. There were individual microphones that could be attached to a shirt or coat. There were plug-ins for the microphones and a button the person could push in order to get a turn to speak. A green light indicated when his turn had come, and a red light that indicated his time was up. There was a yellow light that indicated the end of his time was approaching. I was very happy with everything I saw. We were ready to begin having conference at Camp David. I had translators on the pay role, and we could handle all the Islamic dialects."

Dylan turned off the recorders and said, "What do you think we should do for lunch?"

I said, "On a day like this, I would just as soon eat at home." I left Dylan and went to the kitchen. They said they had lunch ready. I returned to my study, and the kitchen staff members brought in a great lunch. They even remembered the beers. We ate well and talked about the history of the Middle East. Dylan pointed out a couple of points I wish I had known when I was president. After lunch, we decided a second beer would be the best dessert. I looked out of the window, and it was raining again.

When we finished our second beer, Dylan turned on the recorders. I said, "Israel would be a problem I would have to deal with. The modern nation known as Israel is a very small part of the Fertile Crescent. It is about the size of Wales, a part of British land area. It is located mostly in the ancient kingdom of Judah. It has been an important part of three religions. Hebrew, Abrahamic religions, and Christianity were all born in the area known as Judah. Sacred sites of these religions are located in modern Israel. The area was conquered by various empires, and thus, it has been home to many ethnicities. But the area remained mainly Jewish until the Roman wars. With the influence of Jesus, the area became Christian. The Jews became a minority in most of the area. The area became increasingly Christian until the third century. By the seventh century, the Muslim religion became the majority religion. This Muslim conquest lasted until the middle of the twentieth century. It was the center of the Crusades. World War I changed things. The British Conquest put an end to provinces that were part of the Syrian Sultanate and the Ottoman Empire. The British dominated the Fertile Crescent from the end of World War I but did little to bring peace to this area with a long history of one conquest after another. The middle of the twentieth century, the persecution of the Jews during the rule of Hitler, led to the creation of the Zionist movement. The British and the support of the United States established a homeland for the Jewish people. This homeland is the modern nation of Israel. The increase in Jewish immigration to Israel caused tensions between the Arabs and the Jews. About 50 percent of the people who belong to the Jews' religion live in Israel today.

"I felt that the problem was a land use problem. There were too many people trying to occupy the same small area of land. The Fertile Crescent was a large area of land. I had just completed a trip to Israel, Jordan, Syria, and Lebanon. I wanted to have face-to-face talks with individuals I planned to invite to a meeting at Camp David.

THE ISLAND BOY PRESIDENT

"I was back in the White House when I got a call from Tom. He had retired and was living on Sullivan's Island. He told me about a problem he was having with a long-term health-care insurance company. His father had died, and his mother was living at an assisted-living facility in Mt Pleasant. She loved it there. Several of her old friends also lived there. He said everyone needed to read their long-term health-care policy very carefully before they start paying the premium. He said the insurance companies were dealing with an older retired population and knew it. After his mother was found to be qualified for payments of long-term health-care benefits, she had to wait ninety days before they would start to pay. Tom said, 'I have control of my mother's money. The assisted-living facility billed her in advance for the month. The long-term health insurance company required her to wait until the end of the month to send in our bill from the facility and to fill out a four-page claim form. Once they receive the claim-form application, it would take about three weeks to process the form and mail a check. I sent in the bill and the claim forms three days before the end of the month. After about three weeks, the claim was denied because it had been sent before the end of the month. They sent a four-page form that had to be resent to the company. It required a signature of the director of the facility that stated she had been a resident for the entire month. From the time she paid the bill until she received her check was two months or more. In these days of computers and digital data, can you imagine such an inefficient system? I called their Customer Service and got nowhere. The use of the phrase Customer Service is so insincere. It is ironical. There was no service on the part of the insurance company. They used everything they could to delay payment.' I asked Tom for the name of the insurance company and was very surprised by his answer. It was a well-known, and up to now a respected, company. This indicated to me that everyone should read insurance policies carefully or maybe get legal help before accepting the word of some agent. I told Tom I would look up the head of the insurance and call him."

Dylan turned off the recorders and said, "I remember a professor who was head of the Business Department who said insurance was a rip-off. He said one should invest his own money, and he would be a lot better off in the long run."

I said, "I had heard that about life insurance. Health insurance and long-term health insurance have been like sacred cows to me."

After dinner, Dylan and I decided we should work for a while. We went to the study, and he turned on the recorders. He said, "I hope you gave that head of the insurance company hell?"

I said, "It did not take long to get his name. It was Carl Walters. I called and got him on the phone. He was surprised by getting a call from me. It did not take a minute into the call before I knew where the problem was, and it was the man I was talking to. He had no interest in the clients who were paying money. The fact that they were very senior citizens who were proven to be disabled did not impress him. I kept the phone call short. But I was not finished with him. I went over to the Geek Program building. I found Warren and filled him in on Tom's problem. I said that it would not do any good to try to contact the people with valid claims, but we should contact every policyholder and tell them about the problem with filing a claim and ask them to contact the insurance company and complain. We needed to contact people who were buying and paying for Long-Term Health Care and bring them up-to-date. They might be better off changing companies or not buying the insurance and just investing the money. Warren assured me he and the Geeks could make the insurance companies sit up and listen.

"It was back to the Eastern world problem. I invited forty leaders from that part of the world to Camp David for a meeting. I did not invite anyone from Israel. I had talked with them often, and I knew their position on the land use problem. I wanted to get the Arabs and Muslims' position on this problem. The Western world had never been successful in dealing with the Eastern world. I wanted to give the Eastern world a chance to solve its own problems. We had them flown into Dulles and bused to Camp David. Shortly after, they arrived and had time to look over the meeting facility and their rooms. They were very impressed with what we had done. While it is not a custom in their part of the world, we had a cocktail party before dinner. We had found out that when they were away from home and on their own, they liked a drink. I was glad because the conversations were excellent during the cocktail hour. The dinner was well received. I gave an after-dinner speech. I started by saying as unaccustomed as I am to public speaking. This got the laugh that I wanted. I continued by saying the Western world had messed up royally trying to rule the Eastern world. It was time we gave up our unpopular imperialism and gave the citizens of the Eastern world a chance to form their own governments and decided where the borders of the nations should be. This was followed by a loud applause that lasted until I stopped it. This was a good feeling to know we were on the right path to success. I told them that each desk had maps of the Eastern world and of each nation in the area. I told them we all knew the Fertile Crescent is the area where most people will have to live. I said I believed that the Eastern world was ready for an industrial revolution. Energy was not a problem. But the area needed more than oil to support its people. People need jobs. This brought on another loud applause. I said, 'I suggest, but it is up to you, that a few days of discussion can be a good thing. I will not be with you, and you will be on our own. I can promise you this room is not bugged, and your talks will not be recorded. This is your meeting.'

"I wished that Albert could have been there. We had devoted so much time and effort for this moment. I left the room after my speech. I had suggested to each person who was in attendance that they should try to elect their Chairman. The next morning, I joined them for breakfast. They were all very happy, and Abdul Fekuae had been elected Chairman. He was a liberal Iranian. He was a graduate of the Oregon School of Pharmacy and had received his Doctorate Degree. He had returned to Iran and was Dean of Science at a university there. He spoke perfect English and had married an English girl."

Dylan and I both were ready to turn off the recorders for this very long day. We both felt we had covered a lot of ground. We said our good nights, but Jo Anne and Marlene joined us then, so we went to the kitchen for a snack before bedtime. The ladies had a great time and told us all about their day. They had lunch at a West Ashley restaurant I was familiar with. In fact, the owner lived about three blocks down the street. They had gone to Magnolia's for dinner. Marlene said that she was falling in love with Charleston and wished she and Dylan could move there. She added quickly, 'Below Broad, of course,' and we all laughed. The ladies were tired after their long day and so were Dylan and I. We all went to bed.

We awoke to a much better day. The sun was shining in the window. The house sat at just the right angle, so at this time of the year when the sun came up, it shined in the bedroom windows. After I shaved, showered, and dressed, I walked out on the porch. There was not a cloud in the sky. The blue sky and the white sand leading to the ocean were beautiful. We would have no problem working on the porch today. First, Dylan came out, and he was followed by Marlene and Jo Anne. We had breakfast on the porch. It seemed as though we were all mesmerized by the beauty of the morning. There was very little conversation. After breakfast, Jo Anne said she and Marlene were meeting Nancy and Tonya for a trip into Charleston. Tonya was a friend who was a real estate agent, and she was going to show them several houses in the below Broad Street area. She had one that was very interesting. It was built by the sea captain of a clipper ship that made trips to the Far East. He had carried his plans for the house to a contract and told him he wanted the house built according to the plans or he would not pay a penny. The contractor began to say, 'But, sir—,' but the captain cut him off and said, 'Exactly according to the plans' and left on his trip. When he got back, the house built was exactly according to the plans. It was three floors, but there were no stairs. When you entered the house, it was obvious the stairs were an afterthought. We were looking forward to seeing this house. When the ladies left, a security guard brought out our recorders and placed them on the coffee table. Dylan turned them on, and I said, "It is time to go to work.

"Abdul Fekuae turned out to be a great chairman. He was much in favor of a Democratic-Republic government like the United States government for all the nations in the Eastern world. He was in favor of the American Freedoms. The group we had invited had made great progress in three days of meetings. We had a cocktail party each night before dinner, and we had entertainment after dinner. The first night, we had singers with wonderful voices for the hymns they sang. The second night, we had a group who sang Frank Sinatra songs. The last one was 'I Did It My Way.' That pleased every member of the group. After the cocktail party and the dinner on the third night, I met with the group. I was pleased to learn from Abdul Fekuae that the group had reached a consensus. They agreed it was time to make major changes in the Eastern world, especially the Fertile Crescent. They believed difference in populations and religions had not been considered when the current borders were set. The problem of one conquest after another had caused the area to be prone to war and brought warring populations together. They agreed the area could support all the populations, and with the development of industry and business like those that had occurred in Israel, they could be self-supporting. I was very glad to hear that they were very impressed with the United States and the Israeli educational system, and they felt that a good educational system for the populations of the Eastern world was absolutely needed. I told them we would see to it that the Kahn Academy and the Geek Program Internet education would be made available to them. I said we would ship computers and with instructional disk to them for their schools and any schools they built. This information was met with great acceptance. They would go back to their different parts of the Eastern world and do what they could to get the needed changes made. I told them to let us know any way in which we could be of help. They said we were doing a great job and making headway toward bringing Peace and Prosperity for All in their world.

"When I got back to the White House, Albert wanted to know how things had gone at the meeting. I told him, and I think he was as happy as I was. We were not finished, but we had a great start. I remembered John Paul Jones. We have not yet begun to fight. I visited the Geek Program and told Warren and the Geeks about our success. I congratulated them and told them about the need for educational programs for their schools. I told them to remember the agenda for the Middle East. We wanted them to have a strong desire for personal freedom like the American colonist and the French population at the time of the French Revolution. The Islamic world had been left out of the Age of Enlightenment too long. They said they would get to work and would have things going in about one week. They would need software that translated from one language to another. They said they had to move some programs from one place to another. I asked about training people and students to use computers, and they said that would be easy. They would have as many disks in each dialect as I needed.

"I felt it was time to get Israeli leadership to Camp David. I included people from their schools and their colleges and universities. When we finished with our invitations, we had thirty-five people. They were flown into Dulles and bused to Camp David. I used the same agenda we had used with the Eastern world group. The first night cocktails and dinner were well received. My talk was well received. They understood the need for changes in the borders. But as I thought, they were very protective of their borders and wanted more land included in their borders. I asked if they would aid in Arab and Muslim education. They said they would and had long thought that was a major part of the problem in that part of the world. We discussed the Fertile Crescent and its importance to the area. I found they were willing to work with us, but they were not going to give up anything. We had made them the power in the area, and they were going to use. I stressed the agenda of Peace and Prosperity for All. I said, 'When I say all, I mean all. If we leave anyone out, we will not be able to accomplish peace in the area.' Peace in the area was as important to Israel as it was to any other nation."

Dylan turned off the recorders and said we just needed to take a break. He said, "I am going to have to give a lot of thought on how I am going to write this part of your biography. Readers are not going to be familiar with the Eastern world the way you understand that area. They are somewhat familiar with the Middle East."

I said, "Lack of understanding has always been the problem. Our congress did not understand what we were trying to do. They wanted peace in the area but had no idea about how to get it. The British and the French were unfamiliar with the history and culture of the Middle East when they set up the nations in the area. Imperialism has not worked and will not work. It will take education of the people so they can form and operate their own governments."

Dylan said, "I am going to have to work that into the biography." He turned on his record and dictated a note.

When we were ready, he turned on the recorders, and I said, "I was still working on a new constitution for the United States of America, and I wanted that Constitutional Convention in the worst way. Albert and I had made progress with our visits to the states and to their legislature. The governors were no problem. With either Albert's third visit or my third visit, we had the legislatures of the states on our side. They were all benefiting from the mergers of governments in their states and knew we were right about improving the Federal government. I wrote a White Paper and sent it to each governor and the leadership of the state legislatures. The White Paper was well received, and I got answers from them, saying they would place the Constitutional Convention on the next ballot, so the voters could decide if they wanted a change in the method of government.

"Albert and I knew all we had to do now was to wait for the midterm elections. We were not the kind to sit around and wait. I decided to make another visit to the Eastern world. I arrived in Lebanon. I had a talk with two of the people who had attended our Camp David conference. I said that I would like to go to Syria even though it was a hotbed of terrorism. They asked why I wanted to go. I said it was because of the Russian influence there. I said we needed to work with the other world powers to achieve peace. They asked who the world powers were. I said, 'Well, most people say the United States, Russia, and Britain.' They surprised me when they said there is only one world power and that is the United States of America. I said, 'Do you mean that?' They said, 'Not only us, but most people in the Eastern world look upon the United States as the only world power.' Then they really surprised me—they added, 'especially since the beginning of your administration.' They said, 'Your administration has had an understanding of world problems and Eastern world culture and the problems that no one else has had.'

"With that knowledge, I visited Abdul Fekuae. He was very happy to see me and had a lot of information for me. He showed me maps that had been agreed upon by 80 percent of the leaders of the reason. When he explained the reasoning for the borders, I understood why the new borders were exactly what we wanted. He said they all agreed this would make a more stable Eastern world and make most Arabs and Muslims happy. I asked him to keep up the good work, and he said it was his pleasure.

"I returned to the White House and went to see Warren and the Geek Program workers. They were making great progress with getting schools at all levels in the Eastern world up-to-date with Internet education methods. Warren said the teachers had learned fast and now understood how to use the programs to teach students. The students were making good progress. They had been able to reduce the cost of education and had more students involved in educational programs.

"When I was back in the White House, I had been called by Carl Walters from the insurance company. I returned his call, and he asked me if I would call off my dogs. They were leading to bankruptcy of the Long-Term Health Insurance agencies. He apologized for not being more responsive when I called. He said he was now very aware of my concerns and agreed with me that the industry had not done a good job of keeping up with the digital world and had not been considerate of the people who were claimants. They were an older population and disabled. Many had mental problems. They would work to make the claims process as easy as possible. I asked him to send me a copy of their new policy agreement. He agreed to send by fax as soon as we were finished. I said that if the persons who had contacted me about the problem were happy with the new policy, I would make efforts to assist them in their efforts to get more policyholders. He was happy with that, and we said good-bye.

"When I got the new policy, I called Tom and said I would send him a copy to see if it met his needs. He said that would not be necessary. He would have called earlier but knew I was traveling. He had received the new policy agreement from the company, and he was happy with the policy. He thanked me for my help. I said, 'That is what Island Boy friends are for.' He laughed and said he knew he could count on me. I called Warren and told him we had been successful and that the new policy was just what the policyholders needed. He could now get the word out that the industry had changed and were working for the clients as they should. He was happy with their success and said the Geeks would get right on it.

"It was a lucky day when I met Warren Anderson, and we had started the Geek Program. The number of employees in the Geek Program had increased on a regular basis. We had used them to educate the people for success with each agenda item. Internet education was a great tool. Education of the people was the answer to many of any nation's problems. America had become the leading power in the world by having a good educational program that served all the people. We had allowed it to become ineffective and inefficient. But Internet education and administrative improvement was saving the day.

"We were two weeks from the midterm elections, and I needed a break. So I scheduled a four-day weekend at my beach home. Albert and Mary joined us. I had my staff work with Jo Anne and to put an Island Boy party for Saturday night of the weekend. I went down Thursday night and rested up on Friday. Albert and I played a round of golf at Wild Dunes. We spend time on the porch on Friday and Saturday, talking about the new constitution. I am not sure much was accomplished that we did not already agree upon. But the beer was good, and we consumed quite a few.

"When I was back in Washington, I got the word that several nations in the Fertile Crescent had agreed to change their borders and had built new schools, and three new universities were in the planning stage. Abdul Fekuae and the others were doing such a good job that I did not think we would need another Camp David meeting. But I was wrong. We did need a meeting. We seemed to need more meetings to work on the Israeli and Palestine problem. I received a map showing the agreed-upon new borders. Iraq was divided into Shiite, Sunni, and Kurd areas. The Kurd area included part of Turkey. The Sunni area was part of Iran. The Shiite area included the entire form of the nation of Jordan. Syria had been completely removed. Lebanon and Turkey occupied the area that had formerly been Syria. The Lebanon border was moved north, and the land that was part of Lebanon was given to Israel for expansion. This was the area that had been used to launch rockets into Israel. Israel obtained the Golan Heights and a large section of Syria and Jordan. The Palestine problem seemed to be solved by a nation that included the Gaza strip and an area along the Canal on the Israeli side. It also included part of what had been Jordan. The Palestine area separated Israel and Egypt along the Israeli and Jordan side of the Suez Canal to the Gulf of Aqaba.

"The new nations would be governed by a Democratic-Republican form of government like the United States. They were drawing up constitutions for the various areas. I faxed them our plans for a new constitution. I encouraged them to put time limits on the new constitution and try to improve the government after they had been in effect for a time. I suggested a unicameral government in all cases. I said, 'They should consider the organization of the governments within the nations like the city governments. Make sure their population size is adequate to provide the taxes needed to supply the services. There might need to be controls of square miles of area.'

"Another area that was affected was the nation of Kuwait. It was made part of Iran along with some area of the former nation of Iraq. As I talked by telephone and got messages from the areas involved, I became aware that the organization and establishment of governments would occupy the area for some time and provide peace in the area. When I received a call from Abdul Fekuae, he told me not to worry about peace in the area. The leaders of each new nation had agreed to sign a treaty. The treaty required each nation to have full respect for the other nations. If one nation attacked another nation, the nations of the area would defend the attacked nation. They planned to have a peace-keeping military force paid for by each nation. No nation could support or give sanction to terrorist groups.

"They planned to have a Supreme Court for the Middle Eastern nations that would decide legal question between the nations. They would also have the power to try the members of any government that made war on another nation or supported terrorist groups. They said now was the time they would start to work on the Prosperity for All portion of our motto. I thanked him very much for the wonderful news and once again offered any assistance that he might need from me or the United States.

"It looked as if Albert and I had accomplished something that we had wanted to accomplish. I had to see where Israel stood on all these changes. They had not contacted me at all. I made a trip to Israel and planned to invite their leadership to Camp David for talks. When I met with the leadership, I was surprised and pleased. They had not called because they were respecting my belief that the Middle East should have a free hand to establish their borders and methods of government. They said that Abdul Fekuae and the others had included them in the decision-making and the establishment of the borders. They were part of the treaty Abdul had informed me about. Israel would be defended by Arab Nation if it were attacked.

"All this allowed Albert and me to turn our full attention to getting the approval for a Constitution Convention. The Geek program and Raymond and his staff had done a great job of getting the voters of every state fully informed on the issues in the upcoming election. Albert and I had been on every news network. We had been followed by mostly members of the House who wanted to prevent the voters from supporting a Constitutional Convention. Albert and I had been called every name in the book by our antagonist. It was funny because our antagonists were mostly Republicans. We had a very high approval rating among Democratic voters. We had a 78 percentage point approval rating among Republican voters. We saw the upcoming election as a sure thing for a Constitutional Convention."

I then said to Dylan, "It's past lunchtime, and we are still working. Let's take a long break and go to Dunleavy's for lunch." Dylan said that sounded good to him. The security brought the SUV around, and we headed out. Dunleavy's was surprisingly quiet. The lunch crowd had come and gone. I looked at my watch, and it was 2:45 p.m.

Dunleavy said, "You are late today. I thought you were retired."

I said, "When you never do anything, you can retire, but when you are a busy person, you can never retire."

Dunleavy's sister heard us and said, "My brother was born retired." Dunleavy threw a bar towel at her. We had a good lunch, and the beer was cold. We had the security guards join us. After lunch, I was not in the mood to get back to talking. Dylan was also tired. When we got back to the house, we split up, and he went to his and Marlene's room, and I went to my study and looked up a few things on the computer. I turned on the TV and got a game show. I was asleep in my chair in about five minutes.

At about five o'clock, the ladies returned from their trip to Charleston. Dylan and I joined them on the porch and listened to their stories about the houses they had seen while they were with the real estate agent. They thought the three-story home without a staircase was a funny story. They said it was very obvious the staircase was an afterthought. Otherwise, the house was marvelous. The moldings and woodworkings showed the Oriental interest of the captain. We were served wine and beer. Dylan told Marlene about Dunleavy's and the funny remarks that his sister usually made. He told her about how Dunleavy had bought a bar without a bathroom and had to have one added. His sister wondered why she was so foolish to become a partner with someone who would buy a bar without a bathroom. We all had a good laugh. The kitchen staff informed Jo Anne they had dinner ready if she would like to have it served. That suited us as we were not in the mood for going out.

The next morning came early, and I wanted to shoot that bugle boy, but Jo Anne took the gun. I asked her who invented mornings. She punched me on the side and asked me to get out of bed. For a change, we had breakfast in the kitchen. The coffee was very good, and after a few cups, I had both eyes open. Jo Anne said, "You must have worked for a long time yesterday."

I told her, "We went to lunch late. That was the source of Dylan's stories about Dunleavy last night." She laughed again. Dylan and Marlene joined us. We had an excellent breakfast with oatmeal and brown sugar. I had milk on mine. They served a cheese omelet that was folded into a half circle with bacon and toast. The ladies were meeting the group they were with yesterday, minus the real estate agent. Julia, Elly's wife, was joining them.

Dylan and I moved to our favorite spot on the porch. The recorders were in place, and Dylan turned them on. I said, "Albert and I went to work on our constitution. We had about one written, but we wanted to review it over and over until we were sure we had it right. Here is a copy of the Constitution Albert and I wrote."

Dylan took the document I handed him and said, "I have a copy of this constitution in my files. I got it from your library."

I said, "There is a copy of the new constitution that was adopted by all the states under glass and preserved in the lobby of the presidential library."

Dylan said, "I have seen that one also."

I said, "I was very pleased when the members of the convention decided to use the preamble we had written. In fact, they used most of the constitution, but there were some wording changes.

"It was decided by the congress with our blessing that the new constitution should take effect on July 1 of our last year in office. It would take time to get the Senate Districts set up and an office of Director of Elections in place. The Supreme Court drew the initial boundaries, and the governors of the states within the Senate Districts made only a few changes that were acceptable. The governors worked to get the election process set up. The current senators from the districts and most of the House members from the new Senate Districts were candidates for the one hundred Senate seats. The elections went off well in April. We knew who the new senators would be. After they were in office after July 1, the first order of business was the appointment of a president. They chose me to remain until my turn was complete and for Randy Woods, our Secretary of State, to follow me in office. He was to be sworn in on January 20. I wanted Albert to be the president they appointed, but Albert did not want the position and told the members of the Senate he wanted to retire. I would cover Albert and the Party leader position later."

Dylan and I began to read through Albert's and my constitution. It read as follows:

Preamble to the Constitution of the United States of America

We the people of the United States of America in order to form a method of government that is effective and efficient do ordain and adopt this constitution. The government must protect the lives and the property of all of the people. It is the intent of the people to have a government that promotes Peace and Prosperity for All. The rights, privileges, and freedoms granted to the people by this and any other constitutions are timeless. They should be maintained in all constitutions. The

method of government is time dependent and will require change at the proper time.

Article 1: The Rights and Freedoms of All Citizens of the United States of America

The freedoms, rights of the people, and the guarantee of the right for the people to rule is timeless and must be included in any constitution.

Section 1. Freedom of religion and freedom of speech.

The Congress and all other governing bodies shall not make laws that affect established religions or establishment of a religion. Every citizen shall be free to worship as they please. The motto of this nation is, "In God We Trust."

Since the power to govern is given to the government by the people, their freedoms cannot be denied. They have the full freedom to express their desires and their thoughts. No governing body can deny a citizen or group of citizens their rights of freedom of speech. Citizens should remember that freedoms come with a price. Every citizen needs to be responsible for the freedoms of others. There is a personal responsibility that goes with freedom. Without this responsibility and the denial of freedom by anyone can lead to the denial of freedom to everyone.

This constitution grants the press and the media freedom of speech. As part of the responsibility of freedom, the media and the press must exercise every effort to be truthful in their speech and reporting.

All citizens have the freedom to peaceably assemble and to express their beliefs. Each Citizen or group of citizens can petition the Government for a redress of grievances.

Section 2. The right of the citizens to bear arms.

In keeping with the preamble, this constitution supports the method of government that makes law, regulations, and decisions as near as possible to those who are affected by this action. The fifty states are different in many ways. Thus, laws, regulations, and decisions made by the states are more likely to not have adverse effects on the citizens of their state or the lives of people in other states. The right and freedom to keep and bear arms should be made at the state level.

Section 3. A citizen's home is his castle.

This constitution supports the freedoms of the citizens of the United States of America. The citizen's home should not be violated in any manner without the permission of the citizen. The primary purpose of government is and always has been the protection of all citizens' life and property. The home or other property of the citizens cannot be searched and property cannot be seized without a duly issued order from the court involved in gathering and evaluating the evidence of guilt of a crime or a failure to obey a law or regulation. The citizen is innocent until proven guilty by the court.

No person shall be held to answer for a capital, or otherwise infamous crime, unless on a presentment or indictment of a Grand Jury. The citizen is innocent until he is proven guilty; therefore, the citizen cannot be required to give testimony or to be a witness against himself. As it is the responsibility of the government to protect the life and property of the citizen, the citizen cannot be deprived of life, liberty or property without due process of law. The citizens must be properly compensated for any property taken for public use.

In all aspects of the proceeding of the criminal justices system, the citizens have the right to have the assistance of Council. The accused must be informed of the nature and cause of the charges brought against the accused by the criminal justice system. The citizen must have compulsory process for obtaining witnesses in his favor. The citizen has a right to meet a prescribed bail of the court. The citizen has the right to receive a speedy public trial. There shall be an impartial jury. The trial shall be held in the district where the citizen is accused. Only in cases where the publicity prevents an impartial trial and the defendant agrees can the trial be in another district.

After due process in the criminal Justice System the citizen cannot face the same process a second time. When he has been judged innocent, he is innocent.

In no case can the bail be excessive or the punishment be cruel and inhuman.

In every case and every inquiry, this constitution should be interpreted as in support of the rights of each and every citizen.

Article 2: Division of Power Between the Citizens, States, and Federal Government

Section 1. All powers not given to the Federal Government remain the powers of the citizens or the states. In every case the citizens are the source of all powers. When this constitution is adopted by the citizens, it becomes the law of the land. The citizens, and only by a majority vote of all United States of America citizens, can amend or change this constitution. When the majority of the citizens, by vote of a majority of the citizens, express a desire to have a Constitutional Convent to provide a method of government that is efficient and effective, can this constitution be null and void. All previous constitutions becomes null and void when a new constitution is adopted.

Article 3: Legislative Powers Granted to the Federal Government

Section 1. All legislative powers granted by the people to the Legislature of the United States of America reside in a unicameral Senate government. The Senators are elected by one hundred Senate Districts of near equal population. Thus the one man one vote principle is preserved. After the first Senate is seated it should be divided in to three groups. The groups are made by a draw of lots by each senator. At the end of the first two years the term of office of group one is terminated. The senators elected to replace the first group will serve for six years. The members of group two will serve four years. The senators who replace the members of group two will serve for six years. The members of group three will serve six years. When this procedure is complete all senators will serve for a period of six years.

Every senator must have reached his thirtieth birthday. The candidates for senator must have been a citizen of the United States for ten years and must have been a full time resident of the District he represents for five years.

The Vice President of the United States is a member of the Senate. He shall be Chairman of the Senate. He does not have a vote on any referendum unless there is a tie vote by the Senate. The Senate shall elect a Chairman pro tempore to serve as Chairman when the Vice President is not available. The other organization of the Senate and its committees shall be the prerogative of the Senate.

When a vacancy occurs due to resignation or death of a senator, it shall be the responsibility of the Governors of the states affected to call for an election of a replacement. The Governors may appoint an individual to be senator until a proper election can be held.

The Senate will elect the President of the United States of America. The President will serve at the pleasure of the

Senate and can be removed from office at any time by a majority vote of the Senate.

The President will appoint his Vice President and the Secretaries of the Departments of the government with the approval of the Senate.

The President will serve as the Chief Executive Officer of the government. He is the Commander and Chief of the Armed Forces of the United States of America.

The duties of the President are to organize and manage an efficient and effective government. He will propose appoints to the Supreme Court of the United States of America. His propose member must be approved by a majority vote of the Senate.

A majority vote of the Senate is determined by one more vote than half the number of members present and voting. A Senate quorum is defined by at least ninety members being present and voting. Any senator who fails to attend ninety-five percent of the senate secessions or failed to vote when present can be removed from office by a majority vote of the senate.

The rules and organization of the senate must be obeyed by each and every senator.

When the approval rating of the Federal Legislature reaches twenty-five percent or less, there shall be a recall vote for the senators representing the districts.

Article 4: Compensation for the Members of the Government

Section 1. The members of the Senate shall receive a monthly payment of salary determined by the yearly approved budget of the government. The Secretary of the Treasury is responsible for the issuance of all payments. The Senators receive health insurance and retirement income like every other citizens of the United States of America. These payments must be approved by law.

Section 2. Taxes and other income funds such as Import and Export Duties.

The Senate has the power to enact laws that provide income to the government. The Secretary of the Treasury collects all taxes and duties approved by the Senate. He issue payment for all required expenses of the government. Efficiency is the operating word in all matters of finance regarding the operation of the government.

The Finance Committee and the President are responsible for the yearly budget approved by the Senate. The Chairman of the Senate Finance Committee must present the Chairman of the Senate with a balanced budget by the first of May of each year. The Senate must approve a balanced budget before the fifteenth of June. The United States of America's budget year begins on the first of July and continues until the thirtieth of June. There are only two options available to the members of the senate. They can approve the budget presented to the Chairman by the

Finance Committee or they can vote to return the budget to the Finance Committee. There can be no additions or deletions from the proposed budget by actions on the floor of the Senate.

The President cannot change the budget approved by the senate. All taxes and funds collected by the Secretary of the Treasury must be approved by law imposed by the Senate.

Section 3. Constitutional requirements imposed on the senate and the Secretary of the Treasury.

The yearly budget must be balanced and include a ten percent surplus to be used if revenue does not meet expectations. The surplus fund of ten percent must be included in each budget.

The Senate Finance Committee, President, or Secretary of the Treasury may recommend bonds be sold by the government in order to kick the can down the road. Each budget must include the payment on the approved issued bonds.

Since Business, corporation, and industries pay dividends and salaries that are taxed, these organization cannot be required to pay taxes to the government. They may retain a surplus not to exceed operating expense equitant to two years of operating expenses. All other funds earned by the organizations in a year must be dispensed as dividends to stockholders or salary to employees. Failure of the Businesses, Corporations, or Industries to follow

253

this constitutional requirement will be seen as a breach of the law and the officers of the organization can be held responsible of the breach of the law. Punishment must include collection of all funds owed the government and ten year prison sentence for the responsible individuals. This constitutional requirement is intended to insure the Businesses, Corporations and Industries work to insure a full functioning economy.

All citizens must appreciate the economic environment produced by an efficient and effective government. It is their duty to pay a reasonable income tax in order to support the government. Income is defined as any money paid to the citizen from any source. This includes stock dividends, and interest. All income amounts must be taxed at the same tax rate. The senate Finance Committee will establish the tax rates for each income group. The Secretary of the Treasury will assist the Finance Committee with the establishment of the tax rates.

Import and Exports may be taxed. The method of taxation will be by the Value Added tax system. The Finance Committee should use import taxes as a method for leveling the market for United States of American industries.

Article 5: Controls on Travel and Admission to the United States of America

Section 1. The entrance of any individual other than a citizen of the United States shall be controlled by laws enacted by the senate.

Migration into the United States of America shall be controlled by laws enacted by the senate. It shall be the duty of the President of the United States of America to secure the borders of the nation. All illegal immigrants will be arrested and detained in prison until they can be deported.

Section 2. Any person who is not a citizen of the United States of America can only be employed when they have a green card issued by the State Department. All wages earned by individuals with green cards are subject to the same taxes laws of any citizen. All application for green card admission to the United States shall be submitted to the State Department. The decision of the State Department should occur after a thorough investigation of the background of the individual. This action should occur within a reasonable time frame.

Section 3. Upon application to the State Department, an individual can be granted citizenship in the United States. It is the duty of the State Department to create a system for accepting and processing citizenship applications. The senate can and should enact laws for control of citizenship applications and the granting of citizenship. No person with a criminal background need to apply. They will be denied citizenship.

Article 6: Powers Granted to the Legislature and the President

Section 1. It is the intent of the members of the Constitutional Convention to have the power remains with the people. Their representatives in the government should not be limited in their ability to have and maintain an efficient and effective government by the method of government described in this constitution.

After Dylan had time to view the constitution, I said, "The midterm elections went our way. The voters were well informed on the issues, and the new constitution vote was 82 percent in favor. The entire fifty state governors express their desire to have a new constitution. The Republican Party had a large majority in both Houses. As soon as the congress was back in secession, the Constitutional Convention was approved, and the members were called into secession. A new constitution was presented by the members of the Convention. It met every point we had wanted in a constitution to provide an efficient and effective method of government. As we discussed earlier, the congress decided when and how the new constitution would be put in place.

"I was in frequent touch with Abdul Fekuae. He assured me that all the Middle East new nations had constitutions similar to the new United States constitution. Their governments elected by the citizens were in place. He said the new Iranian and Afghanistan governments were being successful at removing the last of the terrorist groups, and the world should be at peace. The new nations wanted to be members of the United Nations. He said the new environment was a great help to their economy. The sizes of their markets were attracting new businesses, and a few corporations were building factories in the Eastern world. A pharmaceutical corporation was building a plant in one of the capital cities.

"John Camp had done a great job. He had all but ridded the executive branch of our government from all its inefficiency. We had the lowest executive budget since the Eisenhower Presidency. The new constitution meant to reduce the legislative budget substantially. Albert and I were feeling very well. A life's ambition was now completed. We decided to take a long weekend at the beach. Mary joined us at the house. Albert and I were sitting on the porch, and Jo Anne and Mary were with us. I said, 'A new efficient and effective Federal government, the state governments, and their local governments at a new efficient working level, peace in the world, and educational systems that have shown great improvement—I do not think we have done a bad job.' Albert said, 'We have accomplished our life's ambition in our working lifetime.' I said, 'You have still got years to go. You will be the next president of the United States.' Albert said, 'Oh no! You have got that all wrong. I do not want your job when you leave office.' I said, 'You are the logical candidate, and the Party leaders will be after you.' Albert said, 'I am happy with what has been done, and I am ready for a life of my own. We have a house in Wild Dunes now, and I want to enjoy the beach and the island life. I know you have missed that life during our working years.' I said, 'I cannot argue with that.' Mary said, 'Neither can I. I am really looking forward to Albert being retired.'

"When we were back in Washington, I got a call from the Party leadership. They wanted an appointment to talk with me. I granted the appointment. When they arrived, they asked me where I thought they should have the news conference, announcing Albert would be the logical person for the new Senate to appoint to the office of president. I asked them if they had talked with Albert, and they said they had not talked to him. I told them they should before they did very much planning. I let them know he had told me he had told the leadership in congress he did not want to be appointed president. He planned to have a letter ready for each member of the new Senate, telling them not to appoint him and that he would not serve. They said, 'He is by far the best candidate, and he should make every effort to be appointed for his sake and the sake of the Party.' I said, 'I know Albert, and when he says something, he has thought about it and made up his mind. He is not the kind that changes his mind.' They said that they would work on Albert, but they wanted to know where they should have that news conference. I said, 'If Albert agrees, I think the University of South Carolina has a number of places that would be suitable for the conference.' I reminded them that he had two degrees from that university and was a major financial supporter of the university. 'But I do not think you will be successful in getting him to accept an appointment if he is appointed,' I told them. They asked me to pressure Albert to become the next president. I told them he was a lifelong friend, and I would not pressure him. They were very disappointed when they left. It was not long before I heard from Albert. They had been to see him, and they told him he had my support and that I suggested the university as the place for the news conference. I said, 'Those,' with a long pause in my sentence, 'you know what. I told them you did not want to be president and that I would not pressure you. They pressured me for a place for a news conference, and I suggested the university.' Albert said that he knew me well enough to know they were just trying to pressure him to work for the position. He said that there was not a change in hell he would accept the position if they appointed him.

"As we had decided when we were at the beach, we worked on the educational system for the remainder of my second term. The Geek program no longer had to devote so much time to the Middle East and the Arab world, so they were free to work on educational programs. I talked with Warren and suggested they develop training programs for various jobs. He said he would contact employment agencies and see where there were jobs available and develop training programs for those jobs. The unemployment rate was 3 percent. That was the lowest it had been in a long time. But maybe we could reduce it even more. The efficient governments had provided funds that improved the economy greatly. The outsourcing program for the government had been a success, and with retirement and resignations, we had found jobs for every person who lost their jobs in government. With these people's contribution to the government with their taxes and not being a cost, we were aiding both our economy and reducing the government's budget.

"I was amazed by the number of corporate board positions that Albert and I received. They knew we would be retired from government, and they wanted us on their boards. I talked with Albert about these positions, and we decided to turn them down. We wanted to enjoy life on the beach. With Albert near and the Island Boys who were our friends, we could enjoy life. Jo Anne and Mary were in total agreement with our decision.

"The Foundation for Better Government would be up and running when we left office. Albert and I had found a building on East Bay in Charleston that was for sale that was perfect for the Foundation offices and space for the staff we intended to have with us. There was a third floor that would be just right for our Geek Program. I was sure Warren would be happy to be near Jinks and his family. Raymond Maul was an old Charleston boy, and he would most likely ride the bridge between Charleston and Mt Pleasant. John Camp had always lived in Columbia. He had family who lived at Myrtle Beach. I hoped he would join us at the Foundation office. I had not discussed it with him, and that was a mistake I had to correct."

Dylan said, "You always plan ahead. This morning's secession sure proves that." We sat back and enjoyed the view. The security guards radioed the kitchen, and our lunch appeared. I asked Dylan if he would rather go to Dunleavy's, and he said he could not pass up this excellent lunch. I must say I agreed with him. The cold beer was good, also. I said, "I wonder were the ladies are having lunch?"

Dylan said, "I am sure it is some wonderful spot in Charleston. Marlene says Jo Anne knows all the greatest restaurants in Charleston." We ate our lunch, and I suggested a walk on the beach. Dylan said he would enjoy that. When we got to the end of the path from the house to the beach, we took off our shoes and socks, and Dylan rolled up his pants. I had on my Bermuda shorts. We waded in the shallow water and talked about the beach environment.

When we were back on the porch, we had our batteries charged and were ready for a long afternoon of work. I turned on the recorders. I did not remember us turning them off. I asked Dylan if he remembered turning off the recorders. He said he had not turned them off. We both realized we had not turned them off, but the security guards were taking good care of us. I said, "With the actions by congress to put the new constitution in effect and to elect a new one hundred-member Senate, all we could do was wait and see who they would appoint to take my place.

"The Republican Convention was held in St. Louis. Albert and I spoke and praised Randy Woods. We pointed out the success of our administration and said Randy was the obvious person for the next president of the United States of America. Every speaker did a respectable job for the candidate and the Party. I knew the Parties would have State Conventions, but I wondered if this would be the last National Convention. The Conventions were expensive, and we were not electing another president. With these events behind us, Albert and I were like real lame ducks. We were spending more time with the people we wanted for our Foundation work.

"After the April elections of the new Senate, we knew who the one hundred members of the Senate would be. We welcomed them to Washington and commented on the members who were very familiar with the working of the government. Their former experience as members of congress made them the logical choice of the voters. They thanked us for our help during the elections. As I pointed out to you earlier, they did not waste time before appointing Randy Woods as president and set up his swearing-in for January 20. They were holding onto some old traditions. But the next swearing-in ceremony would be the last one on a particular day. The president served at the pleasure of the Senate. They could change the person in office at any time."

Dylan said, "I think you have downplayed your position during the election of the one hundred senators and the appointment of Randy Woods."

I said, "What makes you say that?"

He said, "I have read the records in your library. You and Albert made many trips to help friends get elected. You wrote lots of letters and provided material to the media to support them. You also worked to get Randy Woods, your Secretary of State, appointed president."

I said, "Yes, I did spend time working for senators and Randy. Working the elections is so mundane. I guess I forgot how much work Albert and I did during this change period.

"Albert and I had a lot of time back on the islands. He and Mary loved their new home at Wild Dunes, and you know how much I love our home. We were thinking more about retirement than work. But that is when the Devil jumps up and bites you. We had a peaceful almost eight years in the White House except for one weather-related disaster—a hurricane that hit the South Carolina coast. I was in my study reviewing a few letters from friends when I got the call. There had been a shooting at MacDill Air Force Base in Tampa, Florida. This was the base where the Central Command was headquartered. A deranged man had been able to get on the base and into a building with large office areas. There were more than twenty people working in the area where he was discovered. He pulled out an automatic pistol and began firing. He reloaded several times before he was shot and killed. He killed eight people and wounded ten others. This was not the first time unauthorized individuals had been able to get onto the base. In one case, a woman had been found on the base seven times.

"These kinds of events should never be allowed to happen. I remember several that had occurred over the years. We always investigate and try to close the barn door after the mule is out. While the world was at peace, there were individuals and groups that were sociopaths and wanted to hurt or kill innocent people. We need to be vigilant, and when we see something, we must report what we saw. It is up to the people responsible to evaluate all reports. I called the Armed Forces' Chief of

Command and told him I wanted a thorough investigation of the security at every base and embassy. I said, 'While I am only in office for a short period, if another incident like this happened, I would make sure heads would roll.' I wanted him to know I was very angry, so I said, 'Damn the expense! We must keep our members of the armed forces and our citizens safe.' He assured me he was on the matter right then. I said it was too late then as it should have been done before the event. He apologized and said he would do everything possible to prevent this from happening again. I did not put the phone down softly. My secretary and Raymond were in my study. Raymond had an appointment that morning to discuss an upcoming press conference. This secretary worked at the House, keeping up with telephone calls, e-mails, and mails. She said she had never seen me so angry. Raymond agreed. I said, 'I have never been so angry. The purpose of government was to protect the lives of its citizens. We failed in our job under my watch. Failure is not an option. We are always behind in these cases, and people get killed. I want to be ahead and keep the people safe.' Raymond said he would be right on it, and everyone who worked for the government and everyone else would know my feelings and desires. I thanked him, and they left the study. I called Albert, and he had heard what had happened. He was not as angry as I was. I felt we had let our citizens down."

I then said to Dylan, "I think that is enough for today." He turned off the recorders. Our beers were served, and Jo Anne joined us. We decided to have dinner at home. We went into the kitchen, and the meal was ready. We rested and watched TV for the rest of the day.

The next morning after breakfast, Dylan and I were ready for another day. He turned on the recorders, and I said, "We had a wonderful Thanksgiving. We had the family together. Albert invited us down to his house for cocktails, and we were to go to the Wild Dunes Thanksgiving Dinner. The Dinner was served in the Convention Center. This Thanksgiving Dinner had become very popular with the people who lived at Wild Dunes and the communities nearby. The food was excellent, and the wine list was out of this world. Both families had a good Thanksgiving Dinner and a good time.

"The boys and their families stayed with us over the long weekend. Dave asked what I was going to do when my term was up. I told him that I intended to work with our Foundation to provide any nation that needed help to establish and maintain a good government. He knew the people I had picked for staff at the Foundation, and he thought they would be excellent. I said, 'I was sure Raymond would keep me on the road if I let him. He loved to set up speaking engagements for me. Albert and I plan to have Foundation events at Wild Dunes like the ones we have had over the years.' He asked about Camp David and the facility I had built there. I told him I hoped to use it on some occasions if Randy Woods would allow me to use it.

"Don asked David if he would use me to help with the pharmacy business. David said he would love to have me help in any way I felt comfortable doing for the company. I said, 'We can talk about that later.' Jo Anne and the boys' wives joined us on the porch. It had been over eight years since we had downtime together. As we talked, I thought about all the family time I had missed. I said, 'One thing I want all of you to know is I regret all the family time that I have missed, and I want to apologize to each of you—especially you, Jo Anne.' They all said they would not have had it any other way. They said that I had accomplished so much for the nation and the world. They did not know anyone who had accomplished more during their career. They said they were very proud of me and proud to be members of the family. That made me feel good, but I did wish I had not missed so much family life.

"It was Christmas before I knew it. Jo Anne and I had been in Washington since Thanksgiving. I had to get out and shop. Late one afternoon, I went to several stores and picked out presents for the family. I had Secret Service keep them for me and get them to the house on Sullivan's Island. I noticed that Jo Anne and her staff members were spending a lot of time shopping. I said, 'I hope you are doing a good job of keeping our economy in a boom that will last until the end of my term.' I was pleased with the smile that she brought to her face.

"The new Senate passed a couple of new bills that were needed to keep the nation functioning. I no longer needed to sign the bills. But I had to make sure the proper agency or department could handle the workload needed to carry out the legislations. I checked several times to make sure the Department of Defense was on the job and defending every citizen in any part of the world. Randy let me know the State Department was satisfied with the security of their staff, including those in foreign nations. When the Senate adjourned for the Christmas break, I left Washington for home.

"We had a porch Christmas Party for our friends on the island and in the nearby communities. We had forty-two couples. I had bought additional space heaters like the ones I had seen at the patio restaurants in New Orleans. Marshall catered the Christmas Party. With so many people present, Secret Service had assigned additional guards to the house. I did not think that was necessary, but the head of the Secret Service thought it was necessary. The party was like old home week or an alumni reunion. While they were all friends of ours, they formed in groups that were friends and were with each other often. Those groups that had been friends of mine since high school were in the same group as they were back then. Some things never change in a community like ours. We surprised everyone by saying that we had a gift for each of them. The gift was a White House token that was sold on television." Dylan and I stopped for a mid-morning break and had coffee and a sweet roll. It was a very pleasant day. Dylan commented on the day and said he had not had the pleasure of working in this great environment. I agreed that the environment was a great place to work and play.

He turned on the recorders, and I continued, "We went to Albert's for New Year's Eve. We had been invited for cocktails and conversation with a group of new friends of Albert's and Mary who they had met at Wild Dunes. Albert said that most of them lived on his street. The Golf Pros had formed a golf tournament where the neighborhood golf teams played with other neighborhood teams. It was an elimination tournament. They drew numbers to determine who played who first. Albert had joined his neighborhood team. I was happy for him. He was really enjoying life for a change. We all went to the Wild Dunes hotel for a much larger New Year's Eve party. I was glad Jo Anne and I had a security guard to drive us home after the midnight celebration. The fireworks were beautiful out over the ocean.

"When we were back in the White House, Albert said, 'That was the best Christmas and New Year's party I have ever had the pleasure of attending. I think this retirement thing is going to be a ball.' I said, 'It should be for you. You have worked hard since our Civics Class field trip to the State

Capitol. You have more than made your career dreams come true.' He said, 'I can credit all that to my friendship with you. I was glad when you said you would join me in politics. But I did not know you would be the success you have been. There was that big hug that we had come to enjoy. It added to the feeling of accomplishment we both enjoyed.'

"It seemed like January 20 would never come. I counted down the days. The Senate was back in secession, but not much was happening. I called the Chairman of the Finance Committee, and when he arrived at the White House, I told him I would gladly have my staff put together a budget for his use in making the first budget under the new constitution. He was very glad for our help. I got John Camp and a few of his staff in my office and told them to put together a budget that the Chairman of the Finance Committee could use as a working budget for his committee. They went to work, and in three days, I had a budget to review. I was very satisfied with the balance budget they had prepared. It included debt payments that were large enough to make a difference. There were no more deficits and had not been for a long time.

"I read the new proposed budget three times. I just could not believe it. I got a copy of the current year's budget and looked at the last line and the cost of the House of Representatives. I could not believe the new constitution saved that much money. There would be enough savings in the new budget to completely pay off the large national debt. We had inherited the large national debt. For the first time in a long time, come July 1, the nation would be debt-free. Over my eight years in office, we had paid a lot on the debt.

"The Outsourcing Agency had about accomplished enough to put them out of a job. But they began early after they learned the new constitution would have a unicameral government to place the people who would lose their jobs. They started offering people employed by the House jobs they found in the private sector. They were very busy building and aiding individuals with their curriculum vitae. The Geek program helped them get all the information on their computers. They had a software program that compared job information with the curriculum vitae of individuals. I talked with Randy about the importance of the outsourcing agency. He agreed with me and told me he would keep all the agencies we had put in place for as long as they were needed. He was impressed with the great job John Camp had done, and he and John had found someone to replace John when he left to join our Foundation staff. He said John was working with the new person to make sure he was fully up to speed.

"Once again, I thought I had everything lined up. I had all my ducks in a row. My secretary said Montgomery Allen and Gordon Baskin were in the other office and wanted to see me. Montgomery was the new Chairman of the Senate, and Gordon was Proem. I told her to show them in. We had a very friendly greeting. I had not spent time with them in a long time. Montgomery spoke first and said, 'We have polled the members of the Senate, and they want to appoint you to the office of president.' I said, 'I have served two terms.' Gordon said, 'The new constitution says the president serves at the pleasure of the Senate.' I said, 'Indeed it does, but I did not think the Senate would appoint me beyond January 20. Randy Woods looked like the likely choice if Albert would not agree to be president.' Montgomery said, 'Paul, you have done a brilliant job as president. I do not think anyone else could have accomplished what you have done. The new constitution is a blessing, in that, we do not have to change presidents every eight years. We are back in the days of FDR. We can keep the same president as long as the Senate is satisfied he is doing a good job.' I said, 'This has come up as a complete surprise. I have been planning for retirement. You know if this had come up at the time I was appointed interim president until January 20, I think I might have said yes. My family and I had a wonderful Thanksgiving holiday, and I enjoyed Christmas more this past year than at any time in a long time. During my career, I had missed a lot of family life. I planned to retire and enjoy it again.' Gordon said, 'We understand the importance of family life, but your country needs you.' I thought this was going to be a hardball game. How could anyone turn down his country? I thought I would do what both Montgomery and Gordon had done a thousand times. I would kick the can down the road to get time to think. I said, 'You know this is sudden. Can you give me some time to think about this?' Montgomery said, 'You are still true to form. You always give a thing a lot of thought. That is good. That is what we need in our presidents. How about two days?' I said, 'That would be fine. You know both of you have paid me a great honor, and I want you to know I appreciate the honor very much.' Gordon said, 'You deserve it and more. The members of the Senate think you deserve any honor your country can give you.' Montgomery said, 'You deserve every honor and more.' I thanked them and said they were too kind. They left the office, and I had to sit down. I looked out into the Rose Garden and thought, *Now this has sure put a kink in my plans.* They just ran through my row of ducks and scattered them over the lot."

Dylan turned off the recorders, and I said, "Where shall we go for lunch?"

Dylan asked me, "How does Dunleavy's sound?"

I said, "Great." We were there in no time and enjoyed another lunch with the Island Boys.

When we were back on the porch and ready, I said, "I called Albert and said I needed to see him. He said he was in the security room and would be right in. When he arrived, I told him what had just happened. I said they were playing hardball, and they really wanted me to remain on as president. Albert said, 'I wondered why the Senate had not thought of appointing you president. I would have been after you from the minute the new constitution was approved and I was seated in the Senate.' I said, 'You are just as much responsible for our success as I am. You would make a great president.' Albert said, 'I think I might have something to help you make up your mind. Tom Bradley, who was my neighbor and captain of our community golf team, died yesterday. The team wanted me as the team captain. I told them I would be captain. I called Terry, the Director of Golf, and asked if you could be on our team. Terry said that you were a longtime member of Wild Dunes and that he did not see any reason you could not be a member of our team.' I said, 'Albert, I could always count on you to help me keep my head on straight. I am going to retire and enjoy life.' I thought I should call my family and poll them. I knew what they would say, but I wanted to hear it. I called Jo Anne first and got the answer I had expected to hear. She said the decision was mine and that she would support me regardless of my decision. Dave and Don gave me the same answer.

"When Montgomery and Gordon were in my office for my answer, I told them I was burned out and wanted to retire. Naturally, they were not happy with that answer. They told me the country and the Senate needed me for the job of president. I told them the next president and the congress would have the full support of the Foundation Albert and I intended to set up. We planned to keep the key members of our team together. We would be available at any time our council was needed. They said that was just like not having me in the White House. I told them I intended to retire just like I worked, and that I was going to put my heart and soul into retirement. I said I needed a long rest from the stress of the office of president and that I needed time with my family and friends on the island. They saw they were not making any headway, so they thanked me for the time and left.

"I called Randy and told him I was in support of his presidency. He said that Montgomery and Gordon had consulted him before coming to see me. He said he told them that I was the guy for the job and that he would be happy to continue working for me. I told him that I had said I was going to retire the way I had worked. I was going to put my heart and soul into retirement. He laughed and said I would not expect anything different. I told him to remember we were keeping the key plays from our team together. The Foundation would be available to him at any time. He then thanked me for my support."

I turned off the recorders, and we had a mid-afternoon break. It did not last long, but the beer was good.

I then started speaking again. "January 20 arrived, and Randy Woods was sworn in as the president of the United States of America. For the first time, the United States of America had a government that represented the idea of one-man-one-vote. We no longer had a House of Representatives who were elected by a small percent of the population but gained power and affected everyone. Each senator represented nearly the same number of people.

"The Constitution that was adopted in 1791 had put into place a government that was too complicated to last long. They had three branches of government, trying to run the same government. That was too many branches to govern without controversy. The legislative branch was divided into two houses and thus was organized for controversy. The new Senate had full power to manage a government. They appointed a president who was forced to work hand and glove with the Senate. The 435 members of the House of Representatives who were divided into too many small groups that held up important legislation was a thing of the past. We had a government of the people and for the people. I still hated the political party system. It allowed power-motivated individuals to obtain the power of a group. But as long as the people elected the representatives they wanted, we had a government controlled by the people. We needed a population that would maintain an efficient and effective government.

"We moved out of the White House and back into my house on the beach. On the last plane ride on Air Force One Home, Jo Anne and I talked about security. Neither of us liked all the attention the security generated. I called the head of the Secret Service and asked him to take away the lead and chase cars when we went places. He did, and I bought a specially fitted SUV from Ford. It was bulletproof and bomb-resistant. It had three seating areas that were comfortable. It blended well into the traffic. The Secret Service thought the new SUV was grand and lessened the need for the lead and chase cars. There would be two Secret Service members with us—a driver and one in the back seat. When we had more people in the SUV, the second guard would ride with a shotgun. They would not reduce the number of guards at the house. They said that was a target and that they planned to change the appearance of the SUV at different times. I bought a second one so there would be a backup.

"The next thing I had to turn my attention to was the design and building of my library at the University of South Carolina. I sat in my study and drew floor plans for several days. The first thing I worked on was the entrance. That would be the first impression of any guest. I had the arch just inside the doors so everyone who entered would have to pass under the arch that said, *The freedoms granted by the 1791 Constitution are timeless*. The second arch was an afterthought. It was placed where the guests entered a hall leading to the main part of the library, and my office was just to the left after they passed under the arch. This arch was inscribed with the following words—*The method of government is time-dependent.*

"I worked on the design of my office. I wanted it to be a freestanding wing so it could have large windows. The first office was the receptionist's office. My secretary's office was to the right of the receptionist's office and my office was to the left. I had a large office. My desk faced the area near the door. My chair faced the door. There were two chairs on the door side of my desk. Behind my desk and to the right was a sitting area with a couch for four—two comfortable chairs and a coffee table. The couch faced double glass doors that led to a rose garden like the one outside the Oval Office at the White House. Across the room to the left was an old computer desk and a computer that I had in the living quarters of the White House. The chair was where I could look out the window at the Capitol building. Often, when I sat there, I thought of that

Civics Class field trip. The computer desk had three draws on the working side and one draw under the printer. The back of the desk had lots of cubbyholes to put things. That was why I loved this old desk. You could not back it to a wall because you would lose access to the cubbyholes. That desk is the only piece of furniture that had been in the White House when I was president. I took less to do with the main part of the library and the storage of the documents. A first copy of the new constitution was under glass in this area of the library and preserved by nitrogen.

"Albert and I had everything in place for our Foundation. My Chief of Staff was still in charge. Cecil Dempsey had done a wonderful job for me while I was in the White House, and I wanted him to continue in the leading role. Warren headed up the Geek Program, and they occupied the top floor of the building we had bought. John Camp and his staff with Raymond and his staff were on the second floor. The first floor was the receptionist's office followed by Albert's office, my office, and our secretary's office. The back area of the first floor was a library with document storage and the current journals.

"We decided the first job for the Foundation staff would be to inform people about the use of guns. We wanted them to teach people that when they saw something or heard something that did not sound right, they should tell the authorities— that old saying that if you see something, say something. We wanted employees to be aware of their surroundings and the people in government to be aware of things that seemed to be out of place. We were interested in stopping the random shootings of innocent people. I wanted to arm individuals in our State Department who served in foreign offices. The Secretary of State did not like the idea. He said his people were chosen because they were people of peace. He wanted to keep it that way. I agreed with him.

"I suggested a second task that would be to work on energy and its use. There was always that old problem of the toxicity and environmental consequences of the end products of use for all substances. We needed to have a nation of citizens who were well informed on the use of renewable sources of energy and the use of our energy sources like solar energy, wind energy, and hydro energy. Warren said he could not agree more with this agenda. He planned to work on it himself. I thought that was great. Albert said, 'God's speed and favor be with you.'"

Dylan said, "I did not know about the view from your library office window. You can look at the Capital building that started you on your career to improve governments. That is an interesting point for your biography."

I said, "We are at the end of my term. How much more are we going to cover?"

Dylan said, "You have had such an interesting career and term as president that I think I will write two biographies. One will be titled and written to cover your time as president, and the second will be titled and written to cover the life of Paul Harvey Collins." I said that I thought that might be interesting. Dylan continued, "The one on the presidency will be from documents in your library and things you have said. The one on your life will cover the time outside the White House. It will cover your life here on this porch and on the island."

I said, "I could not wait to read them."

Dylan said, "I have my flight reservations for early tomorrow, and it will take me several weeks of writing. I will call you when I am ready to return with the first drafts."

I suggested that we go to Marshall's for a good dinner before he left for a few weeks. He said he would enjoy that. I called the boys and asked them and their wives to join us. They said they would. Davy was driving down from St George, so he would spend the night with Don. I called Donnie, Elly, and Tom and asked them and their wives to join us, and they said they would meet us there. We had planned to meet at 7:30 pm so that Dave and Gloria could get there from St George. We were seated in the Paul Harvey Collins Presidential Private Dining Room. The cocktails and appetizers were very good. We all ordered seafood dishes from the menu. There was a lot of talk about old times and present times. Jo Anne and I always enjoyed being in the company of this collection of family and friends. Dylan was enjoying himself and that was good.

Marshall said, "I am not going to start anything with you tonight. Those guys with guns worry me."

I said, "That is a good thing. I would hate to get your blood all over this nice floor."

Marshall and all of us had a good laugh. Then Marshall said, "The flowers you ordered for tonight is a nice touch."

Jo Anne said, "Do not give him any credit. The flowers were my idea."

I said, "It is always wise to marry a smart and beautiful lady."

Jo Anne said, "I do not have my purse to pay you for those kind remarks." That brought another good laugh from all of us.

Don said, "Dad, I think Mom just got you again."

Marshall said, "Don, he is not hard to get. It was his dad who could always get everyone."

I said, "Praising my dad in the middle of a fight is unfair competition."

Dylan said, "I will never get enough of you Island Boys. When you are together, I have to hold my sides. It is always an enjoyable time."

Dylan left at seven the next morning, right after breakfast. We ate in the kitchen. When Dylan left, Jo Anne sat for a while and had another cup of coffee. She said she had enjoyed the previous night. I said that I had enjoyed it too. I said, "I have a tee time at nine o'clock at Wild Dunes. I am playing in a tournament with Albert's golf team."

Jo Anne replied, "That sounds like fun. They always have good tournaments."

I said, "Yes, and this will be special. We are playing thirty-six holes. Eighteen holes today and another eighteen tomorrow—we play the Ryder cup format, but we only play nine holes in each type of match. We will have dinner with the opposing team tonight at the club. The losers today will pay for the dinner tonight."

Jo Anne said, "I am sure you and Albert will have fun, and Mary and I will enjoy the dinner tonight. Mary and I plan to go to Charleston and do a little shopping. We will have lunch in Charleston. You and Albert can have lunch wherever you think you will enjoy." She left, and I went out to the SUV I was using. I got to the course in time for a little practice before our tee time. We were playing the Harbor Course that day and the Links Course the next day. I chipped and putted for about thirty minutes before going out to the first tee. Albert and I were paired up, and we won both of our matches. Albert invited us to his house for cocktails before dinner at the club.

Jo Anne got home around 5:30 p.m. We were to be at Albert's at six, so there was not much time. She changed quickly, and we were off to Albert's. Mary and Jo Anne told us about their day over cocktails. We told them we had won our matches. In fact, Albert's team had won the first day, so dinner was on the other team. The club was ready for us when we arrived. Terry, the Director of Golf, and Steve, a golf pro employee, of the club joined us for dinner. Steve told me he was watching me today. He said that I was not squaring up the club head at impact. It was always a little open with my drives and iron approaches. He said I was correcting for it by my line up. But I would do better to line up for my target and close the club a little. He said I should go to the range the next day before I tee off and continue to close the club until I hit the ball toward my target.

I could not wait to get to the range the next day. I thought about my grip most of the night. When I was on the range, I used my normal setup, and I hit every shot to the right of my line. I closed the face a little, and I was near my line. I closed a little at a time until I was hitting the ball down my line. The distance with each club improved. I worked on my distance until I had it right for my irons to the pin. I had a better day, and Albert noticed my improvement. He wanted to know what I had done. I told him Steve helped me the night before. He said he had taken lessons from Steve and that he helped him a lot. We won our match, and our team won. When I got in the club, I looked up at Steve and made an appointment for lessons. I told him if I did improve, I would sue him for malpractice. He said I could join the long line of people he owed. His brother had a car dealership. Steve said that one day he hoped he could drive a car that was made in the decade he was driving in. I made sure I paid him well for my lessons.

Dylan called and said he had a first copy of the biography that had been printed. He said it was a draft, and if I wanted changes, they could be made. When he arrived, we went to the porch, and I started reading. The first thing was the cover. It had the following title: What the Nation Needs is Island Boy Leadership. I thought it was a little long, but I liked it. It took me most of the afternoon to read it. I said, "I thought you were going to cover the White House years."

He said, "When I got started, I decided I did not want to do that. I wanted the readers to get to know you as a man and not just as a president." I turned back and reread some of the pages. They were all written well, and they did cover the man and not just a president.

I said, "I do not know about you, but I would not change a thing." I liked the fact he had a copy of the current constitution in the index.

He said, "I will call my publisher and tell him to go ahead with the printing. He will be very happy about that."

Jo Anne joined us, and when I gave her the biography, she laughed at the title. She said, "Well, Dylan, I see the Island Boys impressed you. They have amazed me for years."

Dylan said, "After meeting and getting to know your husband, I could not think of a better title for his biography. I have so much material that I think I will be writing about Paul for a longer period of time. So I will be back with my next book when I get it finished."

I said, "We hope you will not become a stranger, and we get to see you again soon and often."

Jo Anne said, "Be sure to bring Marlene. I enjoy her company."

Dylan said, "That road runs in both directions. You and Paul should come to visit us. We could have a good time."

The security guard approached and said, "Mr. Johnson, if we are going to make your flight time, we had better head for the airport." We said our good-byes, and my biography was about to become a part of history.

When I was alone on the porch I loved, I said to myself, "Paul Harvey Collins, you are an achievement-motivated Island Boy who has done well. Now it is time to sit back and be proud of your accomplishments."

Author's Notes

After I completed this novel, before publication, the government of the United States allowed a shutdown of the government. The approval rating of the Congress fell to 10 percent. The approval rating of the president was at 35 percent. I believe there are three main reasons for these events. The members of the Congress were more interested in party politics than they were in the welfare of the population. There has remained a racial bias in the nation after the slaves were freed in the mid-nineteenth century and the civil rights laws were passed in the mid-twentieth century. The organization and the lack of a chain of command in the current method of government permit small groups of individuals to hold up and prevent important legislation. The current method of government is not organized to be a decision-making and problem-solving organization. The leadership in the political parties lack to desire to be supportive of the people: they are driven by power motivation and party domination.

I have a friend who often says, "Where is John Wayne when you need him." I would like to paraphrase this remark and say, "Where is Paul Harvey Collins when you need him . . ."